THE QUEEN
OF HEARTS

THE QUEEN
OF HEARTS

DANIEL HOMAN

PRIME BOOKS

THE QUEEN OF HEARTS

Prime Books
www.prime-books.com

ISBN: 978-1-60701-204-7

This tyrant, whose sole name blisters our tongues, was once thought honest; you have loved him well; He hath not touched you yet.

—William Shakespeare, *Macbeth* (Malcolm act IV, iii)

I wonder if I've been changed in the night? Let me think. Was I the same when I got up this morning? I almost think I can remember feeling a little different. But if I'm not the same, the next question is 'Who in the world am I?' Ah, that's the great puzzle!

—Lewis Carroll, *Alice in Wonderland* (Alice)

Diamond, club, spade, heart,
So it fell the order of old.
Diamonds for the hillborns who
Hold the world with gloves of gold.

No less potent swings the club
In God-like hands, from words of men,
With fear in life and after-death,
Their holy laws preserved in pen.

Hillborn-fed yet stocked with louts,
The soldier craft's a spade-black hand.
When God's words fail and coffers spent,
Then charge the poor to other lands.

Their mangled mouths, their crippled backs
Their broken words in stops and starts.
They toil daily, how they wait
For noble hands, The Queen of Hearts.

—Lyle

Ante

But one question remains: Did it begin or end in theft?

His polished shoes hit the cold graying cobblestone of a crowded street. Stepping up onto the sidewalk to get his bearings, Renue takes in the faces of strangers and is overcome with panic. Where is he? What has happened? His shirt, in tatters, a flash of remembrance, leaving white gloves, suit, and vest in the forest, but he can't remember why his clothes had been shed like snakeskin.

At least the market is a familiar place, reds and golds glinting in the afternoon sun. Merchants call out to strangers who call out to friends, yet he stands frozen, feeling breath on the back of his neck. No one has turned on him and perhaps no one will. With luck, the louts won't know his face. With luck, the spades won't see his hands. *It's searching for us.* Yes, because there has been murder. And the eyes watch, the ears listen.

Stifling another rush of panic, Renue stares at his hands, blackened as though burnt. The humid sea air carries stray voices, rumors, conversation. He swallows, eyeing the crowd's hypnotic walk, their daily business, running errands, buying loaves of bread, bartering, picking fruits, lost in chatter. Revulsion. He swallows against sickness, watching as the crowd flows down the street.

Suddenly, a finger brushes his elbow, but his mind is dulled as though drugged and he can but let the cold touch remain, though the hairs on his neck rise and beads of sweat collect on his temple. The touch produces a thought; is this a nightmare, or a shadow of his broken memories and dark dreams, or a solitary, strange vision? Although he has forgotten his name and his mission, a single image is planted in his mind, a playing card, but he is caught in a paradox. To address this sole signpost of his past is to look, but to look is to be consumed. And he cannot be consumed again.

♥

He waits as they pass, those lords and ladies, the guests, fashionable hillborns with their top hats, watches, ivory canes. Slamming doors and laughing, the hillborns leave their cars to the valets and amble up the grassy hill towards the Manor. Renue is from the Slants, from poverty, and yet he is at the great gates that lead to the home of Mesmer, the dictator. Does he even dare? Renue fingers the ten ceremonial coins in his pocket. He has been given a charge to win back the deed to his home, with the hopes that the deed will unravel the Pattern. When Mesmer took Ashkareve so many years ago, he placed a design so strict and final, where servitude is life and resistance death. With his secret police and surveillance, he shattered language itself, broke words, snipped tongues so the people were forced to speak in bursts, with blank words, in poems, using fingers, or not at all. Mesmer's agents are always listening for a plot. Even think of escape, let alone revenge, and Mesmer sets Boran's Black Hands loose. Murder, and the black thing will find you, even though none living can say they've seen it. For so long, Mesmer's pet was confined to the nighttime stories parents and siblings tell to frighten young children. An irrelevant myth, many say, as those who kill, whose palms turn black, simply disappear, one way or the other.

Renue hears voices echoing in his mind: Alkor, the leader of the Damaskers, one of the most powerful wielders of the Gift, and Bardon, his second in command.

Just win the deed to Ashkareve.

And forget the names that tag and locate the source of our poor resistance. But remember, even within those Manor walls there is always someone listening.

With the deed and we can set upon unraveling the Pattern.

You're like a son to me.

Renue, the perfect weapon. Our best hope.

Please be careful.

So much planning, years of deliberation, so many lives embedded in the persona known as Renue. In the end, he was selected for two attributes that the other candidates of the resistance did not possess: the absence of the Gift, and his lack of family, as the black thing hunts both. Renue's mother vanished in his infancy and his father was taken years later, on a stale gray morning when Renue's eyes were barely open. Fractured memories remain in his mind, a door opening to the minor rattle of early risers, morning smells, though his father's final words are mute and lost in the rust of childhood sleep. By the time the boy woke, his father was gone. The boy left the house to search for his father, returning hours later to find spades ransacking his home. His neighbors hadn't heard a thing, they said, but none were willing to take the boy in. Left with nothing but fear, he lived in the swarming alleyways of the Slants and Latchtown for almost two years, filching bread with other street kids, making friends with shadows, sleeping in religious houses, pickpocketing, begging. Then, near Feeble Street, on a day of abrupt luck, the boy stole from the right person and was taken in by Bardon, who came to be his teacher, his oldest friend.

Remember. Less risk. Make weakness strength.

He has nothing to lose.

Always have something to lose. Something to lose is something to live for.

Spouting fish adorn the fountain and baying wolves surround an elegant statue of a woman, hand to her brow, facing the twilight forest. How did Renue even get far enough to see the central fountain and chiseled stony steps of Mesmer's home? Dumb luck? Hundreds of others in the resistance are working tirelessly to help him breach the hills and blend into the retinue arriving for the notorious Great Game. Ashkareve is a city ruled by paradox, both order and chance, by the Pattern, the black laws as they're known in the Slants, and poker. In training Renue illustrated his proclivity for cards and beat out the resistance's other candidates, red and black buried in his blood. But it's all in the first hand, he thinks, watching the men and women he has always despised amble towards the Manor. The first hand tells all. One chance to carve out a seat, one chance to dispel a city's collective nightmare. It can't be called life if the threat of death hangs over like constant fog. What is that saying of the philosopher, Pestras? *Fear long outlives its origins.*

Renue sees his opportunity, three unescorted ladies wearing long flowing dresses, blue, green, and gold. "Might I have the honor?" he says, flashing the smile.

The prettiest of the three grabs his shoulder and scowls appear as her two companions faces. They withdraw their outstretched hands until Renue shows them a card trick and soon all are beaming again. Together they walk on an auburn carpet, the ladies giggling, dancing through the great doors that take three men a side to pull. The pullers, while pulling, are spinning a yarn.

"Table's deadly tonight."

"Say he's grown bored."

"It no longer pleases him?"

"Never has."

"But now he bets in lives."

"So bored he'll bet his own?"

"Imagine the luxury."

"Perhaps tonight?"

"Perhaps, perhaps."

Arms round the women, Renue struts inside, his golden-brown hair lit by warm amber light. Beneath a chandelier, he recognizes from the resistance library photos and prints Old Faldor, the once-ruler of Qarash, his shoulder-length gray hair, his studious glasses.

The old man looks up from a ledger. "Welcome, sir. Name?"

"Renue Avatine."

"Perenish?"

"Has my accent betrayed me?"

"No," Faldor says. "But was I correct, sir? Perenish?"

"Yes."

"Perenish—you must have a friend in the Manor."

"One or two."

"Fee?"

Renue hands the old man stacks of bills. "Here."

"Lucky for you, poker is a game in which bias is to your advantage."

"That's what I'm hoping."

The old man scrolls through the opened ledger, fingers crawling over the names of the country's major Potens, names that test Renue's composure. Too soon. He turns away. By the stairwell he spots Rady, the Poten of Ashkareve, a puppet of Mesmer's, yet oddly respected by louts and hillborns alike. The common face, he's sometimes called. Rady narrows his beady eyes, entertaining several prominent men of the city. Where are the other key players? If there were a deck of cards to illustrate the major powers in Qarash, the three, Debeau, Melnor, and Wildcard, would serve as the remaining aces, and Boran and Rady as kings. But where is the ace of spades, the dictator himself?

"Here," Faldor says. "Avatine. Mark here."

Renue takes a pen and signs, a drop of sweat blurring the ink. "I'm sorry—perhaps a fortunate drop. As you noted, I'm not entirely welcome here."

The old man leans in. "There's much to admire of Perenia,

though I would never said that." He straightens. "Welcome to the Game. I trust you know the stakes."

"I do."

Faldor snaps his hands and a porter appears. "Show him to his room."

Only then does Renue breathe a satisfied sigh. The suit is perfect, the disguise exact. Now comes the act.

♥

He sits on his bed and straightens his collar, staring at himself in the mirror. Even the slightest noise from the hall makes him break out in sweat. He closes his eyes and takes a deep breath. The door is locked. Will they come for him? He stares at the white gloves on the night table. Mere days in the Manor and already the taste of stale bread has been forgotten, replaced by summer soups, light and textured, made for more than softening bread. While he enjoys the excesses of the rich, the louts of Ashkareve continue to suffer. *Our best hope.* Renue puts on his gloves and unlocks the door, thinking of his mother and father. He has always risked his life in their memory.

Walking a white hall lined in foreign rugs, Renue studies the paintings and tapestries on the walls. Tonight is the night is the night is the night. The ten gold coins, the opening ante, is to the hillborns and foreign guests a paltry sum, but to Renue, this was once unimaginable wealth. In mere weeks, his well-crafted character has ascended from the murky lower tables on skill. Skill and luck. Once a number, now a face. Once a slum, now royalty. And the bet will come tonight, he thinks. It has to.

"Ah, the newcomer."

The voice startles him, but it's only the countess. She wears an elaborate maroon dress, silver earrings, a silver necklace. But because of the pills he has given her, she never remembers him.

" . . . Renue, is it?"

"Yes, my dear."

"Congratulations! I've heard you've shaken up the house. The youngest in years invited to the Game."

"I was shocked," he says. "My stomach's still upset."

"Too bad about Faldor, though." The countess frowns, holding a finger to her lips.

"It truly is. An unbearable loss." Renue pulls up both gloves, his long dress shirt meeting above the wrist. "How do I look?"

"Young, confident." She winks. "Virile."

"That's just the costume."

She cackles, then shakes her head sadly. "Those *monsters*— the old man didn't deserve such an end."

"No, he didn't," Renue says, drifting back to himself as a boy, and to his father's stories of how the regime took the country twenty-nine years ago. When Mesmer seized the city, all hope withered, his lust for power limitless, his tactics compulsive, calculated, obsessive. The dictator slaughtered all those who stood in his way, betrayed half his friends, branded them disloyal, sent them to the gallows in the plain of day, televised it no less. Then he spread his men through the streets of Ashkareve and Qarash and ate away resistance year by year, until the country was reduced to a poor frame. Mesmer, even the name meant to disillusion, that single name the root of Renue's greatest strength and most profound weakness. Mesmer. The butcher who stole his parents.

" . . . never the same since the war," the countess is saying. She sniffs a purple powder from a vial in her purse and shuffles in her peacock dress. "Well, I should go." Wiping her nose, she staggers, grabbing Renue's chest. Her hand rubs down to his belt and she tugs, glancing up innocently. She bites her tongue lustfully. "Good luck. Oh, and a few of the flowers in the hall are batting eyelashes over you. You might find yourself in a foreign bed tonight. Perhaps mine, if you play your cards right."

"I'll keep that in mind." He watches her stumble across the carpet.

Midway down the hall, Renue pauses at the portrait of a young woman bathed in late afternoon colors, burned-orange skin, a deep lavender dress, light purple flowers spotting her hair. Recognizing the double doors that lead to the table, he exhales. Behind those doors is the man who silenced thousands before they even spoke a word, before first breath. Until now Renue has only seen Mesmer from afar, at the far end of the banquet tables or peering from the balcony above the entrance stairs. Beyond those doors is the table of the Great Game, where cities have been lost and won and countries divided on mere hands, where lives have become betting chips. But the game is merely an extension of how most live, of life itself, Renue thinks. The world in the hands of a few.

Two spades open the doors to escaping smoke. The room is dimly lit and red embers hang from darkened mouths. Renue moves towards the open seat. Tall maroon chairs, ornately carved wood surround the green table. To his left sits Melnor, an aging man with reading glasses, long piano fingers, a white double vest. Melnor controls Belruth and the cities of the west. A man of implacable logic. Renue has heard rumors of the Poten's dissent during the war with Perenia, before the war began to turn. Sitting beside Melnor is a man known as Wildcard, the leader of Valadrine and the eastern cities. Still touched with youth, with long, framing eyebrows and tangled black hair, Wildcard is a prodigy, perhaps thirty, thirty-one, only a handful of years older than Renue himself. Last year, there were rumors that Wildcard bet his own life and lost, though Renue could not say on what conditions Wildcard was pardoned. Beside the young Poten leans a bulky, hooked nose man, Baron Debeau, with his flowing robe and thick red beard. A warrior, powerful but predictable, Debeau holds Grenore and the icy southern cities. Years ago, his father Dregen ran into the thick of battle at full speed, briefly turning the tide of the war with brute abandon for the sanctity of life or the rules of war.

Renue has stared nightmares in the face every day he has spent in the Manor, but his insides freeze at the final figure at the table, the ace of spades himself. Mesmer sits calmly, studying Renue with his piercing eyes, a crooking smile, his long, gaunt face and dirt-black hair. Myths of Mesmer: he came from poverty, a small town in the northeast. He fought in the old campaigns of Faldor and was injured, dug a bullet out of his thigh with only a pocketknife, received the scar midway down his left eyebrow that officials and officers now maintain as a symbol of loyalty. Twin gray wolves are carved into his chair. The dictator pulls up his gloves and stares at Renue. This is the man whose hands must be blacker than infinite space, than the darkness of the sea floor. This is the man who took Renue's mother and father, who plucked his family before memory, in its infancy.

Mesmer wipes his mouth. "Glad you accepted my invitation. Welcome to the Great Game."

"It's an absolute honor. Truly."

Renue feels for his ten ceremonial gold pieces. The first hand must be won. A fifth presence steps from the corner shadows, a striking woman with long blond hair and light blue eyes. She deals the cards, barely glancing up, bows to Mesmer, then abruptly leaves. Renue slides his cards to the edge and flips them up slightly. Jacks high, threes low. Luck? Sweating, he maintains a steady hand and makes his opening. Wildcard, Debeau, Melnor, Mesmer. On equal playing ground, how they fall, they crumble.

♥

"Deal."

"Yours."

"Yours."

"Yours."

"Newcomer."

Two hands, four, hands exchange betting chips, red, yellow, blue, white. Yet the plastic coins trigger innate desires, the sting of hunger as a street kid, mealie and brown beans. Renue composes his voice. "So when does the fun begin? I didn't come all this way just for—"

"And where did you come from?" Melnor says.

"Perenia."

"Lumbar side or Troland?"

"Lumbar's next door."

Debeau clears his throat. "Some have taken to calling you the Joker, have they not?"

"Penchant for bad jokes," Renue says. "Only a nickname."

"Yours." Wildcard deals briskly.

Jack, seven, five, nine, two. Club strong. Loss. King, Queen, ten, six, six. Bluff. Win. White gloves grasp faces, numbers, suits, hearts, straights, flush, double jacks, triple nines. Commanding, powerful, Renue plays the odds, loses when he needs to, wins when he can. Soon, Melnor and Debeau are broken. Cigars aflame, they sit back, puffing, chuckling.

"He's good."

"He's *very* good."

"Too good," Debeau says.

"Determined, merely." Mesmer ashes his cigar. "Spades suit you, Renue."

Wildcard grins. "Worried, meathead?"

"Call me that again and I'll show you black hands, little one."

Renue antes. "What does he mean? I was given gloves but not their purpose."

"Red hands for those who lie, black for those who murder." Melnor wipes his face. "A brilliant accompaniment to order and law."

"I don't trust the Sickness," Debeau says gruffly, glancing over at Mesmer. "But I suppose it has its place."

"That's because even your brain is muscle, Red Beard." Wildcard stares intently at Renue then winks, anteing.

"*Card.*"

"Face it," Wildcard continues. "You distrust what you don't understand. And might I add, that is a hefty slice of the world, my friend."

As Debeau rises angrily, Renue clears his throat. "But we wear gloves?"

"Well, this *is* a gentlemen's game," Melnor says.

"Of course."

Like a disappearance, the deed to Ashkareve comes before it can be imagined, a faded yellowing paper thrown in the pot by Mesmer like garbage. Alkor believes the deed to be infused with the Gift and a means to locate the Pattern, perhaps a way to destroy the black thing itself. Renue fans a handful of blanks, a spattering of numbers and suits that don't match and the weakest spread possible, at least for those who rely on only luck. He presses the other players, deftly throwing the weight of doubt on their minds, bluffing, provoking weaknesses. Wildcard throws down chips haphazardly but Renue has already discovered his tell. The young Poten flicks his hair back when he bluffs. Soon, the others bow out and Renue wins, left with the deed in his pile and command of the table, game choice and ante.

Holding the paper between his thumb and forefinger, Renue fights the urge to flee the Manor, through the forest, downward from the hills to the market to the bell tower and eastward across the face of the city to the Slants and the underground. But it would be too suspicious to leave so suddenly, he thinks. Of course, he must stay until the end of the game. But as long as he remains, the deed can still be won back. Renue takes the next two hands, then loses several times to low stakes. Not his fault, there's cheating afoot. Mesmer or Wildcard. Renue must isolate and break Wildcard. Renue bluffs again and Mesmer folds. But Wildcard is a maniac, a feral bettor, and thus harder to read.

The next turn in, Renue receives three Jacks, and closes him for the day.

"Bullshit!" Wildcard sits back but is clearly shaken. "No one has such luck."

"What are you implying?" Melnor says.

Debeau chuckles deeply. "Not as clever as you thought, eh, *Card*?"

"At least my kind continues to evolve, you bloody barbarian."

"Temper, temper."

Melnor shakes his head slowly. "Calm down."

"*Cheat*." Wildcard sits back and sneers.

"How dare you, sir," Renue says, starting to rise. He has practiced such outrage.

"Compose yourself," Melnor urges. "Without order we fall."

"I *dare*," Wildcard says. "Check his hands for red."

Renue smirks. "This *is* a gentleman's game."

"Then I'll come back tomorrow and crush you." Wildcard eyes the deed. "I wanted that, *Newcomer*."

"Good riddance," Mesmer says, watching Renue.

There have been rumors of the dictator's growing impatience in the recent years, long bouts of silence followed by immediate, harsh actions. In the beginning of the regime, Mesmer appeared in the streets often, at smash ball games, parades, festivals. He traveled the country, the world. But in his closing years, the dictator has become more reserved and secretive. Whispers of these matters splinter polite conversation in the Manor, how Mesmer's doubles stand in for him constantly, how the man himself hasn't left the grounds for a decade or more.

"Renue," Mesmer says, his voice wax-thick. "The paper is, of course, only a trophy. Before you leave, bring it to an attendant and they will prepare a facsimile."

"Of course."

"You'll find Mesmer among the Slants still." Wildcard yawns. "His heart beats for filth."

Mesmer glares. "I'm done for tonight."

Renue watches Mesmer standing in the hallway, staring at the wall. He reaches out to touch something, then moves further down, out of Renue's view. Wildcard, Melnor, and Debeau file out slowly until Renue is alone at the table.

Long after the cigar smoke has settled, he exits the double velvet doors, pausing at the portrait of the young woman midway down. He studies her face. She is blond, with fair skin and a graceful, crane-like neck, somehow familiar. The image produces a thought, and suddenly he is propelled into memories of his boyhood again, always, into his oldest, deepest, most protected memory: a warm, smiling face, beaming from above his infant body rocking in a creaking wooden cradle. Impossible, he thinks, that it could be her. He turns away. He touches the coated tempera paint. He closes his eyes. A coincidence brought on by the stress of the disguise, he decides. Nothing more. Bardon would have told him had he suspected anything. He couldn't have kept it secret all these years. But what grand possibilities lie in the fallacy of memory? It's my mother, Renue thinks, running his hand over the frame. He can still hear her voice, feel her sweet breath on his eyelids. Staring at the portrait, he can remember her smell, a soft, sweet fragrance, honeysuckles. Renue always had a memory for faces, which is why he's so skilled at cards. He runs his fingers down her face. For all his life, Renue was assured both his parents were dead. Had she have been living here all along? He takes a final glance at the portrait, then continues down the hall. Quiet, tonight.

In his room, Renue packs up clothing, fills his suitcase with bills, leaves the coins. But he can't force the image out of his mind: her face, looking down on him, smiling, singing, honeysuckles. In the brittle silence, Renue pictures the sunken living room where he played Saturday mornings, his father's voice muted behind a door, arguing at his mother. Maybe she left him, Renue wonders. Maybe she's alive. After his mother vanished, Renue's father drank constantly, eyes red as a dog's. He can hear the clank of the glass bottle slamming on the kitchen table, an indentation the boy later would run his hand across just before he left the house that last time, trying to picture his father's fleeting movements. It comes slow as a faucet drip, earlier memories trickling in, his father feeble attempts at smiling, at hiding the loss. Where is Mother? the boy asks. They took her. Who took her? It doesn't matter. But. Leave it *alone*, Bren. Why? Let it be, boy. She's gone. Just gone. The hum of a car, backfiring, the sound of sloshing liquor. There used to be photographs but his father hid them all. What happened to them, Dad? It doesn't matter. You burned them. I don't want to see her face anymore. Why? Mesmer took her from us. I miss her. Forget her.

Later that night, Renue walks the lonely halls to stare at the portrait. A shadow is leaving the hallway, but Renue can't tell who it is. Someone else. Thinner, possibly feminine. Alone, he runs his hand over the paint. His mother. Though his mind tells him otherwise, he knows he cannot leave the Manor. Not until he discovers what secrets the house holds.

♥

"Where are you taking me?"

He recognizes her voice, the servant girl, the one who dealt for the opening game. Renue turns slowly and studies her. Beautiful, a graceful face, soft on the eyes. And he was so sure what the touch was before: the black thing, the nightmare that hunts those who murder and never stops, Mesmer's insatiable, invisible assassin. Now, instinctively, because instincts never leave, Renue reaches his arm around her slim shoulders, across her crane-like neck. His words are hardly a stutter.

"I don't know," he says, staring at the crowds in the streets and the vendors and multi-colored garments blurring in swirls and currents. He smells something earthy, a fungus, and then he's in a garden of Mesmer at night where there is no breeze. "It's the forest. I can't remember." Her green dress is torn and her hair, golden, curls just before reaching her shoulders. But her eyes are different than he remembered.

"They're coming for us."

There were contingency plans, though now he can't find them. He finds one word stuck to his tongue. *Thief.* His eyes are surveying the crowd to pick out the reds from the blacks, louts from the spades and secret police. But he knows what he is really searching for, the nightmare, the black thing. Its origin is unknown though its purpose blunt: maintain a city free of murder, deter the foreign powers from invasion, hunt down the Manor's enemies, and ensure that no one can ever depose Mesmer. The Blanks believe the black thing is an ancient god discovered in the Krylight swamps, but many louts whisper it was an assassin who tried to kill the dictator, transformed as a warning, a reminder. Renue spies a curious, bending shadow behind an old man, but when he looks down the street again, nothing still. He breathes in deeply, letting his nerves calm in the salty air. If it hasn't found them already, then the Damasker barrier might be working, he thinks. A voice within Renue cries. *Beware.* He hesitates, wrapping his hands in green cloth, memory corrupted by the purple leaves of the forest. Whom did he kill? Her hands, also wrapped.

"I tried to warn you on the balcony," she says. "Why didn't you listen? Say something—don't leave me again."

He remembers the dim echoes of his training and what Bardon taught him to do when one sense fails: follow another. Touch. Where is the wealth he won? Spilled in the wood, he remembers. It weighed us down. Without coins, they're defenseless. Her dress will attract attention. The girl from the balcony. His sister. She raises her eyebrows. She's shaking, her mouth half-open. Even

21

her tongue quivers. She's heard the stories. The black thing's already inside her. It just hasn't found the body. He tracks her line of sight to a table alight with jewelry, earrings, necklaces, pins shaped as stars. Something to calm her. Nodding, he casts a darting glance in all directions, vaguely aware of what she wants, a silver, heart-shaped locket on the corner of the jeweler's table. She thinks it will protect her.

Harping laughter. Renue focuses on the locket, drawn into himself at seven, his band of street kids deciding on targets to pickpocket, but quickly he assumes the confident mantel of Renue again, stepping down into a stench of bodies, overpowering aromas, clothing and voices swarming. He weaves fluidly through the crowd, focusing solely on the locket. But the louts know a secret, his secret, and their stares singe accusingly. He traded millions of lives for the memories of two. Renue pauses to examine himself. Something is missing. Where is the watch that left an imprint on his wrist? Where are the rings that have fled his slender fingers? The mind may forget but the body remembers.

He moves predatorily past a gabbing lout and in a split second leaps, grasping the silver locket with sleight of hand and tucking it in a crease of his shirt. A memory surfaces, that of a card held by her narrow fingers, quick, so slight he almost didn't see her tuck it from the deck, but then the din shatters his concentration. *Thief.* Why do they call him that? What has he stolen? He studies his hands again, imagining them beneath the cloth, charred black. He returns and pushes the necklace into her palm.

"It'll protect you," he says.

"It will?"

"Come on."

Nearby, two men are gabbing. One smells of the docks. The other has an Inverter's accent.

"Big reward."

"What'd he steal?"

"They won't say—just fled."

"He'll be down there."

"With us."

"Big reward."

"I'll get him first."

"Met too."

"We'll sniff him out."

"We'll snuff him candle out."

Renue shudders, feeling centipedes crawling on his back up his neck. Her fingers. He turns. She takes her hand from his neck and he lets out a faint scream, the crowd turning to watch: images, a green pentagonal table, dueling staircases, a hysterical peacock, Rady, riches, ember smiles, puffing cigars. Once, he could take those stares and twist them around and revel in them, but now his persona has shattered.

"I have something to tell you," he whispers. "Something important. But not here." More images flash in his mind, marble steps, hedges, the central fountain, the portrait of his mother, which pulls him strangely.

"Say he lost big."

"One bad hand."

"How will it end?"

"Don't you know?"

"As always."

Together. "In death."

♥

"It's a beautiful night, isn't it?"

Renue turns as the woman who dealt the first hand of the game steps out onto the balcony. A servant girl? The daughter of some hillborn? The cool air soothes his speculative heart. During each stroll down the long halls at night, Renue has heard his mother wailing. In each room he enters, he feels her presence. Yet in the past days, even with careful questions, he has come up with almost nothing material. Many mistresses in the Manor, countless paintings, all brimming with stories, mysteries of their own. Best not to ask about a tyrant's lovers, a young hillborn advised. Without a trace of his mother, Renue contemplates leaving later in the night.

"Gorgeous view."

"I love those lights," she says, pointing to Latchtown.

He's stalled enough. What is left to make him stay? Mere speculation, unsubstantiated theories about the fate of his parents: his mother, taken from him before his eyes opened, stolen perhaps as Mesmer's plaything. His mother, raped and killed by a spade. His father, part of the resistance. His father, died drunk in an alleyway, too cowardly to raise a boy alone. These thoughts enter Renue's mind and cloud his reason, but soon, a decision must be made. Stay and compromise the mission. Go, and forever lose the opportunity for knowledge of the past.

"So, who are you, Newcomer?"

"I'm no one," he says, tugging on his white gloves.

"And where is no one's home?"

"Nowhere." He grins. "And you?"

"Just a woman."

"Mesmer's?"

The breeze from the sea is carried by the wind. Dusk carries in the air like ice birds. She is young, perhaps twenty, and tall, red lipstick, black tie round her hair, emerald dress. "So you like the view?"

He nods. "Stunning."

"Have you been to the Slants?"

"I didn't have time to tour the city," Renue says. "Perhaps before I leave."

She straightens. "That's where my mother was from. The Slants. What about you?"

"Oh," he says disdainfully, though inside a strange thought occurs. She looks roughly six years younger than him. His father disappeared when he was six. Looking at Latchtown, Renue suddenly feels heavy and desperate. "The Slants, you say?" Keep it lighter, he reminds himself. Work out his suspicions later, when alone. He grins. "So I guess one could say that you're crooked."

"My mother was," she says. "But she died when I was little."

" . . . she worked here?"

"Yes."

"You're a servant, then."

"More a prisoner."

He braces against the balcony. "But you don't know really know your mother, do you? Just a ghost of her. A shade."

"Something like that."

Renue gazes at the city, oddly quiet except for the summer wind. Collecting stories and rumors as puzzle pieces, he forces a fit. Could his mother have given birth in the Manor? Is that what she's hinting at? Could she be his sister?

"How did she die?" he says. "If that's not too rude."

"Poorly. She wasted away."

"I'm sorry."

"Well, money can only buy so much," she says. "My father says he would have done anything to save her, except give her the one thing she wanted. All things have a price, I suppose."

"And yours?"

"Priceless." The lines of her face tighten, as though she's angry. "Most things wither when possessed. *That*, I know."

Renue stares out at the Slants, his home, those poor flickering lights. Her fingernail catches his hand as she turns away: the touch produces a memory, his mother, holding him up to see the Manor, clouds rolling over the mountains, buildings crowded around them. Of his father he has more years to sift through, a chiseled, honest face, his tree-brown eyes, a gravely voice. Once his father told night stories to put the boy to sleep. But in Renue's fraying recollection, his father's face almost always appears eternally dark and drawn. Now he sees a possible plot:

his father tried to save his stolen wife as well as their unborn child. And then the Slants, the mission, fade. There is only one man in the Manor who would know. The table is deadly tonight, Renue thinks. For Mesmer.

"If you think you'll get away with it, you're wrong," she says.

" . . . I'm sorry?"

"He'll never let you leave," she says in his ear. "You won't even remember me. I'm a ghost too. I know what you want, but you won't get it. You know the expression. The house always wins."

"What are you talking about?" He frowns. "There must be some misunderstanding."

"Perhaps. But I'd go now, tonight. Before it's too late." She leaves him on the balcony, staring out at Ashkareve.

♥

Renue's new mission: make Mesmer to bet his life, then force a confession. He enters the room. Four chairs are empty. Only the dictator sits across the table.

"Where is everyone?" Renue takes a seat.

"No one will play with you anymore," Mesmer says snidely. "Didn't you know that? They're all down in the city, celebrating." He shakes his head, tisking. "Deadly luck. Deadly. And here we are, the last day. Between you and me, I think your luck's run out."

"We'll see."

"So cocky," Mesmer says, scratching his chin. "You've done well, squirreled away quite the fortune, my advisors tell me. But only when one has nothing to lose does one bet wildly. I certainly did. Have you heard this story? They tell it in the Slants, now and again, I'm told."

"Ante."

"What's your game?"

"Straight."

"What stakes?"

Renue lays his gloved hands flat on the table. "All."

"All?" Mesmer's cold expression twists slightly. "Let's warm our palate with trifles first, shall we?"

They play furiously, back and forth, two players, alert, hands twitching, eyes unblinking, testing, teasing, smoking, listening. Mesmer's pot is almost taken, the chips piled and piled on Renue's side. Then the door opens and both turn as the woman from the balcony enters. Why is she here? Can it be a sign?

"I didn't call for you," Mesmer says. "Go away. I'm busy."

"Not tonight." She takes the cards and beginning to shuffle.

Cards fly across the table: Jack, nine, three, King, seven, four, Ace, five, hearts, clubs, spades, diamonds, gold, cards, hands, decks, runs, losses, straights, blanks, flushes. Renue lets Mesmer win a few hands so that he will grow overconfident. Now he understands a tyrant's true weakness. Pride. Always.

"Need your pet?" Mesmer says sharply.

"This old maid?" Renue says. "She can go as she pleases."

Renue can't help it but he seems unable to lose. A crawling doubt—Mesmer is wasting time, waiting for something.

"Ridiculous luck," Mesmer says, folding. "You could buy your own country with what you've won."

"I don't care about the money." Renue flicks a chip away. "Deal."

"A final game?"

"Of course."

The woman gathers the cards, shuffling.

"A new bet—blind."

"Blind?"

"Blind." Mesmer flicks his cigar, resting it on the table. The cigar has left a black ring, like worm rot.

"What do you want?"

"I want the deed back." He smiles. "I'm feeling sentimental."

"Why?"

"To remember. One last time before I leave."

"Where are you going?" Renue says.

"I haven't decided, actually. A trip." He lifts his chin up. "To see the gray world with fresh eyes. Lyle. Do you know that poet?"

"I'm afraid not."

"Never mind. The deed—what will you bet for it?"

"I want your life."

"My life? Oh my." Mesmer laughs, sitting back. "You have no idea. No, you don't want *my* life."

"One life for many—a fair trade."

"Death *would* give me a new perspective."

"Death is no perspective."

"Pestras says only the dead can tell true stories," Mesmer says. "You don't think so? Tell you what. Add your life to the ante and we'll continue. After all, I could take yours if I wanted."

Renue tries to read the woman's face, cold and expressionless as she deals. He studies his cards quickly, places them face down. Ace, King, Jack, Ten, diamond strong. Jack of spades. Almost a royal flush. "One."

"One?" Mesmer says with narrowed eyes. "Two."

The reinforcement cards are dealt. King, Jack, Ten, Ace, Ace. "Raise."

"A further bet?" he says. "What would you accept? You've already won so much tonight. No, no, don't say it. Don't say it, poised on the tip of your tongue. The opulence of words." He glances at the deed in the center. "The seat? That's what you want, yes?"

"The seat?"

"Yes. The country, I mean."

"That's not what I want." Renue says. "You must have a very good hand, though."

"What do you bet?"

"I have nothing more of interest beyond money."

"But you do. There is always more to give. Service, for example. Yes, service. *That*, or you must fold."

Renue takes in his cards slowly. King, Jack, Ten, Ace, Ace. Two aces will not beat the house. But under what conditions does a man bluff with his own life? he wonders. "Service?"

"I could use a man like you."

"If I fold, I die?"

"I believe so."

"Then I'm forced to play."

"That's the nature of a game with such stakes."

"No different then ruling a country," Renue says. "Like the lives you've so callously taken over the years."

Mesmer scoffs. "What would you know? What inkling would you have of the sacrifices one must make to rule? I could've had you killed weeks ago, when you first strode so arrogantly into my home. But I'm feeling charitable tonight. So if you fold, I'll cancel your debts. Just leave me the deed. Or, play, and we'll simply see what side lady luck chooses." Mesmer regards the table slowly. Under the sickly overhead light he looks like skin, bones. "I can't eat," he says. "Sleep. Food tastes as ash. My essence is stretched to the breaking point, Renue. All that once held me here is gone. Want to know my secret? I'm already long dead. So if you continue, it's a fair bet. If not, you can leave right now. Leave the Manor. I can summon a car to take you beyond the forest. Leave."

"They do say a true player always plays dead," Renue says. "A dead man can't give anything away."

"You believe that?"

"I'll continue."

Mesmer shakes his head. "Before we show, I must ask. Are you a gentlemen?"

"More than you."

The queen of diamonds is what Renue needs for the straight flush and he's confident he'll get it. She passes a card to him and adds it to the four. She hands Mesmer one.

"Call," Mesmer says. "Show."

Renue spreads the cards, ten, Jack, Queen, King, Ace. A double take, aware of the ice racing through his veins. Queen of *spades*. The death suit. Still a straight, he thinks. A confused expression spreads across Mesmer's face, his cards flipped. Three fours, two sevens.

"Full house, too bad." Mesmer leans forward. Underneath the dictator's confident smirk Renue finds a curious conflict, but before he can beg for his life, a puzzled expression appears on Mesmer's face. He opens his mouth, blood dripping out of the corners and dribbling onto the table, pooling, and the gleam of a dagger as it twists through his chest, poking between pink ribs. A glint of steel surfaces through Mesmer's chest as he sighs. His body crumples. Renue stares dumbly at the fallen man. The woman appears behind the great chair.

"What have you done?"

"Go," she says. "Now."

"Come with me."

Beware, a voice within him cries. The heart lies there.

I

Chapter One

C an you hear me?" she said. "They're all staring at us."
Prickly blond hair fell over Renue's face. He batted the strands away, shutting his eyes tightly. "Give me room," he said.

Multicolored clothes hung from crossing lines, five stories high, and metal green balconies rimmed the side walls. She crouched over him, a few feet into an alleyway. Beyond the buildings Renue could see a blurry, pale afternoon sky. His head hurt. He stood, legs buckling, then flattened against the wall and winced from a dull pain. Reaching to the small of his back, he felt the tatters of his shirt, then his forehead, a long gash. He brought his fingers to his eyes. Dried blood, flaking. A few hours old.

"Are you you again?"

He turned slowly to find a young woman staring down at him. She wore a dark green dress and her hair was shoulder-length and blond, with a slight widow's peak. Then he recognized her. Renue wondered if the Damasker's barrier would be strong enough to hide both of them from the black thing. At least it hadn't found them yet. She continued to watch him, hands pawing nervously down her hips. Could she really be his sister? If he left, she wouldn't survive a second, if she wandered down the wrong street, if she misspoke. And she had black hands. The barrier might protect him, he thought, but not her. Renue glanced over at a broken bottle on the floor. What would it matter, adding another layer of black? He could strangle her quietly, ease her body behind a dumpster and hide it in trash. Wrap his hands around that soft neck. Save her from the worse fate.

Renue looked back at the market piles of yellow and orange spices, then over at the figurines and rusted lamps, an antique stand. No cars. A pedestrian mall. He thought he saw Faldor's face in the crowd but when he blinked there was only a passing businessman tightening his tie. The woman was fingering the heart-shaped locket around her neck. He told her the locket would protect her, but she had to know it wouldn't.

"Where are we going?" she said.

"Somewhere safe." The sweat from her fingers reminded him of dragging her down the marble steps of the Manor and to the forest's edge, her resisting all the while. When he took off his gloves and showed her his hands she had tried to run and he let her go. His sister. That had been the hardest part, letting her go. But when her palms blackened there was no longer any choice and she chased after him and ran the rest of the way through the forest by her own volition.

"What's wrong?"

"Nothing," he said, sickness bubbling in his throat. The nausea meant that someone close by was using the Gift. Secret police. Boran's Black Hands, maybe. Or the thing itself. "Come on." He snatched her hand but she refused to budge. "We have to go."

"Where are you taking me?"

"Somewhere we can hide."

She backed away.

"Don't you understand what it will do to us?"

"It?"

"The black thing," Renue said. "You don't know? It's tracking us. In two ways: marked hands—murderers—and also bloodline. Only a matter of time before it finds us, if we don't move quick."

" . . . black thing?"

"Mesmer's best assassin—the laws? Never mind. Did you see any spades in the market?" She shook her head.

"Spades? Soldiers—police?"

"In the forest," she said. "Not since then. I couldn't wake you. You were mumbling, strange things."

"What?"

"I don't know. Your mother, a pattern. You knit, too?"

"No." They came to a crossroads in the alley and he took a left.

"You passed out once in the market," she said. "When I said I saw—"

"Don't say his name," he hissed, then softer. "*Never* say his name."

At the opening of the alley, the blinding afternoon sun was eclipsed by two drably dressed louts. Renue wiped his lips, taking a thin line of mucus on his finger, the color of gums. He scratched his bare wrist. "Fuck. Bardon's Watch. How long have I been out?"

"This time?" she said. "Just a few minutes."

"Did anyone see us?"

"You fell against the bricks and cut yourself," she said. "Someone asked you something, but the words were all jumbled. Like another language."

"Inverters. Did you say anything?"

"Drunk. That's all. He's drunk."

"Fine," he said, studying the hopelessness on her face. He felt it too. They were both marked and would spend the rest of their lives with the branded Damaskers, if the black thing didn't find them first. "Good." Seeing how afraid she was, he tried a smile. "Really good. Smart. We'll be fine. Don't worry."

She nodded weakly, glancing back at the louts.

"We're coming out on the other side of the market. Don't speak—if you have to, one word, two."

"Why?"

"They're always listening," he said. "I'm being careless right now."

"I don't understand."

"The Ears are listening. Spies. For our safety. Terrorists. Protection. It's all fear, like the thing. Keeps us in line. Watch what you say."

The louts stepped into the alleyway and Renue wondered whether they were Manor agents. He guided her away, their shoulders brushing against the narrow alley walls, the smell of urine pungent and memory-inducing. Wandering the streets. Somehow, it seemed less painful to remember things farther in the past.

The woman stepped through a hollowed melon rind and cursed, kicking it to the wall. As she bent down to remove a piece from her shoe he pulled her on. "Got to keep moving," he said. "Can't stop for anything."

Dulled building shadows fell over the approaching louts. Renue dragged her behind the next dumpster. The sound of bodies slamming against glass made him jump. To his right were two sliding glass doors and beyond them a couple holding wine glasses, whispering.

"Do you see that?" he said. "Do you?"

"No." She was watching him as though he were insane.

When he looked next he saw only bare red brick. An image from the garden, he remembered, just before he met Faldor. "Hallucinations are part of the forest. Are you having them too?"

"I saw . . . him. Back there. That's all. Mes—"

"Don't say that name." She tried to speak but he clamped his hand over her mouth and she struggled as he brought her to the wall. The louts were gone. He studied her torn dress and her hands, barely covered by strips of his dress shirt, a sliver of black on her palms visible. "Got to be quicker if we're going to survive, Lisande. That's your name now. Lisande. It's a long way where we're going. Now, you were saying. Lisande?" He closed his eyes. "I'm sorry," he said. "I didn't mean to frighten you.

But don't say his name—just the Manor. Ears might pick it up. They're looking for us."

She held up her hands. "They're like this forever?"

"Only until it finds you—sorry, sorry. Not us. It won't get us."

"I *killed* him, Renue."

"Don't worry. The man was a butcher. He had my parents murdered."

"He did?" She went quiet, hands to her chest.

The Damaskers had tried everything to overthrow Mesmer, but the one thing they could never do was assassinate him. Mesmer had linked himself to the Pattern; to take his life meant to release the black thing into Ashkareve forever. The final deterrent. Renue would have to tell her, but later, when she couldn't take her life so easily.

"Don't think about it," Renue said. "They say that's how it finds you, some say. Conscience, guilt."

As they approached the end of the alley, Faldor stood at its mouth, motionless. Renue pried her fingers from his hand and wiped his face, tasting sweat. A few spades ran in front of the image and the old man was gone. Only hundreds of busy shoppers. It was still difficult for him to discern what was real, what was manufactured. That was a symptom of Mesmer's forest that the Damasker's barrier was supposed to guard against. The twilight forest was older than even the black thing, the first of a long line of protections made with the Gift to safeguard the Manor against its enemies. With the twilight forest, the only information one left with was what the regime allowed. That was why the Damaskers had set upon stealing the deed. Hard copy. Unforgettable. Renue knew he had been told state secrets while in the Manor, though now even the simplest details eluded him. But Lisande had lived there, he thought. Maybe she knew something of value.

Across the street, a vendor in a smock sold metallic flowers with red petals, and in an instant the passing men and women became a forest of blue leaves and black trunks and Renue could see Lisande and himself running, chests on fire, freeing clouds of petals from tree limbs. He angled his back to the opening of the alley and searched the ground, pocketing a rusty wire. Above, the colored windows of the high market were filtering the light into reds and yellows. He picked up a shard of glass and Lisande flinched as he took it to her hair.

"Easy," he said. "Relax. I won't hurt you. Momentary disguises, that's all."

He brought the glass across her face and blond strands drifted to the ground like a shedding flower. Dirt was smudged under her eyes, now muddy from tears. He pushed her a few feet back into the alley near an open dumpster swarming with gnats and flies.

"Forever?" She flinched as he cut strips from her dress.

"Put these around your hands so the spades can't see. Around your palms." He brought the shard to his thigh, the blood pooling, dabbed the cloth and handed it to her. Then he tore another strip, two for her, two for him, and began to wrap his own hands. "Keep one on my ribs, hidden, like this, the other beneath my shirt, like you're injured or in love with me." He squeezed her hand. "Past the market, we'll come to the bell tower. Then east into the Slants. Hop, skip, jump. It's far, but we can make it. Deep breaths. Ready?" He tugged at her dress but she shook him off.

" . . . I *killed* him."

"I know," he said. "But there's no time." He pulled her dress again and heard it tear. "Lisande, I'll leave if I have to."

"You won't."

He held his forehead. "It was a bluff. But you've come this far. It's only a little further."

"But I *killed* him." She fingered her dress. "He was going to kill you."

"I know. Thank you," he said. "We'll figure the rest out later. I promise." Renue tried to locate himself. The alleyway where they had stopped was perhaps a mile from the bell tower, roughly the center of Ashkareve. If they could get past the tower undiscovered, he thought, they'd have a chance. "This way."

He waited for an opening in the crowd and pulled her out onto an expansive avenue, six lanes wide, brimming with pedestrians. It had to be Saturday. Goramon Avenue was always closed for the Saturday market. Lisande was lost in the sky. He followed her line of sight. Six gray sea cranes were flying south and swooped as a sharp breeze cut across the cobblestone. As he looked downhill, the city he had once known so intimately were now foreign and the buildings and concrete were faded and removed from reality, as though out of a watercolor. Two spades waited at the next street, blocking their path, and for a moment he almost regretted not leaving her in the alley. They would torture her or rape her. He scanned the crowd, searching for an escape route. Two additional spades appeared on the eastern side of the street, now pointing in their direction. A hundred bodies milled about between them. The spades shouted.

"I love you," he said.

She looked at him as though confused.

Then a great cry came from the Manor and a thousand necks cracked to glance up to the hills, then the restless resettling of vertebrae. For a moment pedestrians resumed their conversations but as a second cry came through the air there was an explosion from beyond the hills and the crowd fell silent. All at once the crowd became frenzied, their expressions twisted in fear.

"We're being attacked!"

"Run!"

To Renue's right, an old man collapsed, grabbing his chest, his elbow then stomped by the boot of a tall merchant. Two children were batted in the face by the leather purse of a heavy-set woman scrambling away and huffing. Some of the crowd dropped to their knees and began to plead for forgiveness, crying Mesmer over and over. The spades shouted for everyone to freeze and remain calm. Lisande's hand slipped from his. She reached for him as they were bumped apart. Then in one great push the crowd lurched and Renue and Lisande were almost trampled, he, knocked to the ground, trying to stand, her hand leading him up from the street. He edged them towards the sidewalk but they were pushed back towards the avenue center by a wild current of panicked men and women. Lisande cried out. Blood was dripping from her nose to her chin.

When the third cry reached the streets the crowd stopped, lost in heavy breathing and steady whispering. Shots had been fired and the spades were barking orders. Renue pulled Lisande close. He could smell her breath, stale sweetness, cake. Beyond the tree line a string of smoke billowed into the sky. Someone yelled again and the crowd took off, running downhill full speed. At the next intersection, spades were waiting, poised around a lamppost, ordering the crowd, but when the crowd showed no sign of stopping they fired blindly with outstretched rifles. Renue put his arm around Lisande and dragged her low to the ground. At the lamppost the crowd diverged into two groups and Lisande was thrown to the right and tripped over the body of a bloodied young man. Renue caught her dress, a long rip, and then picked her up, edging the two of them in front of a great stone of a woman with a large head. Jingling beads covered the grimacing woman and they took shelter on her downhill side as she slowly waddled, letting the violent river pass, occasionally clipped by a flailing limb. Renue spotted Faldor again, leaning against a bakery window. Lisande brushed his elbow and he felt a fleeting warmth and sense of purpose, seeing himself back in his room at the Manor, placing her face alongside the portrait of his mother, comparing the two. He took Lisande along the least resisting path of bodies and a minute later they finally broke free, spilling out onto the western sidewalk. The two ran as market stalls became boutiques and soon they were in a wealthier neighborhood of homes with marbles, the lawns crisp and finely cultivated. Stopping beneath the lush branches of a crescent tree, Renue caught his breath as Lisande hugged a limb. Her shirt was brown with blood.

"Are you alright?" he said.

"Don't let it get me."

"I won't." He could hear his mother in her voice. "Why did you really do it?" he said. "Why did you kill him?"

"What?"

"Why did you *kill* him, Lisande?" he said.

She was avoiding his eyes.

"You're hiding something—tell me. No more secrets."

"He was my father," she blurted.

Renue's face paled and he felt incredibly heavy "You're joking—don't lie to me."

"I tried to tell you. In the forest. You wouldn't listen."

"Alright, calm down." His skin itched. He needed to move. "The only thing that matters now is where we have to go." He put a hand to his forehead. "You're his daughter? You're sure."

"Yes."

"Fuck." He spit. "Fuck. Come on, come on. New clothes," he said. "Then the Damaskers. Take advantage of whatever that was. Come on, over here." Across the street was a house framed by two oak trees, shaded and quiet. He led her to a clump of nearby bushes. "Stay put."

"Can I come?"

"Hide. Wait until you hear my voice."

"You'll be back?"

"Don't think about anything. Clear your mind completely."

"Don't think?"

"About the murder," he said. "Just a theory—but the black thing doesn't see like we do. Only the marks and the essence. Part of the Pattern, the black laws—moral stricture. But no one really knows what it is. Some say it assumes the image of the person you've killed before it takes you. We don't really know." He wiped his face. "So many people disappear, it's hard to tell."

"You keep saying that," she said. "Disappear. Taken. What do you mean?"

"Don't you know *anything*?" he said. "The resistance. Against *him*." He lowered his voice. "It's fine. Fine, don't worry. I'm here. An education, that's all. Like at school. When I was a kid, maybe six, my father's best friend was taken—a man named Heron. A doctor." Renue snapped his fingers and she flinched. "Just like that, spades took him."

"I don't understand."

"He made a joke, Lisande," Renue said. "About the war failing and . . . Mesmer being impotent. Maybe it was Boran. I don't remember. But Heron was lucky if they just slit his throat. The Black Hands, they'll boil you, torture you, those long hooked knives, chemicals, poisons. Or the Manor will send you to the mines to work and the tumors will grow in your body like fat white larvae. For a few words. That's what it's like down here. You have to understand."

"Say you're joking."

"Sorry. And for God's sake, don't tell *anyone* who you *think* your father is." Renue picked his teeth. "You don't know any of this, do you? How is that even possible?" He found a street sign, nearly obscured by a crescent tree. Hendrin Street.

"I've never been to the city," she said. "He took your parents."

"We'll talk later," Renue said. "I'll be back. Think about anything else."

He left her and ran down the street half a block, then up three stairs, quickly picking the lock with the wire. Gently, he eased the door open. From the quality of the dining table, he expected to find clothes that wouldn't attract too much attention. Besides, hillborns could mostly go where they pleased, only not

Latchtown or the Blanks. Not that they would. Occasionally, a few teenagers would venture down to the Slants to buy curiosities or for the violent, wild tunes of dockie bands like the Lost Pines. Sometimes, they snuck at night to purchase cheaper drugs, mindbenders and hallucinogens like salva, pop, tryst, or bliss. But it was easy to get turned around in the side streets and dead ends of the aptly named Slants. Once in a while you'd find some smooth-handed youth twitching in a puddle at the edge of an alleyway, stripped of wallet, rings, anything of value. In another time, another city, the youth would have had his throat slit. But not in Ashkareve, not in the city without murder.

At the foot of the stairs Renue crouched, listening to the silent second floor. He climbed slowly, low to the ground. At the top he glanced down the hall and put his ear to the closest door. He opened it, finding a child's room, full of bright colored book piles, toys and stuffed animals. A strange animal, lizard-like, swam in a tank of light green water. Closing the door carefully, Renue skipped the next two rooms and headed for the end of the hall, the master bedroom. Against the far wall was a modest mattress covered in a light orange bedspread. Beside the bed lay a dresser, on which he found a hand mirror with a gnarled wooden grip, a hardcover diary, and a brooch. He picked up a small wooden carving of a ghostly boatman, hands stretching the entire length of the craft. In the top dresser drawer were earrings and necklaces, most false silvers which would rub off on the skin. One necklace with a pale blue stone attracted his eye, but would be just his luck for a pair of louts to mug him for fake jewelry, and all the more likely considering how Lisande carried herself. He rifled through the rest of the drawers, pulling out lemon-colored stretchers, ladies' pants, and hung them over his shoulder. He headed for the closet.

For a moment he couldn't find the light and he was back in the shadows of the garden of Mesmer amongst the rustling trees. Wind slammed against the house. At the end of summer, there

43

were usually clouds in the afternoons and violent winds. The currents were shifting the great clock of the world, as Bardon often said. Even in the middle of summer the sun hid early behind the tall western hills and mountains, and in an hour or so, Renue thought, dusk would come, then dark. Night was when the Hands made most people disappear. In the morning they tossed out the remains. When Renue was fifteen, he found an Inverter in the south fish market whose eyes had been scooped out and stuffed with paper. The man wasn't a Damasker, so Renue couldn't do much more than guide him to a hospital, and even that was risky, as everyone else in the city could be an informant, whether they knew it or not. Turn someone in and you'd get a reward. Say the wrong thing and you unwittingly served the Manor. That was how Mesmer broke you down. Made you suspect everyone, made you watch your words until you couldn't trust even your own thoughts.

Snatching two shirts, pants, a brown backpack, and a pair of shoes, Renue ducked into the bathroom. He took a bottle of hair dye from the medicine cabinet, some bandages, scissors. Then he returned to the closet to make sure he hadn't missed anything.

"Are you father's friend?" Standing in the hallway was a boy of no more than six, holding a cream-colored sheet.

"Yes," Renue said. "I work for your father."

"Oh." The boy scratched his head. "Say, why do you have mother's panties on your shoulder? You don't wear girl clothes, do you, mister?"

"I'm a tailor. Your father asked me to mend some dresses for your mother, for the ball next week. Have you ever been to a ball?"

"No."

"Well, let me tell you, a ball is . . . no fun. You'll have a better time here."

"Mother was supposed to be home by now."

"She'll be home soon, which is why I have to leave," Renue

said. "You should go to your room, I'll bet you've got some toys that you haven't played with for some time."

"Will you stay until they come back?"

"I can't. But you'll be fine."

"I got scared," the boy said. "She said I'm safe though if I wear this." The boy held up a necklace of a howling wolf. "It's special. I got it last year." He pouted. "I wanted a Slippo guy."

Renue reached for the necklace. It wasn't infused with the Gift. Sometimes, rogue Damaskers or charlatans sold false amulets and other protections to anyone desperate enough to pay. They bled families dry when a father or a son came home with black hands, similar to the way lawyers in other more civilized countries chased ambulances. The worst profiteers sold potions in Latchtown, potions they claimed would hide one from the black thing. Most of the Latchies were too ignorant to know better.

He studied the necklace again. "Yes, I imagine this would. Listen, I want you to stay inside tonight. Your parents might be home late." The lines of the boy's face tightened. "Can you be brave, now? Like Slippo?"

"Yes."

"Good," Renue said, patting the boy's head. "It's getting late, be good. Don't tell your mother I was here—a surprise."

"He came home stinking and she yelled last night." The boy stuck his lip out and bit down on his gum. "I get more guys when they fight."

Renue chuckled. "Sure do," he said, remembering a line from the poet Lyle, who had written about the Mesmer regime in its early years, each poem a small rebellion. *A reason to stay, our children, always/New eyes with which to see the grave gray world.* But like most who stood against the regime, Lyle eventually vanished.

Down the stairs, Renue stepped into a memory of a living room lit with the orange glow of a fire, Bardon holding up a piping cup of herbed *matsa*, Renue, only eleven, barefoot, enjoying the sting of cold stone, taking the cup, warmth in his hand. The sky had been mottled, close to snow. In the street, he looked back at the house a final time as the boy waved from the door, holding the cream-colored sheet.

♥

"Remember his weaknesses and all you have learned, and that the Game is all the time, not just at the green table," comes the droning voice of Alkor. "—are you even *listening*?"

"Yes," Renue says. He watches the old Damasker pace back and forth in the center, in between the two rows of stone steps. Here, a year ago, a council selected from five the one who would become Renue, debating the strengths and weaknesses of each candidate. In the end, Renue's greatest strength was also his most blatant weakness, the early death of both his parents, the end of his family tree. Now, the night before the mission, he feels the specter of uncertainty and the gravity of his past accumulating.

"Three weeks will be all that you have," Alkor says, cutting hidden shapes in the air with his gestures. "The more time you are there, the more you will see, the more invaluable you will become, the more . . . "

"Vulnerable I will become."

"Yes!" Alkor says. "Everyone in the Manor is your enemy. Complicity is as murderous as the act itself, and therefore they are all merciless killers. Dead with power, drunk on death—no— wait a minute, dead with death, drunk on power. Such dialectical sayings are not my forte, my speech a plant in darkness, withered and searching." Alkor pauses. "I hope I've made myself clear."

"Always." Renue tries to hide a half-smile.

"Size them up, play them off each other. Abandon the truth

and remember the official history you've studied. Mesmer saved us from chaos, from the bloodshed of Faldor's era. Mesmer is a hero, a god. Yes, my hands, shaking, but I am no actor as you are, as you must be Renue from the eyes to the intestine. But what a fiction, what a masterpiece! Remember, you must despise us openly. Acting at its finest is true transformation, so use your knowledge, your fear, your rage. For god's sake, use your *looks*. Yes, yes, it does not bother me to say that many of the women in the Manor will find you desirable."

Alkor's cheeks are striped with deep rivulets of scars. The head of the Damaskers is a man who has hid in the shadows for twenty-two years, once of the first marked to survive. Some within the resistance have begun to question whether he is still fit to lead, but without the man pacing in front of Renue, there would be no resistance. He was not the first to stand against Mesmer, but he has stood the longest.

"Once we have the deed we can unravel the Pattern," Renue says, remembering the rush of pride he felt the day he was inducted into the resistance, that pure, childlike excitement in discovering a real myth, a movement to topple Mesmer's regime. "The deed is the key of all of Mesmer's black laws. With it, we can win this war."

"Yes. Now, take a deep breath. Consider these three years of your life. Seize the moment's perspective. This is the thick of time, and the mission will make yours a story fat with meaning, so that once day your name will leap from the pages of history and cry out, I mattered! But be cautious. One week in the Manor and you will start to lose your mettle. Who could blame you? I could. I would! There have been many lives wrapped up in your training, lives lost, lives surrendered so that you might survive for this day. There can be no lapses. You are part of a voice that over the years has wavered and fallen into slightness and become lost among the street noise and the daily grind of the city. If ever the time comes when we shrug at disappearance, then strangle me with your own bare hands. This cursed room of light is merely a simulation, a poor metaphor, a reminder of what we have lost. But, to be there when the sun breaks the clouds again. I am not a fictioner, so such are the blunted clichés I wield. Consider, now, briefly, that this brave dream of ours carries a responsibility. For how long can we fight before the spirit which is essential to us has finally been stolen?"

"One day is too long. One hour."

Alkor's face becomes somber as shadows fill the creases of his scarred face. He lights two candles and then turns off the ceiling lamp. The room glows orange. "You are the best that we have. The perfect weapon. No family to burden you, as blood can hinder moral action." The old Damasker holds a hand up to his face. "*Never* forget. They will take everything, but not the brave dream. Kill if you have to, kill if you must." He takes a seat next to Renue and pats him on the back. "One day, perhaps, I will take down that butcher myself. But first, the deed. With the deed we will glean the Pattern. We can better route his Eyes and Ears. We can gain ground inch by inch, one day, up the forest, storm the Manor itself."

"Perhaps it is time to let our best hope rest, Alkor," Bardon says, appearing in the doorway. "Don't you think he's heard enough?"

"Not his fault, old man," Renue says. "I can't sleep."

"I never thought I'd say this, but you've studied enough. How about a walk?"

Renue stands eagerly.

"Do not *leave*—there, there is more to discuss!" Alkor clears his throat. "Spades could take him. The Hands. Some dumb lout might smash a bottle on his head, drunk on Amber. He . . . ."

"Your contempt for louts is comical," Renue says, "considering I am one."

"But you are *more*. The culmination of a movement. You

know I have the gravest respect for any who fight the tyrant—lout or hillborn."

Renue wipes his eyes. "Or Blank?"

Alkor scowls. "You've grown cocky."

"It's just Renue speaking. A transformation, as you hoped."

Bardon opens the door. "We'll be fine."

"Very well, but better to not become the snake who steals out of the chicken coop only to discover that with the egg he is stuck in the wire."

"What does that even mean?" Renue grins.

Bardon shrugs.

Alkor places his hand on Renue's shoulder. "I won't be there to see you off tomorrow. Most likely I'll be vomiting. "

As the two embrace, Renue feels the first moment of truly sinking into the character of Renue, a terrifying lack of emotion. "See you soon, Riverface."

"Good luck, my boy."

In the opening of summer the air is humid and moves in waves, a skeletal mist which coats the sails of ships and obscures the boardwalk. Louts sit, legs dangling, enjoying brews, smoking, big puffs disappearing into the air. Greater ship's masts breach the fog, caught in moonlight. To Renue, this is an illustration of the most profound oppression, when amid murder and disappearance and the Manor's daily errands of brutality, the louts are still able to enjoy themselves. He gazes past the hills to the Manor, silent, watching

"Nice night."

"It is."

A few fishermen cast off the pier into a black sea as Renue drifts into a tangle of memories, hiding in shadows, hard bread, streets and cruelty and coldness. In the docks, he is reminded of the residual loss of home.

"Do you think they'd be proud?"

"Of course," Bardon says. "Is that why you volunteered? I

thought it was because of that girl. Still time to be a farmer, Bren, or a musician. You could always go to the university, study chemistry, perhaps."

"Chemistry?" The sinking feeling grows and Renue imagines breaking the boards of the dock and falling into water. "Chemistry?"

"Well, I've noticed you don't really go on dates anymore. Twenty-six, aren't you? Chemists cherish solitary lives, I'm told."

"Trying to distract me?"

"Always."

At the end of the dock the two men stop, staring out into the passive waters, the gentle lap of the tide, sea gulls gliding nearby. Four months and the ice birds will return to peck the eddies and sip up froth and frost, calling for winter. As a teenager, Renue spent much of his free time watching birds coast over the water to dip their talons at the crests. Something about the joy of constant movement. Something about the inherent loneliness of flight.

"Are you afraid?" Bardon says.

"Who isn't?" The louts on the boardwalk clink glasses, drunk and salty. "I envy them sometimes," Renue says. "Don't you?"

Bardon dangles his feet on the edge of the dock. "After this is over, I want you to take some time off. To travel."

"But I've seen it all," Renue says sarcastically. "In Stelline, bartenders pour warm liquors down ice slabs. In the desert of Wasla, coals are buried beneath the sands to keep the sleeper warm as the icy dew settles. I've already seen the world."

"There's a difference between real life and fiction."

"Is there?"

"I believe so."

"Alkor says—"

"Alkor is not who he once was." Bardon rubs his eyes. "And I overheard him telling you again. Don't kill unless you are forced to."

"He would know better than you." On the boardwalk, a few boys are kicking a bottle back and forth. From a nearby boat a man yells. The boys boot the bottle into the water, then scatter. "Do you remember the time you asked me to get groceries and I stole them?"

"You were young. It was an accident."

"No, it wasn't," Renue says. "I was always an actor. I just never knew espionage would be my stage."

"Well, you were very convincing. You even cried, I recall."

"Did I?"

Bardon turns to face Renue. "I need to tell you something before you leave. I debated whether or not to, but at the end of the summer, Dora, Granges, and I will ask Alkor to step down."

"I understand," Renue says. "I should have asked Granges to come out tonight."

"There'll be time for everything when you get back."

♥

His body was wiry and compact, not muscular like the soldiers she was used to in the Manor. The back of his blue dress shirt was stained with blood. She watched him sprint behind a clump of bushes full of pink flowers, wondering whether he was leaving her.

Lisande climbed further into the bushes, brambles poking and scratching her arms. At least the brambles felt real. She tried to imagine the thousands of faces they had passed, the smells of the alleyway, sparkling jewelry, anything other than the murder, but as soon as earlier memories seeped in she felt sick, not illness-sick, but queasy. She could hear him shouting to her as they descended through the forest, black trunks peeling bark like skin, blue leaves blurring her senses. Five minutes in the woods and she had forgotten the soft sheets of her bed, and with each brush of the nocturnal leaves she lost something else, a memory of her mother looking up from her rocking chair, needles in hand, her father's mysterious smile when unveiling a birthday cake shaped like mountains, peppermint bushes and misty frosting, Faldor clomping through the high snow piles behind the Manor. As she and Renue ran through the forest, hand in hand, she wanted to let go and collapse, so painful was the feeling of memories ruthlessly plucked from her brain, until half-way down the hill she couldn't have said who he was, what she had done, why they were running at all. Renue had moved like a man possessed. As she fled, she saw the back of her father's coat, a puncture mark through velvet, a dark substance that seemed too thin to be blood and too dark to be earthly, and then that curl on his lips as he fell and the spark dulled in his eyes. She had fought against the feeling and held her chest tightly, convinced her heart would bolt away if she let go.

Lisande crawled further into the bushes, her palms pressing against dirt, shoulders rubbing between the myriad of interwoven branches. Vines with small white flowers threaded through the bush, smelling of honey. Finally she reached a wall dotted with ferns and rested, back against the cool stone. She could no longer hear the sounds of the market or the main street, only gunfire and the scream. From her window in the Manor, Ashkareve was always expansive but insignificant against the backdrop of an infinitely stretching ocean, only illusorily contained by sharp amber hills and Little Wolf Peak in the west, and the more jagged Wolf Mountain to the east. Her breathing was slowing. She sniffed, smelling blood, and wiped her nose. She spit onto her torn dress, she rubbed her face. She felt her legs. They were prickly. She needed to shave. She almost laughed at the thought, but then went quiet as she saw her father through the bushes, walking the empty street. Swallowing against a parched throat, she tried to calm down, heartbeat loud in her ears. She wanted to call out to him, but the image vanished in a sunbeam sneaking through the tree ceiling. She unclasped the necklace and dropped it in the dirt. Her hands were shaking, as though they belonged to someone else.

Lisande closed her eyes and tried to imagine the ocean she had gazed longingly at on warm summer nights, when she was little and her mother was alive, the two of them on the balcony, stretching their hands toward the city. After her mother died, she would often feign sleep until after the Manor lights were out, lift the window latch and listen for her mother's voice in the ocean. Sometimes, if she tried hard enough, she could still see her mother, leaning again out over the balcony, telling her about sea birds and ocean currents. Lisande heard a voice yelling and opened her eyes. When she tried to remember her mother next, she saw only a gravestone.

"Lisande? Lisande?"

At first she did not recognize the man peering at her through the wall of leaves. Her chest rose in short, stabbing breaths. She watched as he got on his hands and knees and crawled toward her through the sticking bushes.

"Lisande."

He leaned towards her and she lunged at him with a broken stick. "Stay back," she said.

"Easy." He reached for her shoulder gently. "It's just the hallucinations—it's me. We have to go." He brought up a necklace from the dirt but she wouldn't take it. Then he opened her fist and pressed it in her hand, a silver drop hanging over a black pit. "It'll be okay," he said. "A nightmare, that's all."

"It's you."

Renue took the locket, undid the clasp and put the chain around her neck and fastened it. He brought the heart up to her eyes. "This will protect you," he said. "I promise."

"No, it won't. You were lying."

He took the clothes he had stolen out of the bag. "Put these on quickly."

"Turn around."

"Okay."

After a few moments she handed him her stained clothes. "The only thing left from the Manor is my panties," she said.

"There's probably more, I think."

"It was a joke."

"Oh."

Together, they crawled out from the bushes. It was dusk by the time they reached the market but there were no bodies in the streets. She hoped the entire riot had been just another hallucination. But she could still hear the voices. Renue led her across the sloping, twisting street. Stepping over a child-size pink sandal, Lisande covered her mouth with her shoulder. Her hands were slimy. They continued across the expansive avenue and then southwards towards a rising bell tower. At the tower knelt three women with their hands folded, murmuring prayers as the bells sounded. The ringing hurt Lisande's chest. The sun was now behind the hills, casting the city lamps and stones in a reddish, purple shadow. Nothing seemed real to her. She kept her hands tucked closely to Renue's side, feeling his heartbeat, a controlled, slow rhythm. Hers was wild. The bell struck again as they headed east. In the distance she could see strange tilted buildings, but as she stopped to watch, Renue pulled her sharply to the edge of the street, across a line of shops with darkening windows, strange forms and shadows moving inside.

"I feel nauseous," she said, pressing her stomach with her elbow.

He embraced her as a group of soldiers trotted south along the sidewalk, followed by a black van. After they were gone Renue pulled her down to the end of a side street where they squeezed between two old stone buildings. He was walking more confidently now, she noticed. It was difficult for her to believe he was a lout at all, at least not the way she had heard them described by guests. Briefly, she wondered whether this was all a ruse to kidnap her, something her father had often warned could happen if she left the grounds. Maybe Renue had enchanted her. Maybe her father was still alive. She considered turning herself in, but how could she explain her hands?

Lisande's shoulder rubbed against a rough wall and they came out into a thicket of buildings. When she looked up at the sky it was dark. Streetlights were beaming. Renue turned to say something but his eyes were glassy.

"What?" she said. White light swept across the darkening buildings, illuminating windows tacked with restaurants menus and posters of jewelry sales. "What's the matter?"

She tried to hold him up but his body was heavy so she eased him to the ground. A piercing scream came from over the wall of buildings, then again, and she struggled, grabbing his shirt, and pulled him towards the closest building. Ten feet and her arms were already sore. She could hear his teeth clicking together. The buildings across the street went dark and there was only a lone street light at the center of the thicket to guide her. She dragged him towards the closest door and pounded but no one answered. The scream came again, closer, just on the main row of shops they had passed. Her hands felt raw, like she was grabbing sand. The sky was turbid. The scream came again and she propped him against the door, turning the knob with one hand, and they fell through a matt of cobwebs. She kicked the door closed and latched it shut. The room was empty. Panting, she collapsed on top of him. The last thing she remembered was a scraping against the door.

Chapter Two

Renue shuts the hallway door and mutes the hum of guests inside, the shrill peacock laughter of warm-voiced northerners, the guttural drones of stiff-throated southerners. He steps into a length of shadow on the corner of a veranda, nervously fingering two small vials. Old Faldor, the once ruler of Ashkareve, has appeared for the Great Game almost as infrequently as Mesmer. An overdue meeting is about to take place, in the garden of the Manor where the old man walks nightly.

In the past weeks, Renue's wild tales have captivated audiences and won allies, yet he senses a deep change welling within as his manufactured memories squeeze out those from his childhood. Renue, the character, has seen the world: a bar called The Steadies in the Trolish city of Stelline where warm liquors are poured down ice slabs to youthful mouths; the desert of Wasla, where coals are buried beneath the sands to keep the sleeper warm as the icy dew settles. To Renue, storytelling is merely a tool to elicit certain responses, excitement, fear, wonder, bewilderment, loyalty, but each fiction he weaves contain slivers of his own life, just small enough to ring true without arousing suspicion.

Renue has learned the rhythms of violence and the culture of excess, how opulence leaves hillborns unstable and vulnerable. Once, he thought that such lows could be found only in the Slants, in honest poverty, but the countess sleeps with four men a night to hide her weakening estate. She dreams of suicide often, and has shown Renue her collection of pills and poisons. In fact, he has stolen the most dangerous vial from her tonight.

In a city without murder, poison becomes an art form. The scientists of Mesmer's regime have designed concoctions that mute voices, shrivel skin, induce coma, blind, deafen, cripple the mind, seize the body, and send one into a state of endless nightmare. And hillborns are born, live, and die in this culture of poison. Such are the risks many take for a chance to sit at Mesmer's table, where all is bet, won, and lost, risks Renue now considers as he threads a needle and dips it into the vial, then replaces the cork.

Drunken giggling comes from nearby, a couple. He peers through the window to the long hall as two young hillborns bang into the glass door and Renue almost drops the vial, barely palming it in time.

"Shh, he'll, he'll . . . " the woman says, slurring. "Let's go to the room."

"Stupid bitch."

"He's sick. Can't hear."

"Shut up. Come on."

They push off the glass and disappear, leaving a pair of fading handprints.

The truly careless guests, those who have no hope of ascending the ranks or are simply too drugged or drunk to contain themselves, gossip about how Mesmer has not set foot outside the Manor for years, how he increasingly relies on his doubles, how, through his arrogant mistakes, the country is failing and will never recover from its forfeited war. Even rich in Krylight, the economy crumbles. A new campaign must be on the horizon, so the rumors go. Qarash has nowhere else to turn but war. Mesmer cut out the intellectuals, the scientists, the Damaskers, the Drailers, the engineers. He surrounded himself only with loyal men, the fuel of abusive power. Inevitably, late at night, these guests whisper of the black thing, the lone deterrent for a country begging to be conquered and plundered.

Time stretches as Renue's fictions grow, as the distance between his past self and the character of Renue widens, engulfed by deceit, by constant and consuming acting, with the sharing of succulent fowls and slow-cooked steak, cherry pastries, rosemary bread, ancient wines, new potatoes. He feels sick with guilt from the sheer joy he receives when sampling the finest foods, cuisine which his mind has stopped fighting, meals that no longer taste of cinders. The charade must end quickly.

Renue readies the poison, then slips the vial back in his pocket. As he leaves the corner shadow, someone else passes by the door. Renue feigns vomiting and spits on the ground. He closes his eyes. Careless. He hasn't slept much in the past few days and his concentration is thinning. Footsteps. The hall is empty again. He wraps the thread around his index finger, needle barely poking beyond his fingernail. Then he steps out into the garden.

Where has the old man gone? Faldor is the most exposed seat at Mesmer's table, and Renue has poisoned Faldor drop by drop the last two weeks, just enough for the old man to grow sick and bow out. But the once-ruler of Ashkareve is more resilient than Renue originally assumed, and there is no more time for subtlety. The vial Renue stole from the countess tonight contains *vespas*, an augmented poison of the viper fish that paralyzes the muscles and eats away the mind, yet extends and preserves life: the nightmare poison, it's sometimes called. Renue has dreaded the act of murder since the day he was selected for the mission, even though the Damasker's historical account of Faldor's final days in power is not kind. When Mesmer and his ilk challenged Faldor's power thirty years ago, he made a deal and immediately backed down. Faldor failed his country, valued only his own miserable life, ordered soldiers still loyal to lay down their weapons. In such a manner, Mesmer's regime was engineered to appear legitimate, when it was simple, pure theft. Soon after Faldor stepped down, the butchers went to work. Faldor did not take Renue's mother or father with his own hands, but he still bears responsibility for their death. But there are worse things than death, Renue thinks.

Vespas, for one.

The voices come again, reverberations of that night before the Manor.

Do what you have to do to win the deed.

No murder if it can be helped. To kill is to become someone else.

Pah, useless sentiment, Bardon. There is no life without death, no death without life, and no Gift without both. It is a natural thing, death.

To die, yes, Alkor. To kill, I don't agree.

One death for a country's life is not so grave.

Murder unravels even the strongest.

One would think you supported the black laws. But what would you know? You didn't fight in the old war. A dose of nightmare for the coward. Faldor traded a million lives for his own. He deserves no less.

Debeau, if you have to. He's the one who truly haunts my dreams. Debeau or Wildcard. Find out what you can about Faldor as well. For Mesmer to keep him alive, he must hold something valuable indeed.

Night and the garden is in bloom, a jungle hidden within the great walls of the Manor. In his training, Renue was given a rough layout of the grounds, barely a contour, the long halls, the parapets, the basements where prisoners hang in darkness like bats and are conditioned to become Ears and slip back into the city. Blanks are the exception to the rule, preferring suicide to strings and cables, and they are rarely captured.

Poised at the edge of the garden, anger and self-doubt eat away at Renue until Bardon's final words give Renue confidence. Sometimes the memory of a loved one is all the strength that remains.

Once you enter the Manor you must become someone else. The character we have crafted is essential, so do not let them glean, even for a second, your true identity. The only way to do this is to hide yourself. Embrace Renue. Cocky, arrogant, clever, unfeeling. All of the things you are not. But those are the attributes men of power will respect. Do you know how many I've trained? And no one has succeeded. Why? Pestras says the loss of self is death. But if we're successful, you will have given the people back something that will never be taken again. That, I promise. Like a son to me.

The dirt path disappears behind a line of thick bushes. There is no maze of clipped hedges, no finely cultivated grasses. Unlike Mesmer's rule, the garden is not ordered but mysterious and wild. Trees of purple bulbs sway gently from stretching, twisting limbs, and the sudden peace Renue experiences makes him recoil, though the softened wind cools his neck as he watches the tall, dark-green leaves dance, almost black. Midnight trees. Renue remembers their name, seeing his fingers some months ago pause on a page of resistance history.

He smells *vespas* on the tip of the needle. When poisoned, a man can live a decade before death, enough time to deceive even the black thing. The basement poison, it's also nicknamed, because a victim is often stored deep below to dampen his cries, if the tongue is not cut out. Renue sniffs the *vespas* again, a sweet, tangy odor for a slow, bitter death. For years, he was confined to mildewed cellars, thumbing through the history of the resistance, each chapter a different face of Mesmer's regime, mere pages a movement, a paragraph, even a sentence, the summation of a life: a lout who reached the forest, an Inverter who charmed a hillborn, a latchie who crashed through the Manor gates in time to see the gatekeepers. But most lives are a single word, if not blunt punctuation. Period. The end. It's rare if one's life can mean something to future generations. Renue also knows that the possessed cannot last much longer. Something irretrievable dies in a person after so many years of captivity.

He passes beneath the midnight trees, plucking a purple bulb and squeezing it with his fingers, juices oozing. Spring fruits crush beneath his heels. From somewhere behind the bushes comes a hacking cough. *He walks the garden alone, a man trapped within the shell of his past,* whispered the countess earlier in the night, her olive-skinned body pressed against Renue's. He shivers. Her skin was colder than her voice promised. The countess is from Grenore, Debeau's city, the Hard City, frozen in the South. Debeau, a name often found within the mere paragraphs that are lives.

Ahead, green glowing lanterns hang from tree limbs. Krylight, hidden deep within the earth, was first brought to life by the Madsas, the people of the swamp. Krylight, on which many things already run, mysterious, dangerous energy. *Glow,* some call it. Volatile, but brimming with potential, like Renue's position in the Manor. He winces, feeling the penknife strapped to his thigh dig in. How many nights did he stand opposite the doors of Debeau's room? How many nights, out of the view of the grand hallway window, watching through the glass and curtains, did he wait for a moment to take Wildcard? Two men whose lives he would rather end tonight. But each time an opportunity to kill the cocky young Poten presented itself, random fate would swallow up the chance, so inconceivable and timely that it could not be coincidence. It is no secret that Debeau and Wildcard both want to succeed Mesmer, but Wildcard is the more dangerous, as he is still bathed in youth, with many years left to achieve his vision.

Renue spots Faldor standing beneath the midnight trees, their long-armed branches stretching to the ground like waking sleepers. The old man walks into a shadow. It is a tainted, tortured life that is to be taken, Renue tells himself, readying the needle between his fingers. Faldor is the unfortunate, rotting link. Merciful. A mosquito lands on his arm. He swats it with his left hand, bloodless.

"Who's there?" comes a gentle voice.

"Me."

"Me is not a name I know—unless I'm talking to myself, as old men are wont to do."

Renue follows the voice's trail, ducking beneath a limb, feeling the silky leaves brush through his hair. Faldor has paused beneath a swinging lantern, the promontories of his once stone-chiseled features illuminated, his edged cheeks, his time-folded forehead, his sharp nose, spring green in the Krylight, as is the shoulder-length gray hair which bounces with each step. Faldor's grayish eyes peek from withered skin. Renue has seen a more youthful Faldor from paintings and prints. Once stocky, the old man is now gaunt, almost emaciated.

"A friend," Renue says, aware of the coldness instinctively hiding the welling emotion in his voice. He's been trained too well.

"Ah, the Newcomer. Come to join me for a walk?"

"Yes," Renue says. "For a conversation, yes."

Faldor steps out from underneath a lamp, darkness spreading across his face. The night sky is clouded. "Anything to dispel the shadows."

"Something troubling you?"

The old man holds his hand in the air as though toasting. "When you're as old as I am, may your dreams remain untroubled." He frowns. "Your gloves?"

"I wasn't sure what they were for." Renue extends his hand and Faldor shakes it softly. "Damn mosquitoes." As Renue bends down to swat one, he slaps the old man's exposed leg with the needle. "Got it."

"Thanks. I can't reach my toes anymore." Faldor rubs the back of his leg. "My body's stiffening by the second. Take some advice, my young friend. Never grow old."

"That could be difficult. But those who love deeply never grow old," Renue quotes. "They may die of old age, but they still die young."

"Pestras," Faldor says. "I studied him when I was your age. A brilliant philosopher."

How long will the poison take? Renue wonders. It will no

doubt spread more quickly if Faldor walks. Renue slides the needle in between the fabric of his boot, then holds up a crushed mosquito. "Damn bugs." He flicks the body away. "I can't wait for winter."

Faldor scratches his leg again. "That little bugger took a lot."

"Yes, he did," Renue says. "You mentioned the gloves—do I need them for something?"

"I should say so. Have you not heard? That seems unlikely."

"Red hands lie, black hands die. Yes, yes, I listened to some children singing it while skipping rope. Is it normal for kids to sing about such grisly things? I don't mean to offend you, it's just that where I'm from, we deal with criminals differently. Trials and laws. I still haven't gotten used to your system."

"We have laws," Faldor says, coughing into his chest. Staring at Renue, he shields his eyes with a hand. "You're familiar. Do I know you?"

"I don't think so."

The old man claps. "Well, would you like a tour?"

"Why not? I just wanted to get a breath of fresh air. Those halls are clogged with perfume." Renue studies the old man intently for the first sign of the poison taking hold.

"As though perfume could hide everything ugly."

Faldor leads Renue away from the faint yellow lights of the Manor and the green lights of the lanterns. A small stream gurgles into a hidden drain. Earlier, a drugged servant told Renue that tunnels connect the Manor to the Slants, and long ago Mesmer walked the streets at night, in disguise.

"God, these trees are *magnificent*. The passion of a gifted gardener at work." The old man points to a patch of purple bulbs. "Isn't the forest stunning this time of year? Beautiful."

"I slept through it," Renue says. "They gave us a pill. Strange dreams. I think I became a talking vegetable of some kind." There is little greenery in the Slants. The Vines, where the Drailers, the female practitioners of the Gift, hide, are covered and green and the hills of Ashkareve bask in Crescent trees and ivy, but the soil of the Slants, the stretches yet unpaved, are covered only in weeds. "The most beautiful thing I ever saw was a glacier at night," Renue says. "It crackled, boomed, like those old cannons they sometimes shoot off during ceremonies."

"Was it the Beldian Glacier, by any chance?"

"Yes . . . you too?"

"Ages ago. Majestic."

"Like a blue coal, burning."

"And a poet too!" Faldor grins. "I *like* you. You have a certain, amiable curiosity that reminds me of me. Are you enjoying your stay here?"

"Of course, but I'm afraid I'm leaving soon. Now, you were speaking of this red and black."

The old man stops. "I'm sorry?"

"The hands, the gloves."

"Yes . . . " the old man's voice drifts. "Ah. Yes. Come, come. This way."

The two men stop in a small clearing hidden by walls of water-bursting green vines draped over the red, tangled branches of Blood trees. Renue can't remember their scientific name, but the bark and sap are used to heal a rare familial illness and to prevent the passage of infection. As the last edges of Krylight are swallowed by the thick growth, only fragments of light from the high parapets sneak through. In the poor light, Renue squints, watching the old man's movements. The absence of *vespas* physical signs is both disconcerting and relieving. Could Renue have tipped the needle with the antidote in his haste?

"You *really* should wear your gloves," the old man says. "Even in the Manor. The red laws don't work much nowadays. Only gross lies. Red hands. I could tell you stories, though, of ladies who forgot their gloves and were asked about weight and sexual questions." Faldor chortles, wiping his eyes. "There are some things a man just doesn't want to know."

"God, yes," Renue says. "And the black?"

"You've heard of it, yes? The black thing. The nightmare." The old man's voice betrays a hidden fear. "Don't worry. It can't enter the Manor, I believe."

"Belief? Surely the laws of murder must also be a science."

"But law is not science. After all, what could be more inconsistent than men deciding the fate of other men?"

"I agree."

"That *look* on your face. Yes, I know that foreigners call the laws inhumane, even cruel, but they know nothing of its necessity. No sane man could argue that murder is beneficial."

"Only if the laws are equitable. I mean, who do these gloves protect?"

"Only a few."

"Those on your side."

"Those on the side of law and order."

"Ah, a distinction."

"The laws have kept the peace in the Glittering City," Faldor says stiffly. "The black thing has saved lives. Trust me."

"Ashkareve's called the Glittering City? You're joking."

Faldor's fist rest on his chin. "You're strangely ignorant of certain things for a man who's traveled so."

"I'm goading you, old man, that's all. It's just that, when *I* arrived, there were some sections that didn't exactly glitter."

"Well, no name fits perfectly."

"What about murder?"

The old man stops to inspect a leafy fern, pulling the petals off in strips. "I don't understand." He sprinkles the petals onto the ground.

"Don't men kill others here—with poison, for example? But poison is expensive, while a gun is not. That's what I mean by equitable. Besides, isn't some killing justified?"

Faldor laughs deeply. "No, I don't think so. How? No, of course not—"

"Now wait. Say, for example, I knew you were going to kill my father. Wouldn't I have a right to stop you? And what if I did? Under your laws, my family would suffer for my actions. What kind of society does that inspire?"

"We have police here—you could put me in prison, if you had proof."

"You killed my father. My mother, too."

"Show me the evidence, I would say. Besides, we *have* laws," the old man insists. "Think of the Pattern as more of a safety net. Rarely used. More a deterrent. Like capital punishment, only automatic."

"But what if you owned the prison? What if you were responsible for the deaths of millions? What if I poisoned you here, tonight, in this garden?"

"Have you poisoned me?"

"Oh, of course," Renue says. "That goes without saying."

"But you just said it."

"Did I?"

"How much time do I have?"

"Well, your cock will probably fall off in an hour." Renue smirks. "So, you might want to find that slutty countess while you still have something to show her."

"Unfortunately, your poison will do little. Another product of old age. But I prefer your company."

Renue pats Faldor on the back. "There's a strange aura to these gardens. I feel very safe here." No sign of the poison, but the symptoms could be blending with Faldor's already shaking hands and trembling lips. Renue feels for the penknife, his hands slippery.

Faldor smiles aimlessly. "Yes, that's why I like it." He lifts the stem of a blue flower and sniffs it, staggering back. "Come here. Now, don't breathe *too* deeply. You could lose your good name."

Renue kneels by the blue flower and takes it gently between in his fingers as the old man bends beside him. "What does it do?"

"Makes you forget," Faldor says, taking another breath. "Empties memories."

"Forget what?"

"Does it matter?" The old man's face appears to sadden as he tries to stand, almost falling, but Renue catches him. "A bit too much. Oh, too much." Faldor holds his nose and sneezes.

"How much do I have to sniff to forget the woman I was with the other night? God, she was fat." Renue stands, wiping his nose. "At least when I leave, people will still just say I'm well-traveled."

The old man touches his brow and winces. "A fat woman's sitting on my head right now."

"You took a tumble with the lard lady too? I'm kidding. Are you alright?"

Faldor sighs. "May I confess something? I'll warn you—it's a heavy thought."

"I already confessed, so you might as well."

"This might sound silly, but I lost something, long ago. Something important. Faith. In humanity. If Pestras says loss of self is death, so is the loss of faith." Faldor swallows, a bitter expression on his face. "You met me at an odd time, Renue," he says, wiping his face. "Melancholy, deep with dream. But we deserve no better."

"You really believe that?"

"That is simply a fact, my idealistic young friend."

Renue turns off the path and unzips his pants.

"And further—what, what are you doing?"

He looks down. "I *believe* I'm pissing."

"Pissing?"

"There's no law against it, is there? What color will my hands turn?"

"Pissing. In the garden of the most powerful man in the country. Pissing." Faldor shakes his head. "Unbelievable."

"If Mesmer were behind me," Renue says, aiming at a purple flower, "you can be sure I'd let him have my spot."

The old man snickers into his chest. "I *like* you. You're unpredictable. Oh, why not. An old man's bladder has no patience."

"We do have the entire garden to ourselves."

Renue contemplates his alternatives. Beside him, urinating, is the man who opened the door for the most brutal tyrant in history. There should be no hesitancy or guilt, yet his heartbeat quickens at the thought of taking the old man's life. The persona of Renue is cold and calculating, yet there is something undeniably inhuman about extending the pain of an old man so close to natural death.

Faldor zips up and backs away. "Youth." He continues down the path. "Aren't you coming?" he calls. "How much did you drink tonight?"

"Not much," Renue says, running to catch up.

"Dammit."

On the snaking pathway he finds Faldor on the ground. The old man is whimpering, holding his leg. "Faldor?"

"Damn," the old man says. "Damn, damn, damn. Careless—I twisted my ankle." His voice cracks. "I'm a hopeless addict."

Faldor grunts as Renue takes his weight and helps the old man to his feet.

"Are you alright?"

"Yes . . . " The old man's voice trails off. "Listen. I want—I wanted to tell you, why the laws are necessary. I want you to understand."

"It's not—"

"I need to. *Please.* Years ago, there were terrible riots in the country. Factions upon factions. They called Ashkareve the Suffering City then." The old man's breaths are growing short and labored. "Made a mess by fate and the meddling . . . of foreign powers, by conquest." Faldor tries to stand but his legs fail. Renue watches silently. "You're well-read, I'm sure, but to read of war is never the same as experiencing it. I went to Perenia . . . once. A peaceful, fortunate place. But if you lived in the Ashkareve I knew . . . " He winces. "My hand is tingling—did you really poison me?"

"How does it feel?"

Faldor struggles to breathe. "See? Individual morality is the most dangerous kind. Murder erodes society. The Pattern . . . " he spits, "is a re . . . realignment of the moral center." The old man grabs his heart, massaging unconsciously. "My brother Lundus was killed by a Blank. We never found him." He's crying now. "I never knew my brother. Can you imagine it, wondering all those years?" Faldor tries to stand. "You're right to ask questions, but if some freedom must be sacrificed, it's a small price. Still, a difficult . . . innovation to live with, like a painting or song that inspires. War. Beautiful and perfect, but destructive, damning."

"Most great inventions do. Most beautiful things, too." As Renue helps the old man to his feet, wonders whether Faldor could also be acting. "Take the women that walk these halls. Like marble statues, but with fangs."

The old man limps into a narrow beam of light, holding a hand to shield his eyes. No section of the Manor is visible from their location, only walls and walls of darkness. But everything about him is slowing, his walk, his breaths, voice. Faldor pauses, shaking violently again. "God, I miss the . . . " The old man falls to the ground as Renue rushes to his side. "I'm fine—fine. Just let me rest a moment." He squints at Renue. "I *loved* Ashkareve. The music of the docks, the harsh . . . Blank beers. Versumes— do they sell that still?"

"I wouldn't know." Renue sits beside him. "I'm a stranger here, remember?"

"I forgot." Faldor's expression freezes, haunting, pained.

"Even the stink of the fish market. That particular odor. It must sound odd to you."

"We all have our fetishes."

"Not fetish," the old man says softly. "Love. Long lost love." In the light, his gray eyes catch.

"Did you love it more before the black thing, or after?"

"Before was the only time I knew it. I haven't set foot outside since." To Renue's surprise, the old man gets up, limping along the path. Renue follows and the two tread on a path of mulch.

"Where were we going?" Faldor says. "Oh yes, to the statue! I wanted to show you the statue."

"Perhaps another night." The poison has clearly failed and worse still, Renue has given too much of himself away. "Murder, society, black hands," Renue says. "I prefer my dreams peaceful and full of skirt, heaving breasts, and—"

Faldor stumbles, falling hard to the ground. A light from the parapet illuminates his wincing face. The old man coughs, shaking his head. Bending down, Renue reaches for Faldor's armpit, but the old man stops him.

"What is that?" Faldor says, pointing to the line of brown thread that falls over Renue's bootlaces. " . . . a loose thread?"

"String, actually."

"Perenian? I thought they . . . made better boots than that." Faldor reaches, tugging at the thread. The needle sneaks out of the crease and the old man lets it dangle.

Renue's stomach cramps. "I wasn't joking, I'm afraid."

"What is it?"

"*Vespas.*"

"*Vespas* . . . " Tears pool above Faldor's lip. "Please, no."

"Do you have regrets?"

Faldor is trembling. "But why?"

"You know why, Old Faldor."

"Old Faldor—haven't been called that since . . . I was a young man."

"A name they used to call you in the Slants," Renue says. "You gave the country away. To a monster."

Faldor closes his eyes, crying. His voice is barely audible. "We would have been slaughtered. We would have . . . "

"We supported you, *loved* you."

"So many would have died."

"If order is worth human life, then so must be freedom." Renue props the old man up against the nearest tree. "Goodnight."

"Don't go," Faldor begs. "Please. I'd rather you kill me . . . outright."

"That's how we feel, but the laws—you understand." Renue swallows, feeling heavy, feet sinking into the mulch.

"Stay with me, boy. Please."

Renue turns. "Why didn't you try to *escape?*" There's surprising anger in his voice, and confusion. He's choking. The words come in bursts. "Why didn't you *fight* him?"

The old man turns slowly to face Renue, his expression distorted. "He's kept me alive because of who I once was . . . and the things I know. But he keeps me close. Very close." A stiff wind blows over the garden as Faldor shuts his eyes. "That's his breath on the back of my neck. Do you feel it?" His legs and arms have begun to convulse.

"I have an antidote." Renue fishes in his pocket, pulling out the vial—perhaps something could be arranged. Faldor tries to reach for it but his fingers seize as his hand drops. "If you help us."

"Too . . . late," the old man says faintly. "Did . . . did I know you?"

"In a way. As a friend long forgotten," Renue says. "Long betrayed. And the lives of others should never be gambled with."

In the extreme of quiet, when the wind dies softly and the leaves do not rustle, the knife falls into Renue's hand. Under the slim cover of shadow it touches Faldor's chest and sinks into his heart, so silent, so breathless, that it does not seem real. The old man's eyes grow soft as the blade within twists.

"I'm sorry, old man," Renue says, holding Faldor upright with his hand and shoulder. "You should have left while you could."

Faldor gurgles as overhead a bird cries. "Sophia . . . " He grips Renue's shoulder. "Don't . . . " he says. "Or the dream truly . . . " His face relaxes as he falls to his knees.

"Sleep well," Renue says, resting the old man in a thick of bushes. "We remember you." Only then does he become aware of the garden, alive, listening. He takes off his gloves, out of the light, easing Faldor deeper in the shadows. He brings his hands up, watching silently as they turn black.

Chapter Three

Sunlight came through the bottom crack of the door. In the dimly lit room, Lisande watched Renue thrash around until suddenly his head hit the wall and blood surfaced on his forehead. She crawled over and lifted his head into her lap and he mumbled a few broken words. Her stomach hurt with hunger.

A few hours ago, she'd woken with the city for the first time, bells ringing, barking dogs, jingling pursues, vehicles racing down distant streets to the pop of combustion. She was relieved to be firmly awake again, though her body still ached from lack of sleep. It had taken every ounce of her willpower to get through the night. Her mother used to tell her to think of happy memories when she couldn't sleep, but last night Lisande found she could only conjure up disconnected images, a warm cup of milk and cinnamon, a budding twilight forest, a fire, her mother, asleep in her knitting chair, murmuring, fresh snowfall. Most of her few pleasant memories were from her early childhood, before her mother became sick. Back when they were a real family. Finally, she remembered a time when her parents had let her stay up a whole night next to a crackling fire and they took turns reading out of a hard yellow-covered book of fairy tales. She had woken when the sun was rising to see her mother's head cradled by her father's shoulder. That was the last time she could remember both of them smiling.

Renue opened his mouth in a mute scream and Lisande repositioned herself, stroking his hair. "It's okay," she said. "You're awake now." Slowly his eyes opened to that same look of terror she had seen in the market the day before. "It's me. Relax. Just a bad dream. Think of something good."

He jerked back onto his hands. Then he stood and patted his body down, fell onto his butt awkwardly. He was laughing, a different, more musical laugh than the one she remembered from the poker tables.

"Are you alright?" she said. "What's funny?"

"We're alive." He pulled at his hair. "The barrier worked—I didn't think it would." A brief smile appeared on his face and he hugged her, head to her chest.

"You saved us," she said.

He glanced around the room. "How did we get here?"

"Well, technically *I* saved us."

"Where are we?"

"I don't know," she said. "You're not the best guide." She pointed to the door. "We came in through there, if you're wondering."

Renue got to his feet and approached the door, running his hand around the frame. "There's a barrier, I can't tell whose." He ran his hand over the door a second time, pausing at the knob. "It's old. A strange imprint." Squinting, he surveyed the room again. "I thought I knew all the safe houses in the city."

"Imprint?"

"The Gift's like a thumbprint," he said. "Makes Patterns. Maybe this barrier's left over from the old days, when the Gift wasn't against the law. They used these detectives who could track the Gift. Now they have the thing, of course." He rubbed his temple, wincing. "I still can't keep my thoughts straight."

"And you were so cocky in the Manor. But that's not really *you*, is it?"

"Not exactly."

"I feel fine, if you were wondering. Hungry, though."

"Some people are more susceptible," he said. "I had to train very hard to build a resistance." Renue touched his eyebrow and smeared blood. He wiped his pants. "You said we passed the market."

"Yes."

"That's right. There was this boy, in the house where I stole the clothes. I remember him."

"A boy?"

"Yeah. And I remember the locket," Renue said. "And the boy. Definitely. In the house. The boy. I didn't tell you?"

Lisande ran her hand over her nose. It was slightly swollen, but she had rubbed all the flaking blood off earlier when she woke. "Where are you taking me?"

"Somewhere we can hide from the thing," Renue said, stretching his arms up to the low ceiling. "Don't worry." He dug through the backpack and brought out a vial of hair dye.

"You were having bad dreams?"

He unscrewed the vial. "Yes."

"Of what?"

"It's not important."

"Tell me."

"I'll save the good dreams for you," he said. She frowned. "Okay? Not this one." He held up the vial. "We've got to change our hair. Is there a sink?"

"It's dry. I already checked."

"Lean back." He maneuvered behind her, put her head in his lap. Then he poured the dye and spit into her hair.

"Gross."

"Sorry." Renue started to massage the dye in, brown swallowing up the blond. "Your roots are dark." He cleared his throat. "What color was our mother's hair? Naturally, I mean. I saw the painting, but I'm just curious."

"Our mother?" she said.

"Yes. Our mother."

" . . . our mother."

75

"Our mother," he said. "Yes. Our mother. Lisande. *Our* mother."

"No." She tried to get up but his hands weighed on her, rubbing the dye through her hair. "What do you mean, *our* mother? Why are you saying this? Are you testing me again?"

For a few minute neither could speak. Renue moved the dye through her hair. "My mom disappeared when I was an infant. I can't even remember anything about her, just her face from a photograph I saw as a kid. Maybe I made it up. The rest were stolen when my dad was taken by the Manor. Your mother is my mother, Lisande. That's why—that's why everything. Why you killed him. To save me, right? The things you said on the balcony." He paused. "I'm not making this up."

"Your mother," she said, moving a few feet away from him. "You're obviously confused. My father *might* have brought women to the Manor. I don't really know. Maybe your mother was one of them. But my mother didn't have another child. I'm sure. My parents used to fight about it."

"But on the balcony, you said your mother was from the Slants."

"My mother *was* from the Slants, Renue. At least that's what my father told me."

"Mesmer." He rubbed his face. "Mesmer's your father."

"Why are you *looking* at me like that?"

"I guess I didn't believe you." He handed her the bottle and lay down as she propped his head up. "Do mine." Renue felt the dye sink in. "We'll find out for certain when we get to the underground." He turned. "Tell me about our mother."

"She's *not* your mother."

"Then your mother," he said. "Just a little."

"Why?"

"This might be the only chance I have to know."

"Where are you going?"

"Please, Lisande. Just a little."

"But she's not even your—" Lisande stared down at Renue. He was so helpless and vulnerable, so different from in the Manor.

"Please."

"Fine." She sighed. "My mother rarely slept," she said, rubbing the dye through his hair in streaks. "She had a very wild mind. She was always painting. Very exciting, very passionate. This one time, my mother almost set the house on fire. She had fallen asleep knitting and the wax dropped unevenly on the counter. She didn't like electricity—or Krylight. Only candles. My father was furious. She was so gentle."

"Gentle," he said. "Tell me more. Just a little."

"She wove tapestries. Beautiful tapestries, big, small. My father would order the threads from Valadrine. Miles and miles of thread. They were gorgeous. Once, I came downstairs for my birthday and there was a river of them, lavender, canary yellow, green-blue, flowing down the stairs. Boran and my father popped out of the string and scared me. I think it was my—what?"

"Please don't mention them," Renue said.

"Who?"

"Boran. Mesmer—you don't know how it sounds."

"And how does it sound?"

He stared at her. "A monster. Boran's a monster. And your . . . and Mesmer . . . "

"Maybe *you're* the monster," she snapped. "I mean, you've got black hands. You *know*, Renue. It's hard to talk about my mother without talking about my father." She squeezed her temple with a hand. "God, I must be in shock. Why don't you just leave?"

"I can't."

She watched him eye the door. "You want to go though, don't you?" Taking a deep breath, she smiled maliciously. "Maybe mine is a family you're better off not being a part of."

"You don't understand."

"And you keep saying that. If you want to leave, leave. I'll be fine by myself." She raised her eyes defiantly. "I'll just go back."

"You can't," he said. "Lisande. They'll kill you in a heartbeat. I'm sorry, that was a stupid thing to say. But you can't go back. I'm sorry. Please."

"Tell me something about you," she said. "Something *real*. Your family."

"They're gone."

"Cards. Why do you like cards?"

He quickly began packing the dye and clothes in the bag. "Means to an end."

"Mine hasn't dried yet—you put it on too thick."

"I don't even really like cards," he said. "Not really. It was just the best way to get at the deed."

"Why does it matter, this deed?" she said. "You were saying it in your sleep. Over and over."

"I can't tell you." He touched his throat and made a sour face.

"Big surprise." She scoffed. "Fine, cards. You must like something about them. While the dye dries. You owe me."

"I used to like bluffing," he said quietly. "That's all."

"Bluffing."

"Yeah. I'd wish for a bad hand. I like that, that you could win if you just studied your opponent. I was always good at reading faces."

"But you won the deed a few days ago," she said. "I'm not stupid. You're some spy or something. But why would you—" She closed her eyes. "You stayed for me. That's it, isn't it? You stayed for me."

He nodded.

"Do you regret it?"

"Not if you're my sister, I don't."

"Who did you kill?"

"One of your father's men," he said. "On the way out. Is yours dry?"

Lisande checked her hair. "Why don't I turn myself in? I won't tell them a thing."

"You can't," he said. "No one knows you exist. I mean no one. Please, Lisande. They'll kill you." He got up, rubbing his hair. "How does it look? It is even?"

"More or less."

He bent down and touched her hair. "It'll work. Is there a back door? We shouldn't leave the same way we came."

"There's a hallway," she said. "But it's dark."

"You're scared of the dark?"

"Is that alright with you?"

"Come on."

He took her down the nearly pitch-black hall and turned the corner, entering a small room that was empty with the exception of a few, broken wooden chairs. Spider webs hung from the ceiling corners and a fanlight in the center was shattered. They approached the room's single box window. Lisande could see a street below, riddled with potholes.

"Stay close," he said. "Listen. There are things you need to know. Survival things—just in case we're separated. Head east until your stomach feels really sick, then ask someone for Riverface. Say Bren if they won't take you. Don't mention anything else. Try not to speak if you can. Got it?"

She squeezed his hand, watching a group of louts milling in front of a mailbox across the street. "Yes."

"And you can't let anyone know who you are. Ever. Understand? Make something up. You have no idea what people would do to you."

"But I didn't *do* anything."

"It doesn't matter," Renue said. "And another thing. No one can know that he's dead. Do you understand? No one. Where I'm taking you, you'll be safe. The Damaskers won't turn you away." His hand washed down his face, then he grabbed her arms and faced her. "I would have come back for you. I couldn't have just left you there."

"I believe you."

"We're just above Farrow," he said, pointing past the gray buildings on the south side of the street. "Do you know the city at all? No? Well, Farrow Street cuts the city roughly in two, east-west. Goramon Avenue runs through the market we were in yesterday—north south. The two meet at the bell tower. Spokes on a wheel. Then Farrow veers east into the edge of the Slants. West, it borders the Vines and Inverts, roughly splits them, then curves downwards to the Blanks and docks. The Slants start there, past that row of sharp buildings. Got it?"

"I think so."

"This way." He walked to the door at the other end of the room, revealing an unlit stairwell. "Here it goes."

After wrapping his hands with a thin beige stocking, he handed her one. Together, they proceeded down the stairs, brushing past hanging cobwebs. Lisande sputtered, picking one out of her mouth. At the bottom of the stairs Renue opened the door and reach for her hand.

"We'll be fine," he said. "Stay with me."

On the far sidewalk, a man was selling greasy meats and onions on sticks. They walked quickly past brown quilts weighed down by timepieces and vials of colored sand. An old woman hobbled in front of them, talking to herself. In the middle of the next intersection, an old brown dog was struggling to sit up. Children were throwing pieces of apple at the dog. It had a cancerous bulge on its stomach, and when it tried to get away, the bulge rubbed against concrete. Renue guided Lisande shoulder behind a pair of louts swinging their arms in awkward arches. Because their accents were harsh and cut off the ends of words prematurely, she struggled to understand what they were saying.

"I swear."

"Where?"

"*Who* saw? Not you."

"No, but Elsa, last night."

"The Scream, they're calling it."

"Said we was attacked."

"Who?"

Lisande did her best not to stare at the louts, but their shifting eyes and unshaven faces made her nervous. In her teenage years, when she had begged to be allowed to go to the city, her father often lectured her about how dangerous the louts were. He had even made jokes about her mother being a criminal once, causing one of the most vicious arguments that Lisande could still remember. Renue paused, halfway on the sidewalk, and squinted as though trying to hear some hidden voice. She tried to avoid passing louts, eyes planted at her feet, listening.

"Where *were* you?"

"For what?"

"For what?"

Blowing air.

"What else?"

"Latch."

"Where in Latch?"

"Cofsties."

"You old boot!"

A whisper.

"Lucky."

They paused at the next street in front of a bank. Renue talked with a merchant who spoke from beneath an expansive mustache and beard. Next to the bank was a metal staircase where three louts huddled together on the steps. Two were shorter with knobby, exposed knees and the third taller, with a lean, unhealthy face and intense and beady eyes.

"No, tore 'em," the shortest of the three was saying.

"Really?"

"Yeah."

"Until?"

"Bodies. Limbs. Arms."

"You *saw* it?"

"No one's *saw* it."

"It's *hungry*."

"Famished."

Whispers.

"What have we done?"

The tallest one wept.

She turned as a lout tapped Renue on the shoulder and pointed at her hands. Realizing she had tugged part of the wrap off, she quickly tucked her hands in her dress but the lout was still waving his finger at her.

"Why they wrapped then?"

"Fetish," Renue said. "Fucked, I know."

"Sicko." The merchant patted him on the back. "*And* a hillborn—dangerous skirt."

Renue winked and, putting his arm around her, led them across the street and southwards. Soon they were dwarfed by masses of metal and concrete and shadows covered them. They passed a boy selling newspapers and another listening to the radio before turning onto a less-crowded street. Lisande tried to concentrate on the concrete in front of her. When she looked up next, the buildings appeared to be leaning towards the ocean. At the following intersection she saw a five-story building. From the middle floor, two people were yelling at each other, then papers drifted out of the window like square sheets of snow, landing onto a bum curled around the entrance steps. From her bedroom window, the Slants had always resembled the jagged teeth of a mouth. She couldn't believe her mother had grown up here. It made her miss her mother, seeing buildings that long ago her mother might have walked by in her youth.

They crossed the street and passed into a residential area of smaller houses with tiny fenced yards, blues and greens on one block, reds and purples on another. In the distance she could hear someone banging on garbage cans. She coughed, an itch in her throat. The air smelled dirty. Cutting through an abandoned concrete court, Renue and Lisande passed several young boys who hid their cigarettes and watched her suspiciously. She glanced back and one winked, licking his teeth. Past the courts they reached a thin road that wove in and around islands of small shops, a mechanic, a shoe repairman. In the center of the street, two old men were pointing behind them, into the sky.

"It's right there, old coot."

"Oh, I see . . . what is it?"

"Fuck if I know."

"Can't be good."

The two louts shuffled by as Renue dragged her on. Within minutes they crossed a scraggly, overgrown park, syringes and paper cups littering the grass. At the top of a small dirt mound at the end of the park was a statue of her father, standing with a sword in one hand and a gun in the other. Several cats were sunning themselves at the base. Lisande felt cold watching the steely expression on her father's face.

"Come here," Renue said. "Quick."

He had already started down the hill, heading straight for a short lout wearing a faded orange shirt and shorts who had appeared from a shop across the street. The lout was twisting back to the shop and shaking his head and almost bumped into Renue. As the lout tried to run away Renue grabbed him violently.

"What happened?" Renue said.

"Nothing," the lout insisted. "Let me go."

"What happened, I said?"

"I'll call the spades."

"No, you won't."

The lout shifted nervously. "No, I won't."

"I will if you don't tell me."

"No, I won't." The lout bent close and opened his mouth, teeth crooked and yellow-stained. "Another," he said, exposing a mouth nearly empty of teeth. "Found another."

"Another what?"

"One yesterday, two today." The lout fought against Renue's grip, his voice wild and excited. "Bomb fucked the Manor— Perenia's attacked. We can *see* them now."

"See who?"

"No, I won't," the man said, struggling.

Renue let him go and the lout fell in the dirt, scrambled to his feet and disappeared beyond her father's statue, dispersing the cats.

"I need to see something," Renue said. "Real quick."

"No." Lisande held the heart-shaped locket beneath her grimy hand cloth, rubbing the cold metal between her fingers. "Are you crazy? No."

"I have to."

"To what?"

"See if the Pattern's failing," he said. "Maybe that's why it didn't find us."

♥

Lisande almost choked from the stench of a small crowd of louts quickly pushing past one another towards the back of the shop. Renue motioned for her to stay at the door but she continued past the counter where a woman with candy-red hair stood. They made their way to the far corner bunches of green and blue-tipped dyed leaves were stacked alongside glass pipes, incense holders, cones, candles, and jars of tobacco. To her left, a wall of louts watched a man who stood in a sunken section several yards away. Two shelves had topped to the floor beside the man. He leaned on a sledgehammer and wiped his white dust-coated face, then heaved the hammer and swung at the far wall, sending more drywall into the air. The half-circle of louts watching backed up slightly, sneezing as the air filled with white dust.

"Get the fuck out," the owner screamed, but the louts in the room seemed hypnotized and only inched closer to the wall where two bulky louts were prodding at something in the corner.

"Here," one said.

"Is it listening?"

"How can ya tell?"

"Ask it."

"*You* ask it."

"Get the fuck out of my store," the woman behind the counter cried. "Now or I'll call—"

"Shut up and no, you won't, you dried fruit."

The louts laughed and moved closer. Lisande watched as the crowd parted for a lout holding large garden clippers.

"We can go," Renue said. "Lisande? Let's go."

"I want to see," she said, putting a hand on his shoulder. "Like you said. An education."

A man held a dropper, leaned into the wall, and something hidden screamed, sending a collective shiver through the crowd. Then an arm limped out of the hole in spasm. Seconds later a white body fell to the floor, twitching. Lisande watched as the body writhed on the floor like an exposed earthworm.

The few louts who remained were cheering and giggling.

"It's an *Ear*."

"Another!"

The body twitched again. The crowd stepped back as the Ear wailed.

"Mercy," it croaked.

Someone kicked the body and chipped teeth fell out of its mouth.

"Spades," someone yelled.

"Hide it."

Renue grabbed her hand and they bolted for the entrance. The last thing she heard was a snap, followed by pitiful sobbing.

Outside, she watched his eyes scanning the nearly empty street. At the top of the dirt mound seven spades had appeared. The spades fired and the louts scattered as Renue pulled her violently and they cut though the block via a narrow alleyway a few feet from the shop. Midway down, he opened a groaning steel door and she started to enter but he pushed her beyond it, then kicked the door, grinding it into the brick. At the end of the alleyway they hugged a line of buildings shaded by a wooden awning, running through the streets. A few minutes later, he looked back briefly, then tugged her behind a dumpster and leaned against a steel wall, coughing and spitting. She caught her breath, hands gripping the hot metal dumpster rim.

His face was flushed. "Are you alright?"

"Is that what it's like down here?"

"No. No one would ever . . . something's wrong. I don't know." He coughed again "That didn't bother you?"

"Only a little."

"Why not?"

She shook her head. "I sort of expected it. From what my father told me about down here."

"I think we lost them," Renue said. "Come on. We should go."

Beyond, in the valley of the city stretched a crude, endless smattering of shining metal roofs. As they descended into a neighborhood of tall apartment buildings, someone yelled to stop. At the corner of the previous intersection were four spades. Renue and Lisande took off down another street and cut in front of a line of honking cars. He guided her through a garbage-filled alleyway to the next street but a wall of impassable buildings forced them south. They tried to head east at the next intersection but now a mesh of warehouses and buildings encircled them and within moments they were stopped at a dead end. As Renue and Lisande tried to backtrack, six louts sprang off the walls, cutting off their escape.

"Lost, Faces?" A lout with a thick black beard stepped forward.

"Get the hell out of my way," Renue said. He pulled out the rusty wire and the louts oohed and stood their ground.

"You can't be serious," the bearded lout chucked as his men closed in.

"Don't come any closer," Renue warned. "I'll call the spades."

Lisande caught the lout staring at her. "Please help us," she said. "Please."

He scoffed as the others exchanged glances. "From what?"

"The soldiers. Please."

The lout studied her again. "Shit," he said. "Fine. After me."

He barked orders to the louts, who hurried back the way Renue and Lisande had come. To her surprise, Renue made no complaint as the lout led them through an unmarked door that opened into the back of a darkened bar. The bartender tossed him a small key and the three continued around the corner and into a smaller room. The bearded man locked the door behind them. At the end of the room they came out into a thin alley, the sun directly overhead. A pair of rats were rattling around, half exposed from inside tin cans.

"Piek," the lout said, extending his hand. "You?"

"Lisande."

"Lisande." He bit his lower lip. "Lisande. Very pretty." Three louts came from the other end of the alley and Piek met them halfway, conferring for a moment. "They want you bad," he said. "Relax, tough guy. Couldn't turn in that pretty face—not yours, hers."

The louts laughed.

"So, what'd you do?

"Nothing," Renue said.

"Sure, sure. Running from the guard's good for the heart. Exercise. How much can you pay?"

Renue fished through his pockets. "Empty."

Piek turned back to the louts and cleared his throat. "So, what'd ya do, or we turn ya in?"

"Nothing."

"I won't repeat myself."

The louts stared silently as Lisande unwrapped her hands. Two took a step back. Another whistled.

"She's marked."

"Fucker."

"Damn," Piek said. "Don't scare her. Easy, girlie, easy. You're fine. Don't cry." He dug into his pouch and brought out a broach, a small metal butterfly made from a dull copper tinged with blue. "Have it—come on. I have plenty. Make 'em for borns and blazes. An artist."

"Ya stole it, fibber."

"Honey-tongue poet."

"Let them go. She's marked."

"Shut up. Nice going, Kors." Piek grabbed Lisande's fingers. "Don't worry," he said. "They're not gonna find ya—not if I can help it. I'm promise. Don't cry. Please. How about something to get your mind off of it? A magic trick? You like magic?"

She sniffled.

"I'll take that as a yes. Here we go. One trick, coming up."

"Thanks for your help," Renue said. "But unless you want the thing on you, just show us the way out."

"*Show* em, Pieky," the youngest lout said. "Show 'em, show 'em."

"Shut *up*, Benny," Piek said. "Captive audience, right?" He brought out a cent and a twenty-five cent coin and handed them to Renue. "Thing's busted, just like the Ears, I'll bet. Besides, I like a little risk. Now, put one coin in each hand and show 'em around. Only need two questions to find the coin." The coin in your left hand—times it by two." Piek waited. "Got it? Okay, now multiply the coin in your right hand by thirteen."

"Thirteen?"

"Yep. Now, skirts and louts, prepare to be dazzled." Piek's fingers moved dramatically in waves over his head. "The twenty-five cent is in your . . . " He snapped. "Left hand." Renue opened his hand, revealing the twenty-five cent coin. Lisande clapped weakly as Piek bowed. "Get them some water, okay?"

"Is there a bathroom?" she said.

He pointed down the alley and two of the louts ran to escort her. Renue began to follow but Piek grabbed his shirt. "Easy. She'll be fine." He cupped his face with his hand, then bit his bottom lip again. "I'm not stupid."

"Neither am I," Renue said. "You asked those questions to see how long it'd take me to multiply. I used to do that trick when I was a kid—"

"It worked."

"It made her happy."

"You're taking her to the Maskers, aren't you?"

"Yes."

"They can fix her hands?" Piek said. "I heard they can, sometimes."

"That's just a rumor, unfortunately."

"She yours?"

"My sister."

"Oh." Piek glanced down the alley. "Well, now. I can protect her better than they can."

"Not from the thing."

Piek stepped closer. "I can get her out. On a boat," he said. "Tonight. Or through the mountains. For the right price. Come on, don't go to the Maskers."

"You're a smuggler."

"Of sorts."

"No, thanks."

Lisande returned, the louts trailing behind. "Your brother's a good guy," Piek said. He took her hand again. "I'm sorry. Really sorry. If you need anything, just ask for me." He pointed down the alley. "Door at the end. Put ya back on Burnick." He kissed her fingers. "Sorry I couldn't help more. Good luck."

As the door closed Lisande could hear it lock. The wind was kicking up dust and wrappers. "Last leg," Renue said as she shielded her eyes. The conversations of pedestrians were lost by the great gusts sweeping the streets clean. He led her across the street and through a snaking alleyway, the path ahead of them obscured by thick steam rising from the sewer. The alleyway led to another, and they seemed to be passing through blocks and blocks of buildings.

She held her stomach. "I don't feel well."

"It's just the barrier," he said. "No, don't turn around. You'd forget the way if you walked back on the street. The homeless who live around here have no memories. There's a poem by Lyle about them." At a T junction in the alley he paused, as though trying to remember the way. "Don't tell them your name. Don't say anything."

"I hear voices."

"We're walking through lives," he said. "That's what you're feeling. Each essence."

"Lives?"

"It took a lot to hide this place."

As they approached the end of the alley she saw two shapes coming out of slight cracks in the wall. Renue ran his finger through her hair and kissed her forehead. "We made it." A few feet further he doubled over and vomited on the wall.

"Are you alright?"

A guard stepped up to Renue as he wiped his mouth. The guard had dirty blond hair and a hawkish nose. "Where the fuck have you been?"

"Who is it?" the other said in a high-pitched voice which to Lisande sounded like the whine of a violin. "Check them, Granges?"

"You, the girl. Me, the Puker," Granges said. "Go on."

Lisande felt so nauseous she was barely able to stand as Granges' fingers outlined Renue's body. "No Gift." He smirked. "You, Dale?"

"No. Nothing."

"Move over." Granges stood in front of Lisande and his hands raced around her curves briskly. "Yes, she does. She's just hiding it. There's a barrier." He spat. "If she were a Hand, we'd be dead by now. Try to sense it again. Got it?" He turned back to Renue. "I'll bring you in of course, old friend. But not her."

"She has to come, Granges."

"You know the rules," he said.

"Then we'll wait for Bardon."

"Will you? You've missed a lot the last few days," Granges said. "He's doing damage control. Besides, her stomach will have bled out by morning. Few Latchies did already—gone in the head."

Renue undid the wrapping on his hand but Granges' face only hinted surprise. Dale exhaled nervously.

"Take her to a quiet room, Dale."

"Should I—"

"Call for new guards," Granges said briskly. "Looks like I'm escorting Puker here personally."

♥

The four walked down a sloping pathway for several minutes until Granges stopped at a cross corridor and Dale led Lisande to the left. "Relax, *Renue*," Granges said. "She'll be fine." He extinguished the Krylight lamp and followed markers invisible to Renue. Before the mission, Renue had navigated the halls with ease, even though he had no natural talent for the Gift. It was one of his greatest disappointments, that he had no such affinity: Bardon's words had always stung, "a well long dried." Throughout his training, Renue often resented the advantage others had and worked doubly hard to rise through the ranks of the Damaskers, fighting the inherent bias of the organization, proving, gradually, that intellect and effort could be just as effective as the Gift.

Granges paused. "So what happened? They're saying the Perenians attacked—obvious bullshit." He cocked his head. "Alright, I'll try again. Why the smoke? It's been pouring out of the Manor since yesterday. Thought you might have set the Manor on fire."

"No idea."

They continued on through the next corridor and took an elevator down two flights. "They should have sent someone with the Gift," Granges said. "Not in the mood to talk today, I see. And Renue was always such a talker. "

Though the skills Renue had learned were numerous, only language ever came close to reaching what he imagined the power of the Gift to be. The true strength of words were in their ability to invoke symbols, and the pliability of those symbols to quickly invert. A mere name could transform whole groups into monsters one night and heroes the next. In Qarash, a few words uttered from Mesmer had birthed a war, and with another pair of words that same war ended. Like the Gift, words were slippery and frightening in potential, but only the Manor had perfected the art of both. Bardon's dad always argued with Alkor that the essence of their struggle was terminology. The term Manor itself recalled the middle ages where peasants were locked in an inescapable system of oppression. Blanks, worthless cards. Louts, thieves. The Sickness, something only to be handled by the regime, too dangerous in the hands of anyone else. Even though Renue went on the mission, he sided with Bardon, who had long argued that the essence of their resistance was a war of words and definitions, a war that the Damaskers were clearly losing.

Granges opened a door and gestured for Renue to enter. "Wait here."

"Thanks."

"I should have gone," he said. "And you know it."

"I wish you had. You wouldn't believe what I saw."

Granges shut the door. The room contained only a cot, a bookcase, and a desk. Renue lay down on the cot and took off his shoes, feeling the arches of his feet for blisters. He couldn't get the portrait from the Manor out of his mind. Placed the image next to Lisande again. Renue wondered whether he could have been mistaken. Before seeing the portrait, it had never even crossed his mind that his parents could exist anywhere outside his few memories of them. But if his mother had been alive throughout his childhood, Bardon must have known. He had headed the section of the resistance dedicated to finding missing persons and collecting testimonials of the tortured. He could find anyone. Sometime later Renue fell asleep and dreamed of Faldor. When he woke he stared at his hands and felt sick.

He sorted through the blue bookcase, hoping to find a copy of the poet Lyle's collection, "The Suffering City," Renue's favorite, but there was only the resistance code and other histories. He ran his fingers along the edge of the shelf. Blue would always remind him of a girl who had briefly attended the Helmek Academy where Bardon once taught. Renue's first day of school, eight years old and only months off the streets, the girl had sat next to him, with Granges to the other side. The girl was petite, with mousy features. She was gorgeous, though curiously, her ears were always hidden behind her crow-black hair, pinned tightly with two silver clips. Renue would steal glances at her between strategically timed questions. The other boys in class teased her ruthlessly about her ears. For some reason, he wanted to see them too, but he would still defend her. Granges himself dealt Renue his first black eye on the playground, and continued to tease the girl because her father was rich, or had been until the Manor shut down his newspaper, *The Sentinel.* Most of the instincts Renue learned fighting Granges would later propel him to the top of the mission list, skills he earned defending the girl with the topaz earrings, to whom he never spoke, not even to say her name. Near the end of the school year, after a particularly vicious taunting session, the girl pulled back her hair to reveal her ears. They were perfectly formed and beautiful. Renue always wondered why she hadn't revealed them sooner.

That summer was spent on wax battles, imagined stealth missions to the Blank neighborhoods, and sneaking out at night to sit behind Ember's on the docks to listen to fiddle stories or sneak into shows. When the fall semester began, the girl was gone. On the playground, the boys began to speculate. They took her, Granges said at recess one day with uncharacteristic regret in his voice. The spades find the rabbits but Mesmer makes them disappear. Why? Renue had asked. Doesn't matter, they'll never tell us. Why'd you have to tease her so much then? Granges pushed him. Fuck off, man. I loved her. And now she's gone and it's too late.

In the years that followed the girl stayed with Renue: the texture of her voice, her curious inflections, her hair flickers, her long dark eyebrows, as though she simply refused to fade from his memory. He thought of her when the first icy blue winter moon would rise above the ocean, and during the times when he missed his father and mother the most. Most of his peers moved on and forgot her but he remembered. Renue's teenage anger was directed not at Bardon, the closest he had to a father, but towards those who shrugged off the disappearances easily. Most people, Renue soon learned, invented reasons and justifications for those the Manor took, or ignored the disappearances altogether, as though the person who had disappeared had simply left for on a long trip. *Across the sea* was the expression. One day the grocer was gone, replaced by her older brother. Where'd your sister go?

Renue had asked. Better not to question things. Don't you care? Questions get you into trouble. Why? You never know who's listening. She was your sister. Don't come back here, boy.

Bardon's house was often full of teachers and students, but at night when they were finally alone, Renue continued to press him on the girl's fate. He could find anymore.

I'll tell you when you're older.

I need to know now.

You're still a child.

She was a child.

You don't need to be troubled by such things yet.

You don't trust me?

Of course I do. But you're young.

Not in Ashkareve.

Renue continued to study at the Helmek Academy and he and Granges became close friends, but most his classmates gradually accepted life under the regime. But Renue never forgot the girl. It wasn't exactly stubbornness. He simply couldn't forget her, though he tried. Maybe it was the mystery of her disappearance, the sleepless nights spent speculating. Once, Renue overheard Bardon explaining to Alkor that the loss of the girl had simply replaced the loss of his parents, that the boy had exchanged one loss for another. But that wasn't true. It was her voice. Renue heard it often, in the summer when the wind died down, in the winter when storm light and the ocean turned the snow blue. He heard it in the Manor. Lying on the cot, he let the voice wash over him but now he felt no calmer.

Happy birthday. Today you're an adult.

What happened to her?

Unwrap your present. This is supposed to be a joyous day.

It's not even my birthday.

You don't know that.

Neither do you. Tell me. You know how to find everyone in this city.

I've always cherished how stubborn you are. Since you were a little boy you were never satisfied with what people told you. It's one of your most admirable qualities.

You're stalling, Bardon. Tell me.

Her father was put to work in the mines, Bren. I'm sorry.

Why?

He wrote things the Manor didn't like, published transcripts of the tortured but tried to pass them off as fictional stories, for foreigners to read. A truly brave man.

What happened to her and her mother, then?

I don't know. I tried to find out for you. I truly did.

Mesmer. I'll kill him.

Don't be foolish. There are other ways to grieve.

I don't have the Gift. You said so yourself.

Times change. We need people without the Gift. Quieter people.

I'll do it.

Think about it for a month or two. You're too compulsive. Enjoy the summer.

You're right. Take me tomorrow.

♥

Renue was sprawled on the cot when the old Damasker charged into the room. "Where is the *deed*?" he demanded.

"Alkor." Renue sat up.

The old Damasker slammed the door. "What are you hiding? It was a week ago when we heard the deed was won! How *overjoyed* we were. *Finally* a successful mission. Already I began to calculate how the Manor would have hidden the Pattern, started to work on it like a puzzle square. I couldn't sleep, couldn't eat, I was so God-damn happy." Alkor grabbed a heavy volume of history off the bookshelf and hurled it into the corner. "Well? What do you have to say?"

"Where's Bardon?"

"Always, you turn to him, like a spoiled child. When Faldor was killed, I was just beginning to recover from the exhausting task of getting you through the woods, myself and twenty others, the sun room putrid with vomit. Then we heard you had the deed. You know I am not an exaggerator, but that, *that* was the happiest day of my life." The old Damasker flexed his gloved hands. "I wept a day straight, and into sleep, dreaming I wept, and when I woke I had saline thoughts, as though I had been soaking in the sea of memory. I wept at our luck, at the break in the clouds. Finally, a chance to end that bloody dictator's rule." Alkor frowned. "Then, two days ago, you vanished, with something stolen from the Manor. Something important. Something even Boran could not hide. But I would have felt the deed once you broke free of the woods, so steeped in the Pattern it must be. So what have you taken?"

"I don't have the deed."

Alkor snarled. "Well, *something* had changed, as though suddenly each color of the world was made its opposite. The Manor is quiet. The Manor is silent. Clearly the Pattern is deteriorating. There are spades on every corner of this city, taking people for so much as sneezing. So what happened?"

Renue swallowed. "He's dead, Alkor."

"Pah, Faldor, I don't care! He deserved it. Where is the deed? Where is the fucking *deed*?" The old Damasker grabbed Renue's shirt then slowly let go and backed away. "It's still in the Manor, isn't it?" he said softly. "You left it like a fool."

"He's dead." Renue said, showing his hands. "Your barrier failed. I'm marked."

"What?—No, but *Faldor* is dead! Don't say it. No, tell me now. Who? Who else has been killed?"

"Mesmer."

Alkor whipped his head around. "You? *You* killed him?"

" . . . yes. Then I escaped, with her help."

"Her? Who is this *her*? Not one of ours." The old Damasker stumbled back, his face distorted, and leaned against the wall. "How can it *be*?" he said. "That our best hope has led to this? I believed, *believed* that this time we would cast off that mongrel's hands from our neck and breathe free air for the first time in almost three decades. All but an ungenerous sliver of my life, trapped in this gutter." He scoffed. "You were supposed to be perfect, but you're just a lout after all. Well, you'll get no protection from me." Alkor pointed at the door. "Get the fuck out."

"Listen," Renue said. "Just listen. There's a chance—"

"—a chance? A *chance*? You arrogant little prick. Because of you, the black thing is forever free," the Damasker said, his voice falling into whisper. "It's already happening. The Scream. Perenia. They've found a way to start another war, further sap our strength. Just as in Shilogh, the black thing will destroy Ashkareve." He stared past Renue. "The city quivers. Even animals feel his death. *The black thing*. If Ashkareve is lost, our neighbors will soon find out. Five different nations will feed on us like carrion. Our country will be stripped to the bone." He held his hands to Renue's face. "Do you realize what you've done?"

"She's Mesmer's daughter."

The lines around Alkor's face tightened. "Mesmer has no daughter. Did you check her blood? Of course not! After all, *you* don't have the Gift, *lest* we forget! No, don't play games with me. When Mesmer's sons were killed, *that* was the end of his bloodline. Our one miserable victory. A daughter—I think not." The old Damasker coughed violently, holding his chest. "The Gift draws its source from the dead and the living. Without death there is no life, and without life there is no death. Without both, there is no Gift, the intermediary between the two, the sickening embrace, the melancholy dance. To be a truly powerful Damasker, the Gift is always the ultimate sacrifice."

"What are you saying?"

"Blood is life, the Gift is blood," Alkor said. "Such powerful enchantments come at a terrible price. It took two to make the thing." He held up a pair of fingers. "Valan and Mesmer. The black thing's progenitors. But when Mesmer's sons were killed, *that* was the end of his line. God, that stupid look of yours, as though you would ask a question you already know the answer to. Fine, I will say it into the open air, and with words that even a lout like you can understand. Sterility. Infertility. Barren. Salted loins!" Alkor sneered. "Mesmer could have no daughter."

Chapter Four

You're wanted in the library," came Granges' voice a few hours later. "Now."

He led Renue down a passageway and as group of Damaskers walked by, Renue hid his face. At the central chamber, a few more Damaskers sat in the mess hall, their conversations drifting as they turned to stare.

"He's waiting in the library. Come on, Puker."

"Does he know?"

"What do you think?"

The library contained the history, records, and torture testimonials of the Mesmer dictatorship, as well as stolen interrogations carried out by the Boran's secret police, the Black Hands. After Renue was inducted into the resistance, he scoured the torture records for mention of his parents. What he had read chilled him far beyond the disappearances and street gossip he had known as a teenager, as torture had evolved into a high art during Mesmer's nearly three decades of rule, with the body the canvas and poisons and chemicals the palette. *Bite*, taken from stalker scorpions, would paralyze the spinal cord while *Leach* slowly ate away at muscles. *Bliss* could sharpen the brain to sensations and make you more attuned to the pain, until even a prick of the finger would leave a victim screaming for days. Granges often told new inductees about a blind woman he found on Fallow Street. Mesmer's scientists had enhanced her sense of hearing so that even a stiff breeze would send her into fits. She died from the laughter of children, Granges would say, to illustrate that Mesmer's methods for instilling fear exceeded their own nightmares, and that it was better to take your own life rather than be captured, as the Blanks practiced. The regime had truly made an art out of human suffering.

They walked beneath the arch of stone ivory that led to the library, a poor joke for a place without no natural light and little plant life. Above the double doors, the motto of the resistance was inscribed in stone: *Be performers of the word and not listeners.* Through the windows were younger Damaskers sitting at long wooden tables. Across the study area was a small meeting room where Renue could see Bardon waiting.

"Good luck, Puker," Granges said.

As the door closed, Bardon put down a small, leather-bound book and hugged Renue. Bardon's cheeks were gaunt and his hair peppered gray. "Have you slept any?" he said, taking a seat.

"No."

"I heard they have nice beds in the Manor."

"That's not funny."

"Poor taste, sorry. So what happened?" Bardon gestured for Renue to sit.

Renue wiped his face. "I had the deed in my hands," he said. "But there was this . . . painting."

"Painting?"

"Of my mother." He studied Bardon's face but found his old teacher's expression unreadable. "I remembered her face—I know. You'll say something scientific, like no infant could remember his mother. But it was her." Renue clenched his teeth. "When I saw her, I lost my composure. Of all the possibilities, all the time I spent wondering what happened, it never occurred to me that she could have been taken as one of Mesmer's . . . women."

"Would it have changed anything?" Bardon said. "What could you have done?"

"Did you know? You suspected." Renue found himself unable to contain his brimming anger. "Is that it? How long ago did she die, Bardon? How many years did I spend down here when I could have gone after her?"

Bardon sat back and folded his hands. "Say this theory of yours was true. How, exactly, might your life have changed? What would you have done differently?"

"So you knew?"

"How far would you have gotten, Renue? Or shall I call you Bren?"

"I'm not Bren anymore. You were right about the murder. But don't change the—"

"How far would you have gone, had you tromped up through the hills at the tender age of nine, ten—even eighteen? What could you have done that thousands before you failed to do? Are you so clever, so talented, that you could skip to the forest unseen without our help? Slip into the Manor. And then what? Murder him? For whose benefit? To what end?"

"I could have done *something*," Renue insisted. Through the window, he could see a group of Damaskers watching him. "I could have tried."

"And you no doubt would have wasted your life, and those with incredible talent such as yourself have a responsibility to others." Bardon sighed. "I tried to teach you that all those with the ability to improve the lives of others *must*. What happened? Was it Faldor? I warned you."

"If there was a chance to help her, I would have taken it."

"Then you certainly *have* changed. More Renue now than the boy I raised."

"At least I could have made the decision for myself." Renue's voice wavered as he met Bardon's eyes. "Did you know, God damn you?"

When Bardon refused to answer, Renue stood and kicked over the chair, then shoved the bookshelf into the side table, sending a lamp to the floor. Bardon simply watched. Slowly, Renue knelt down and began to pick up the fallen books, restoring the shelf to its previous position. His teacher stood and silently, the two men slotted the remaining books. Renue bent over the fallen lamp. The yellow glass had shattered.

"Sorry," he said. "I don't know what . . . "

"Well, you've made some promising points," Bardon said. "As eloquently as Debeau or Rady. Now, if you're done being an ass, sit down. Sit down and listen." From his pocket Bardon took out a pair of gloves and handed them to Renue.

"No."

"Put them on—the others say it helps."

"Fine."

"Now just listen," Bardon said. "I want to tell you about something I saw once, Renue. A child. He was perhaps six, seven years old. It was in Latchtown. I was going to meet an old friend, but I stopped to watch the boy. He was playing with a paper ball. As I watched, a gust fell across the flats and the ball started rolling. The boy took off after it. I followed him through the streets, though I couldn't say why. I was younger then. Everything is easier when you're younger. I followed him from Emores, all the way to the bell tower, around the market, south to the gem district, simply *delighting* in this little boy's enthusiasm. He darted through the crowds, a wide, joyful expression on his face. Perhaps he was simple, a victim of the dousings, I thought. It didn't really matter, though. The happiness was genuine. Almost magical. Often, the people this little boy dove in front of for that silly paper ball stopped to watch, as though the boy had, by his mere presence, elicited some ancient feeling, some lost comfort they had forgotten. But others were clearly troubled by him and attempted to block the boy, to slow him down. But the boy was too quick. I followed him south of the bell tower, to Frake Square, past the fountains. When we neared the Blank neighborhoods, I thought for sure the child would look up and realize how far he had gone, but he showed no sign of slowing. With luck, and a bit of handling on my part, the breeze changed on Bennett Street and the paper ball led him east back to the Slants."

Renue pushed the glass shards with his foot.

"I can still hear it, that laughter," Bardon said, smiling. "A strange, curious laughter. How far the paper ball had brought him, dancing around puddles and from beneath the feet of businessmen. All this the boy somehow *expected*. It was the Gift in the truest sense of the word. When we neared the docks the wind was blowing more forcefully than I can even remember. The little boy could barely keep up, and then suddenly the ball was whisked into the air. He continued after it, following all the way to edge of the docks. The wind carried the ball out over the water. Without a second thought—"

"—he jumped into the water," Renue said. "So determined was he to get that ball, and he drowned. Or you saved him. Is that it?"

Bardon shook his head sadly. "No. Like a damn fool I jumped into that frigid water and dragged the cursed ball out onto the dock. The boy stopped at the edge, staring at me, laughing. I placed what was left of the ball on the boardwalk and then we sat there for some time, he and I, looking at what was now only pulp. Then he just left, without a word. But you're right, there *is* a moral to this story. It's *worth* it to chase dreams, Bren. But you must choose the dreams you chase wisely." Bardon put his hand on Renue's shoulder. "Your parents are gone. I'm sorry. To never truly know where you came from is an unspeakable loss. I'm fortunate that I knew both of mine. My mother lived a natural life. My father died in Faldor's war. I can see the pain in your face, but the past is only a liability if you so choose. And, like it or not, the privileged, we who hold the lives of others in our hands, are often faced with difficult decisions." As Renue tried to protest, Bardon silenced him with his hand. "*Furthermore*, this poor resistance has already put an extraordinary amount of resources into your upbringing, so much so that many would say it is not your life to be risked anymore." He picked up the leather-bound book and handed it to Renue. The code of the underground.

"Not if I was lied to."

"This is war, not contract law. I'll defend you, of course, should that prove necessary, but for now we should move on to more practical considerations. The murder of Mesmer. In your own words, tell me, calmly, what happened. Who is the girl and why are her hands black?"

"She's Mesmer's daughter," Renue said. "Alkor says it's not possible, but I believe her. I think she's my sister—half-sister, too. She came after me, saved me, apparently. Her mother was from the Slants."

"Your sister?"

"That can be discovered by the Gift, can't it?"

"Yes, but it will take some time. Now, how was Mesmer killed? You are an accomplished liar, but I just can't believe you would be foolish enough to kill him."

"It was the last night of the game," Renue said. "Mesmer knew my father. I think he also knew about the mission, who I was."

"And what proof do you have?"

"None, really. But he knew my—"

"—so you've become someone who values belief over proof?"

Renue closed his eyes, seeing again that curious expression on Mesmer's face right before he died. "She came to the table. I lost the hand. Then she killed him. I don't remember much. Because of the forest."

"She killed him. But why?"

"I don't know. I'm not sure she does. She said something about Faldor."

"Well, she refuses to speak to any of us," Bardon said. "And the Manor is certainly searching for her, if quietly. You must find out what you can."

The young Damasker had led her to a room with a mattress covered with stiff blue sheets. It was the smallest room she had ever been in. A few minutes later, he returned with a change of clothes and a plate of white fish with a sour sauce and buttery potatoes. After her stomach calmed down, she ate ravenously. Then the quiet set in. Inevitably, she began to compare her new world with the Manor: the softness of the sheets, the richness of fowl with raspberry sauce, the texture of voices, smooth and clear. The lout accents were ugly and stunted and assaulted her ears. The air in the hills was cooler, fresher, on the Manor grounds but the city it stank with odors, sweat, garlic, onion, salt, blood. Even her body felt different. She had been running for so long her legs still felt in motion.

Lisande tried to sleep but sudden sounds from the hallway would make her break out in violent sweats. When she closed her eyes she saw her father. She tried to block out the image of the knife piercing his back, the final breath, his body slipping from the table. Briefly, she found memories that calmed her, picking fire spikes with her mother in the field behind the Manor, flying her purple and yellow kite under the shade of the mountains with Faldor. But he was gone. That night, more than ever, she wished her mother were still alive.

Because there was no clock, she couldn't tell when morning broke and soon she lost track of how many days had passed in the small room. Some time later, a Damasker knocked and told her to get dressed and after she had done so, Lisande followed him eagerly. The Damasker was younger than she, perhaps eighteen, and very short and thin. His body reminded her of bundled twigs. A lantern dangled from his hand. The two turned down a brown brick corridor and at the next intersection the Damasker paused, took a few steps down the right, then came back.

"Sorry," he said. "One sec."

"What's your name?"

"Lev."

"Lev, you haven't told me where we're going."

"This way. It's this way." He gestured to the left. "Sorry, but I can't say. Rules and all." A few Damaskers walked by, stared at the two, then continued down the corridor, whispering.

"Where are all the women?"

He snickered. "You from the farms?"

"I can't answer that," Lisande said. "The rules, you understand."

The young Damasker took a few hesitant steps down the hallway. "Drailers? None here." He grinned. "Sucks, I know." He extinguished the lantern and continued to lead her down the dimly lit corridor.

"I don't feel well."

"It'll pass. Just a moment."

"The Sickness," she said. "Is that—"

"We don't call it that here."

"The Gift, then. When did you know you had it?"

"Hmm . . . suppose that doesn't matter," he said. "And these halls are lonelier if you *don't* talk. Since I was a kid, I guess. First time was probably when my sis fell ill. I was sitting by her bed and I wanted her to be better real bad, so I just thought, you know, about her being better and the evil spirits in her skin and organs. Boy, I was *dumb* then. Evil spirits! Didn't even really know about germs or viruses or any of that small stuff. Now I know lots. The doctor, he told my ma my sis wouldn't live through the night."

"And you saved her? Can the Gift really do that?" she said. "Save people?"

"Sometimes—I threw up the next day," he boasted. "And I went and asked Alley about it. She's an oldie who lived down my street, until they took her across the sea." He frowned. "You probably don't get so many taken, living in the farms. Plus, the nasty doesn't really come out there, right? Must be nice." He sighed. "Across the sea."

"I want to go there someday."

"You . . . you do?"

"Soon, I hope."

Against the dull glow of the Krylight Lisande could see Lev's smallish teeth. She licked her own, straight and flat except for one space near the top back.

"He has a lighter touch where you're from?" he said softly. "Huh?"

"No," she said. "Not really."

Pausing next to a yellow wall lamp, Lev chuckled nervously. "Crazy, now. Everything's changing so fast. Manor said the Perenians attacked us, trying to sabotage the thing. I don't believe it." The young Damasker started to turn back the way they had come. "Shit . . . sorry. Been so forgetful lately. Wait. I've got it! Okay. Here." The passage he had chosen sloped upwards until they came into a relatively large mall that led to several different rooms. "Here we are! Sun room." Lev opened the door for her. Polished white rock bleachers lined two of the opposing walls, and in the center of the room was a beam of light coming down from a hole in the ceiling. "Real light," he said, pointing to a marble sundial where the beam focused. "Sometimes, they put colored crystals there and the whole room glows like a big, sparkling river. Beautiful. Keeps people sane, I think. A lot of the oldies are marked. That means they've murdered—I'm not saying you're dumb or anything, but I just didn't know if you're know what marked is, 'cause you're from the farms and all."

"I know."

"Well, so, *yeah*. The barrier hides them from the nasty."

"Nasty?"

He bit his tongue. "The thing? *The black thing?*"

She shut her eyes.

"So you *have* heard. Well, the barrier protects them down

here. A lot of them haven't been above ground in *years*. I'm talking twenty so years, on account of that's when the dark nasty first appeared. Seems like the worst thing in the world, to be trapped down here. I mean, you find things to like *anywhere*. But I'm just saying, to not be able to sit on the pier drinking Ramsden's—man!" The young Damasker's face suddenly froze, as though he were listening to a far away voice. "Gotta go, sorry. It was nice meeting ya."

Paintings were neatly spaced along the walls and a large print of the bell tower hung in the center, bristling with people and green, black. Above the print Lisande recognized the Qarashi flag, red and green and black, overlaid by an image of a gray wolf. One of her mother's tapestries had contained a similar wolf, but it had been standing across a frozen stream, with blood at its feet. The tapestry had frightened Lisande so much when she was little that her father took it down and only displayed it when heads of state visited.

"Lisande," Renue said from the door. Though his hair was finely combed, he was obviously exhausted.

"Where have you *been*?"

"I wanted to see you sooner, but they wouldn't let me." He crossed the room quickly and hugged her. "Are you alright?"

"What do you think? They've been keeping me in that small room like a lout. No, I'm not alright. I don't like it here, Renue."

"At least we're safe."

She sat on the stone and rested her chin in her hands. "I don't feel safe. I'm as much a prisoner here as I was there. And no one will speak to me. It was better in the Manor."

"But those people are monsters."

She sighed angrily. "Well if I have to choose between living with monsters or being alone, I'll choose monsters."

"Everything's going to be alright," he said. "Trust me."

"But we can't ever *leave*, right? Never?" She flattened her hands against the bleacher.

"Not necessarily. The laws are linked to Mesmer's blood, Lisande," he said. "Which means yours, if he is your father."

"You don't believe me either?"

"I do. Maybe you can help us," he said. "Then Alkor will find a way to unravel the Pattern, and we'll be free. *You'll* have freed us."

"Don't say that," she snapped. "Don't just assume I didn't love him."

"But you killed him."

"Who did you kill?"

He looked down. "I think you know."

"I had to figure that out for myself, though, didn't I?" she said. "You couldn't just tell me."

"You would have left."

Lisande rubbed her head. "You let me believe my father had Faldor murdered. He was more family than my father ever was. I loved him. I don't know why my father kept him around. Maybe he knew Faldor made me happy." Renue put a hand on her back but she scooted away. "Don't touch me."

"I know this is hard for you to accept," he said. "I can't imagine what this all must be like for you. But your father was a murderer. He tortured thousands. Alkor wants to show you the confessions. Maybe then you'll see what your father really was. But, Lisande, it was Faldor who sold out the country. He made all of it possible."

"No."

Renue took a deep breath. "You need to accept what your father really was. On your birthday, he probably ordered tortures, sent a hundred thousand off to war, and then helped you blow out candles. And you had to know. At least a little."

She watched as the beam in the center of the room began to fade. "Are you done?" she said. "If you had just listened to me and left, none of this would have happened. Even if what you say is really true, which it isn't, then I killed a tyrant. You killed an old man. Which blemish would *you* rather have?"

"Stop." He tried to grab her hand but she yanked it back. "We're family."

"That warms me like a match in winter." She watched Renue tremble, but sensing he was about to break, she softened her voice. "I'm not your sister," she said. "But you're so sick you can't see anything else. Besides, you think that's the answer? Family? My father and I shared the same blood, yes, and it only pushed us further apart." Her voice became even fainter. "So what makes you think it'll be any different with us." She headed for the door. "Well, it doesn't matter now," she said. "I saved your life, Renue. You took mine."

♥

He sat on the stone bleachers for almost an hour, replaying the conversation in his mind. Renue watched the light slowly empty from the room. Normally, it was filled at dawn and dusk with the marked ones who had made a daily ritual out of watching the natural light grow and fade. Now, he wondered why no one had come to join him. In the darkness, he thought of Lisande and Bardon, his two worlds, collapsing. Renue put on his new gloves and left the room, navigating the dark hallways. When a light would approach, he hid in the shadows. He knew all the passageways and how to make himself invisible. No one would expect him to leave because of the black thing, but whether it took him no longer seemed to matter.

When he emerged in the Slants, Renue took a deserted street down into Latchtown, its squat homes barely visible under flickering lights. Because the streetlights were few and spaced at such great distances there was almost complete darkness for large stretches. He found this comforting until he heard a woman crying. The cries came from a metallic shack just off the road.

Like most of Latchtown, the shack was little more than two crude windows surrounded by an assortment of scrap parts. To Renue, Latchtown was the heart of the city, the poorest section of Ashkareve. The only real money came from the black market, smugglers who docked in the salt marsh further to the east or dealers, or the gangs who controlled the streets. To Renue it was the home of his second chance. Only a few blocks away, as a boy, he had tried to pick Bardon's pocket. He must have been desperate then. If you pickpocketed from the wrong people in Latchtown, you'd end up dead, and the person who'd slit your throat would be a gang member who snitched or double-crossed someone. You'd die and he'd get black hands. Two deaths. But if he hadn't tried to steal from Bardon, his life could have ended far worse. The priests only let street kids sleep in the back yard of their religious house a short while. They only considered you a kid for so long. Eventually the spades would haul you off to the swamps or the mines. He'd been lucky, of course, but now thinking of Bardon made his mouth bitter.

The woman cried out again and Renue crept closer to the shack. Inside, a glass broke. To either side of the shack he could hear the grumbling of neighbors too close to avoid hearing the beating. She was sobbing. But even a wall removed was far enough not to care. Inside the shack, a man was beating his wife, but no neighbors would dare call the police. Community was non-existent in most of the city. Mesmer had seen to that by transforming everyone in Ashkareve into unknowing informants. Still, this troubled Renue. It always had. Husbands ruled homes, making slaves of wives and children, merchants cheating people out of hard-earned wages, jewelers selling fake gemstones to the ash-faced mine workers who had scraped together months of a salary to buy a gift for a loved one, people too dumb and desperate to know better. How was it that people who had lived under the shadow of Mesmer all their lives and knew a hundred different faces of cruelty still chose to cast shadows of their own?

As the sobbing died down, Renue left, heading across an overgrown field, scattering a pack of stray dogs that disappeared in the weeds. Along the field ran a metal fence, and halfway across the weeds cigarette embers hovering in the dark like glowing eyes. For a moment Renue was afraid but he fought the urge to run back to the underground. It was a necessary experiment, a game of chance, to test whether the laws still held, similar to how the Blanks would jump into ice-blanketed waters with steel-tipped shoes. They'd break the ice, plunging into the frigid waters, then scramble to find the opening before frostbite set in. The Blanks were a rigid, dogmatic people, but to their credit they had fought Mesmer in pockets all across Qarash, and even in Ashkareve. But the rift between the Blanks and the Damaskers had long been too great to acknowledge their mutual struggle. Had the two groups joined together, Renue thought, Mesmer's regime might have been toppled years ago. But the Blanks despised the Damaskers perhaps as much as they despised the dictator himself.

At the far side of the field, Renue heard the woman wailing once more. Then a harsh wind overtook her cries. He considered returning to the shack. Eventually the neighbors would step in and, if not, at least the husband would stop short of death. The regime's supporters called this evidence that Mesmer's laws worked, but Renue considered it proof that they didn't. He doubled back and passed by the shack again but she was quiet. All Latchtown was quiet, as though holding its breath.

Cutting northwards on Hork Street, he passed a few lit homes but most were dark. Latchtown was where his life as a street kid had ended, and now he realized where he would naturally head: the docks, where he had become Renue. He climbed uphill and across a winding street bordered by a rambling brick wall, near where the Ear had been caught. To his surprise, he heard the faint sound of drunken laughter and followed it down a lonely street. A woman with a baby strapped to her stomach darted quickly into an apartment, watching him suspiciously. After she went inside, he heard the laughter again, coming from the thin alleyway halfway down the street.

Four louts huddled in the near dark tossing cards onto a wooden box. Blue lamplight shone down from the fire escape. As a stiff breeze fell across the alleyway, the four louts held their cards tightly. When the wind died down, the louts resumed their game and now Renue recognized their voices.

"Shyyyy!"

"Dego almost lost it."

"Pieky's the lout!"

"Thought I had it, Benny, ya bastard."

"Playing like a pansy, Pieky."

"Say that five times fast, Kors."

"Loser's still crushing on that marked hillborn."

Renue stepped over some empty cans and a half-broken fiddle as Piek leaned away from the light. The other three louts looked up in alarm and reached to their sides, but Piek quickly held up his hand.

"Easy, boys," he said. "Easy."

"The Face?" Benny said. "Right, Pieky?"

"Didn't expect to see you again," Piek said, putting down his cards.

"Same here."

"You and your sis want out?"

"No."

"Cost us a bit to convince those spades we hadn't see you two—care to make a donation?"

"No."

"Come for another trick, then? Watch—"

"I'm not really in the mood."

"Is he a Masker?" Dego said, tossing a card into the pile. "You find out?"

"Sure is," Piek said. "Right?"

"That's a dangerous accusation."

"Not here." Piek gestured grandly across the alley. "Hillborn privacy, tonight."

"*He's* a Damasker?" Benny said, shuffling nervously. "Really?"

Dego threw down his bottle. "Lousy fucks. You're all talking too *loose*."

"Why shouldn't we? It's a holiday. Like Rady just said on the radio. Always remember the Scream."

"Always remember," Kors scoffed. "Maskers probably did it."

"Couldn't have. They're weak."

"Weak?" Benny said, dealing. "They can move minds. Bend wills. Make you shit yourself in the middle of the day."

"Shut up, Benny."

"But I saw it."

"Ma clean your underwear, did she?"

The other louts snorted.

For a few minutes, Renue watched them play. The presence of the four louts comforted him strangely.

"Manor!" Dego said, laying a card triumphantly on the box.

"So how's your sister holding up?" Piek said. "Fucking Maskers."

Kors tossed his last card onto the box. "Hillborn."

"Fuck the Maskers—let's talk about something else."

"The *old ones* were alright," Piek said. "Then they lost it."

Benny nudged him. "Come on, your *turn*. My ma'll find bed melons any minute."

Kors pushed Benny. "My little Benny, oh, the blackie'll get you. Make you shit yourself in the middle of street."

The others chuckled.

"Why don't you like the Damaskers?"

"Here's the thing, Face," Piek said. "Black thing's scared of the Gift. That's why Mes outlawed it. So if *I* had the Gift—"

"—you'd enchant some girl to bone you," Dego said. Piek lunged over the box and Dego fell back over a bottle, crashing into the wall. He returned to his seat, holding his arm. "Softy."

"Maybe, but I'd fix some things first." Piek collected the cards and began to deal. "When I'm running Ash," he said, "thing's are gonna change."

"Ah, shut up and play," Kors said, laying down an eight.

Renue took a step closer. "What game is this?"

"Faldor," Dego said, fanning his cards.

Benny sighed. "I'd be a Masker, but I—"

"Shut *up*, Benny."

"Faldor?"

"Used to be called Lout or Latch," Piek said. "You try to lose all your cards. Manor, Hillborn, Lout, Faldor's the order. Play in pairs, in singles, triples, up to Ace. Red twos cancel the deck, Black two's the black thing, kills the deck." He spit. "When Old F kicked the bucket, we named it in honor of him. Finally lost it all—hey, where you going?"

"I don't know," Renue said. "Goodnight."

"Yeah, night." Piek threw his cards on the box. "Hey, if you and your sis still want out, I'm your man."

The louts began to sing as Renue walked away.

"Drink the drink that drinks the night."

"Drink the drink that drinks the night."

"Work all day then out like lights."

"But take our hearts and then we fight."

"So drink the drink that drinks the night."

"Faldor! Faldor! He lost his cards, he lost his wife, he lost his freedom, then his life."

♥

Renue drifted down through the empty streets until he reached a long, continuous boardwalk. Larger vessels anchored

116

on the western side of the docks in the distance and smaller ships, sailboats, rowboats, fishing barges bobbed in their shadows. A slow breeze swept across the waters, pinching the ocean into broad, rolling waves. The large ships barely swayed at all, just an occasional creaking or groan. As Renue approached the spot where he and Bardon had met the night before he left for the Nanor, he heard a faint rattling from a small building framed by two fish stalls. The sense of the boards taking his weight calmed him some. Early on in the dictatorship, the docks were the sight of mass exodus because the airways had always been closed to civilians. Many had tried to leave the country by ship, but those who didn't have the Manor's consent were usually discovered. Often the spades impounded vessels for weeks on suspicion, and though some people escaped, it soon became known amongst traders the price Mesmer exacted from those who prospered from human transport. He held onto everyone he could. New medical graduates were forced to remain in the country for the war, their degrees held hostage. It was almost impossible to escape the regime. While Renue wondered what it would cost to get Lisande out, he knew Alkor would never let her go.

On the nearby dock sat an emaciated young woman, kicking her toes at the water. She wore a dark-colored dress, and Renue watched her for several minutes to be sure she was real. Then she waved slowly. When he was a few feet away she gazed past him out to the ocean, humming a dumb little tune, repetitive, somehow sliding in between the rhythm of the music coming from the bar. Finally, the young woman faced him.

"I'm the tallest in my family," she said, bobbing her chin up and down. She had a drowsy way of speaking, as though each word found the next by surprise.

"You're very tall," he said.

"Do you think so?" She crooked her head into her shoulder

like a dove and extended her hand. "I'm Mallery, but people call me Mally. It's the 'Mal'—that makes it Mal—and the 'ly' just makes it sound nice, I think."

"Should you be out so late?"

"Oh, I don't know."

"Do you live around here?" he said. "It's not safe for you—even if you *are* the tallest."

Mally let out a small, embarrassed laugh. "Ma'd be *mad*," she said. "I wasn't gonna stray, I really wasn't. But then I heard this thumping and I followed it and it was nice. It's nice, isn't it? You like it? The music?"

"Very nice," Renue said. "But you really should go home. Be with your ma tonight."

"Cause of the Scream?" she said. "Where were you at? I was on Glocker. Glocker and Emir and I got pushed down." Mally rolled up her sleeves and showed her bruised arms.

"I'm glad you're safe."

"Thanks. I don't really remember much." Her lips puckered. "Do you think I'm pretty?"

In the low light he could still make out the many indentations on her face, and across her left cheek was a brown dead patch of skin. Her nose was knotted and appeared to have been broken several times. But her eyes were the most curious part about her, blue and mysteriously vacant.

"I'm the tallest in my family," Mally said. "Ma says, I heard her, she says to Mumbly Pierson, she says, shadn't worry Mally about her brains cause she's pretty. Do you think I'm pretty?"

"Very," he said.

She giggled. "Do you have a girlfriend?"

"No."

Mally beamed, purring softly. The music had died down and it was quiet enough to hear clinking glasses and conversations coming through the windows of the nearest bar.

"Would you like to lay with me?"

His body suddenly felt heavy. "Oh, you're too beautiful for me."

"Come *on*." Taking Renue by the hand, she led him down to the end of the dock and dangled her feet again. "Take off your shoes. The water's cool on your toes. And those gloves too. It's summer!"

"I can't."

"Ooohhh. It's *just* right." After a moment she pushed him down on the dock and scratched his chest. "Are you alright?" she said, scooting closer to him. "You seem a little sad. Not a lot sad, but maybe a little sad?"

"Maybe a little sad."

"Ma says it's okay to be a little sad sometimes." Mally's eyes shallowed. "I came home today but Joggy wasn't there. He's my brother, Joggy is. I came to find him but then I forgot when I heard the nice music."

Renue faced her. "I haven't seen your brother." He sat up. "This is no time to be out, Mallery. You really should go home."

"Fine. The music's gone anyway," she said, hopping to her feet. She put her hands to her lips. "Joggy. Joggy!"

"Don't yell, Mally. Just go home."

She reached out with her hand and he shook hers. "Your hand is cold."

"That's why I wear the gloves," he said. "Cold hands."

Suddenly she looked afraid, but then she showed her teeth and grinned. "Oh, *funny*. I get it. What was your name? You probably told me but I always forget names."

"Bren," he said. "Go home, Mally."

"Okay—I hope you get less sad," she said. "Even a little. You're a nice guy. Wow, this has been the longest conversation I ever had with a man. I must be good at conversing."

"And you're the tallest in your family," Renue said.

As she walked down the boardwalk, he dipped his hands in

the water. His skin was slightly chilled by the sea air as he sat on the dock, imagining that he and Lisande were in a cottage somewhere in the north. They sat by a perfectly still lake, inventing stories about growing up together, retelling the stories until they became true. For a while he listened to the ocean breeze in a rare peace, in and out of sleep.

"Is that him?"

"Sure is."

Renue propped himself up on his elbows. Three men were poised at the edge of the dock and although they were wearing lout clothes, their presence was unmistakably that of Damaskers.

"Night, Puker," Granges said, tapping the watch on his wrist. "Past your curfew."

"I just needed some air. I was going to come back."

Granges stepped forward. "How about a welcome *back* party?"

"I don't think I'm up to it."

"For the record, I wouldn't have fucked up," Granges said. "Bardon and Alkor made a mistake choosing you."

"Well now I'm paying for it." Renue held up his hands and the two other Damaskers froze.

"Holy shit, he's marked."

"Let's just get him . . . quick."

"Relax, thing's is fucked for the time being," Granges said, shaking his head. "You had it in your hands, Puker."

"What would you have done in the Manor?" Renue said. "Can you say for sure?"

"I would have done my job."

The blows fell quickly and Renue made no effort to resist. After they were finished, he groaned, laying flat on his stomach.

"Remember," Granges said. "There is no nightmare, other than to be living in this city."

"Get a bite before we take him home?"

"Let's roll him in the water."

"Sure. Back in a few, Puker."

With their feet, the Damaskers nudged Renue into the water. The cold woke him. He stayed beneath until Granges and the others were gone. As he came to the surface, Renue pushed a layer of grime from his eyes. He rubbed them vigorously with his hands, then pulled himself up out of the water. At the end of the dock, a soap-white man stood, wrapped in a gray cloak. For a moment, Renue thought to slip back into the brackish water but he found his body unresponsive and could only stare at Faldor, the image of him fixed as a stalled projector. When Faldor showed no sign of moving, Renue got to his feet, his vision cut in fours by the high lights of the market. The apparition had vanished. He ran, stopping halfway down the dock, squinted, and took a step back. His shadow was projected in thin strips on the boardwalk and now Faldor stood in front of him.

"Let me see her one more time," Renue said. "Please."

A hard breeze blew across the docks and his ears were filled with white noise. All he could hear was the lapping waters. Faldor had vanished. Renue exhaled. He felt something on his shoulders and turned. For a second he saw the apparition of Faldor, then the image disappeared, replaced by a fogged black mass in the shape of a human. Renue pled for mercy. On his knees he begged. *Lisande* was the last word to escape his lips.

II

Chapter Five

The dusk sun reddens the bell tower stones and the city is awash in a strange light that paints streets and faces, signs, buildings. Ashkareve has been whispering all day. In a nook near the tower, three louts lean against an old mural of Mesmer, overgrown with weeds.

"He's scared, I think."

"Why?"

"Had the thing."

"And now?" the thin one says.

"He doesn't. Maskers fucked it."

"It was the Blanks."

The thin one sips. "Perenians, I heard."

"These are drinking times."

The three louts raise their bottles.

"Don't know what I do . . . " the fat one sings.

The others two join in.

"Without Amber's Honey-Brew."

The louts clink glasses softly, sipping until a fourth man approaches, holding onto the stones for support. As the man falls down, they laugh gently.

"Some left," the thin lout says, holding up his bottle. "Want it?"

The fat one sings. "Drink the drink that drinks the night. Amber Brew is good at night."

"Shut up," the man yells. "Shut the fuck up with that singing."

"Don't need to be rude," the fat one says. "Ya rell me?"

"I don't care anymore." The man snatches the bottle from the thin lout's hand. "They're gone. All gone."

"Gone?"

"The boy."

The ashen-faced lout cranes his head. "Not the boy . . . how?"

The man drinks deeply, resting his teeth on the bottle mouth. "Trampled."

"When?"

"When it spoke," the man says. He reaches for another beer but the ash-faced lout blocks him.

"Dumbing your thinker's not the answer."

"Been thinking too much," the man grumbles. "That's the fucking problem."

"Easy it up."

"Here," the thin one says, handing another bottle to the man.

The man opens it and drinks greedily. "What does it mean?"

"What?" the fat lout says. "What was what mean?"

"Anything." The man gulps. "What does anything mean? Keep calm, they say. Join the army, they say. War again, they say." He coughs. "How the fuck can a man know what's real anymore?"

"Be patient."

"Says they."

The fat one tugs at a vine on the wall. "Scream wasn't the Manor's fault. Sabotage—Perenians."

"Blanks."

"Maskers."

"Bullshit," the man says loudly as the louts shush him. "It's always war."

"Stop."

He glares at the thin lout. "I was in the war. Too old now, but not you. No," he says. "Not you. You, you're fucked. Oh they'll come for you, ribbon on your door. Still have mine. When they come, you're fucked. Can't hide. Not from them. You'll see."

The thin lout bit his lip. "I don't want to *die*," he says softly.

"Then join the army."

"I don't *want* to die."

"Then don't join the army."

The thin lout shifts on the wall as the man chuckles darkly.

"Stop it, you're scaring him."

"So? He should be scared," he says, grinding his teeth. "What's the point? What is your fucking point?"

"Some good left," the fat lout insists. "Come on, you're scaring the kid."

The man stands, tries to maintain his balance but falls against the mural as the louts try to catch him. He shakes them off, tearing vines from the wall, revealing an eyebrow with a scar down the middle, crow black hair, Mesmer's smile. "You fuck." He kicks the bottle against the mural and it shatters.

"Easy, bud. Quiet," the ash-faced lout says.

"M'tired of the thing," the man yells. "Tired of the Manor."

The fat lout puts a hand on his shoulder. "Sit down."

" . . . treat us like mules. Fuck us while we . . . "

"*Quiet.*"

"But I can't *sleep*," the man says. "It's not right. They just keep taking." He wipes his eyes. "Taking."

The ash-faced lout stands. "Let's get our boy home."

"Boy," the man yells. "Boy."

"Shh."

"Ears might be deaf, but spades're still out."

"My boy . . . get your fucking hands off me." The fat lout holds the man's shirt as he struggles. "They killed the boy," he says, eyes red as a dog's. "The boy." The other louts wrestle him to the ground and the man is frenzied and sobbing, "I don't care. I don't fucking care."

The fat lout smacks him across the face. "There's more—"

"I'll kill Mesmer." The man lunges at the mural.

Stepping back, the fat lout shakes his head sadly. "Gone crazy."

"Get your fucking hands off me," the man whimpers against the concrete. He bats the ash-faced louts away. "What's the point?"

"Friends?"

"Brew?"

"Rady's giving some away at the speech, I heard."

The man spits. "More to life than drink."

" . . . maybe he's right," the thin lout says. "I mean . . . "

"I'll strangle him. I'll slit his throat. I'll blow his fucking head off."

"Go home," the ash-faced lout says. "Before it's too late."

"But maybe he's right . . . " There's a sad expression on the thin lout's face, captured as he glances into the streetlight and squints. "I always wanted that fancy cheese." He licks his lips. "Never will afford it—maybe I'll just *take* it."

"That's right, that's right," the man slurs. "Take what you want. Take it all." He backs away, pulls a flask from his pocket, tosses the flask back, then tucks it under his armpit. "That's what they do. They take and take and take and take." He takes a final drink, hurls the flask against the mural.

The ash-faced lout approaches hesitantly, placing a hand on the man's shoulder. "Known you fifteen years. Please go home. Please."

"What changed?" the fat lout says. "Everyone goes in the end."

"When they took the boy," the man chokes. "Family tree died. Too old. Never had that thinking until now."

As the man staggers away, the voices of the louts fade. It's night and the city appears only as a contour, thin sketches of charcoal smearing against blue, red, purple lights. He takes off down a crooked alleyway as the wind picks up, snapping clothes off lines. The wind is screaming.

"Anyone there?" he says, his voice thick. "Nah. Thinker's busted, that's all that's all that's all. And drunk. You're drunk." The man can taste the boy in the night air, the smell of his dirty knees, his milk-sour breath. The texture of his boy's voice, still sharp in the man's mind. That voice, peppy as a pinpoint. The boy's habits, asking two questions so one would be answered. For a time, he and the wife told the boy stories, but then they tired out, drank earlier, slept earlier, let the boy into the city. Just not the Blanks, he'd tell the boy. And not the Damaskers. The Blanks, the Damaskers, as long as you stay clear of them then you'll be fine fine fine, he'd say to the boy while patting his curly black hair. Everything will be just fine.

There's a gritty feeling in his heart, a hissing anger. Stopping at a window, the man knocks and after a moment it opens. He leans in and hands a crumpled bill, receives a bottle, takes it, uncorks it. The liquor smells like oily rags. Walking up Goramon Avenue, he grips the warm bottle, wondering where his son fell. He takes a drink, then another, drifting down into memories long buried, his wife, whisked away by an artist—the shameful ones, they're called by the Blanks—but the man hates the Blanks too. Zealots. Artists, what's the difference? The lousy prosers fight torture and death with words, like fighting the sea with a bucket. The Blanks used to bomb buildings, but they killed as many innocents as spades. What does it matter? Now no one rages against the Manor. People fall in line, strung together with remembered fear. This law, that law. Nothing's left but booze and sex, sex and safety. There's no such thing as family. They took it all. In the city without murder they kill every day, just slower. Some have escaped, he thinks. But you need money to escape.

The man stares up at the darkened hills, wondering where Mesmer is at that moment. Even if he got past the forest, which he couldn't, Boran's Hands would stop him. Maybe he'll kill somebody else, anyone else. Take a life. Lots of spades around. How many can he get, he wonders? As he steps into the street, an image of his boy lays in the gutter, crushed by a lout, his arm double-angled. Not even ten. God, the man had wept. Only a week ago there was order at least. Order and law and no trampling. People were more careful. Life was precious. Good, honest work. Clean, peaceful lives. Cold, winter order. Dead, yes, but quiet, and if not peaceful then at least safe. His son, snuffed before he even knew the country was rotten. Always asked two questions. Voice, peppy as a pin point. He had loved the boy. Just didn't know it until late.

The man sits on a stoop just out of a street lamp's eye, seething, planning, voice lubricated with thick poison. Suddenly, his breath freezes. His essence appears as a coal in pure black night, smoldering, escaping from his body as the man's final breath disappears with the screaming wind.

♥

Bardon opened the door to the room where Renue's body lay and Lisande approached the bed. Gray hair budded from Renue's scalp and his breath came so faintly she had to strain to hear. His wrist barely had a pulse, like the end of a drying water faucet.

"We had a fight," she said. The slight whistling from his mouth made her shiver. "That's why he left."

"You had nothing to do with this," Bardon said, closing the door. "We should never have sent him. It was a mistake—my mistake."

Lisande took a seat in a chair and adjusted the lampshade on the bedside table so the light wouldn't hit Renue's face. Above the frame was a print of a small humming bird poised at the tip of flower, and another of an older woman. "Who is that?"

"Dora. She heads the Drailers," he said. "I've known her since the beginning."

Lisande studied Renue's pale face. "He was willing to risk everything for a memory," she said. "For me."

"Are you alright?"

"Two murders in one week?" Lisande said. "Sure, I do this all the time." Crossing a leg, she leaned on her elbow. "Being down here reminds me of my mother. Until I left, I hadn't thought about her for a long time."

"Oh?"

"She was sick for a long time. And she died in our basement."

"Do you find you're remembering more now, Lisande?"

"Yes." She swallowed. "I wish I had known that when my father buried my mother, he was really burying the memory of her too. That's something they don't tell kids about funerals." Lisande watched Renue for as long as she could stand, then turned away, swallowing against a dried throat. "After the funeral, he tried to forget her." Lisande pulled at her hair, removing a few tangled strands. "That's all this place is good for. Thinking too much."

"Very true." Bardon leaned beside the bed and held Renue's hand.

"I can almost hear his exact words," she said. "His voice. *I hope with time we forget how poorly she went.* That's not what you *say* to a little girl. To your daughter. You're *supposed* to say, she's gone to a better place. Everything will be fine. Not, she died in pain. Not, your mother suffered."

"Do you regret taking his life?"

"He took mine," she said softly. "But now my mother's gone forever. So I took her memory too." Bardon seemed exhausted. "Are you okay?"

"Not at all," he said. "I suspect I feel a bit like you do right now."

"Do you have any family?"

"Only Renue. And Dora, in a way."

"If I hadn't said those things, he'd be alive."

"It was nothing you did," Bardon insisted. "You can't keep things from those you love, not even to protect them." The Damasker paused at the door. "I should go. I'm no good to you right now."

"Stay longer," she said. "Just a little."

"Can you find your way back?"

"Yes."

"Then goodnight, Lisande."

She watched Renue for a few more minutes, then went to the bathroom and washed her face, studying herself in the mirror. In the drawer she found a pair of scissors. She closed her eyes as heavy strands fell into the sink. Even the cutting sounded like her father whispering.

Chapter Six

Three men sit in wooden chairs at a townhome on the hill overlooking Ashkareve. Holding a glass of lemonade, Melnor watches condensation bead and drop onto his fingers. A long, impatient scowl spreads across Debeau's face as he plays with the poker chips strewn about, reds, blues, whites, yellows. A Krylight lamp swings overhead. Across the table, Wildcard studies both while plucking at his long, framing eyebrows.

"Can we change that?" Debeau growls. "I want natural light."

"Technically," Wildcard says, "Krylight is natural light. Electricity is manufactured."

"How very interesting—just fucking change it."

"Always on the quest for knowledge, aren't you, Red Beard? No, don't touch it, Melnor." Wildcard's greasy hair glows green. "I like Krylight."

"You would," Debeau spits.

"Is that really necessary?" Melnor says.

"You should get used to it, Red. All the lights of the world will burn green before you can say shave."

Debeau stands. "I am getting tired of your tone, little one."

Wildcard shakes his head. "You know, there's this thing called a contraction, and it's not only for women." He jumps out of his seat as Debeau lunges for him. "Ah, tut tut tut. No Manor walls to protect you now. Wouldn't want black hands, would we?"

"Will you two stop it?" Melnor says. "We have serious matters to discuss."

"Yes, we do."

"Like what, Card?" Debeau picks up a brimming handful of chips and lets them fall between his broad fingers. "You've never been serious. Not a day in your pampered, brief life."

Wildcard puts his arms around his shoulders and feigns shivering. "The sound of your voice is so . . . melodious. Like springtime flowers. Like the cry of a dying hooker."

"Why am I wasting my time here, Melnor? I was just about to return to Grenore."

"No one should leave before the matter of ascendancy is settled."

"What?"

"Allow me?" Wildcard says, turning to Debeau. "Ascendancy's a tough one, so I'll translate to save time. Melnor, unlike you, is not so dense. He knows Boran's ruse won't last long, as Mesmer is already worm chow. Further, Melnor fears we're plotting against him, which we are. He believes he should take over because he's the oldest of Mesmer's guard still alive. But you don't agree, Red Beard, do you? You fancy those trunkish arms of yours are brawny enough to hold up the entire country. And I think I should rule because . . . " Wildcard smiles. "Well, because I'm a fucking genius."

"I want what is best for the country." Debeau says. "Nothing more."

"Always draped in patriotism, aren't you? Then again, we should be lucky you're wearing anything at all." Debeau rises but Melnor's hand quickly falls on his shoulder and reluctantly he sits. "So, Melnor wants to know whether we can decide who will succeed Mesmer civilly." Wildcard grins. "Or have I misspoken?"

Melnor taps a finger to his cheek. "And the sooner, the better. Practically all of history illustrates that unrest in one city can quickly spread to others. Especially in a country ruled so . . . tightly."

"Well, I assure you, my cities wouldn't touch Debeau's cities."

Wildcard makes a sour face. "That's how you spread diseases. Grenore is the whore of Qarash. And it even *rhymes*!"

Debeau stares down Wildcard, then turns his attention to Melnor. "You want the country, but without the struggle—is that it, Melnor? Well, get on with your deal. I have a woman waiting."

"Then we're doing the young lady a favor, if you ask me," Wildcard says. "More time to escape her bonds." As Debeau starts to rise, Wildcard tosses chips at him. "Oh, sit down. That wasn't even a good one."

"We play for the seat." Melnor takes a sip of lemonade and purses his lips. "Too sour."

"Fine."

"Sure," Wildcard says. "Why not?"

"Now?"

Melnor tosses cards on the table but Wildcard pushes them away. "No, it was a fucking joke. This is a country we're talking about. Besides, aren't you two tired of poker yet? What about Hearts or Spades? Oh right . . . we'd need a fourth. Rady? Boran? Treta? Red Beard, what do you think? Who would you rather climb into bed with? What I mean is, if you had to screw one of them . . . "

"You're a stupid fuck," Debeau says. "Do you know that?"

"I'm just saying."

Melnor rolls his eyes. "Cut it out. The Pattern is failing. That much is obvious. Boran estimates less than half of the city's surveillance is non-Sickness."

"I hate the Sickness," Debeau grumbles, flicking the Krylight lamp. "Worthless."

Melnor clears his throat. "Our most immediate threat is the black thing. Boran claims he doesn't know where the Pattern is located."

Debeau scratches his beard. "Give me a thousand men and I'll find it tonight."

"And how do you propose to do that?"

"It sees murder, doesn't it?" Debeau says. "Make someone kill a deck or two of louts. Draw it in. Then . . . kill it."

Wildcard cackles.

"What the fuck is so funny?"

"Oh, nothing."

"What?" Melnor says. "You're the only one with the Sickness."

"I prefer the Gift, thanks." Wildcard takes a deep breath. "Debeau, it's just such a stupid idea. You call every smutty coal of a thought a diamond. It's a wonder you haven't been assassinated by now. Oh, right. All of your citizens are in jails."

"Watch your tongue, fairy."

"Half your city's in prison, you brute," Wildcard says. "Can't you be nice? Here's a new word for you. Compromise. Or diplomacy? Ring a bell? Give me some paper. I'll write them down."

"I'm getting—"

"Wildcard, could it be controlled?" Melnor says impatiently. He picks up the lemonade and puts it to his brow. "Did it answer to only Mesmer, or—"

"Would it answer to one of us?" Wildcard says softly. "Now *that's* interesting. All of a sudden too, as though the thought came naturally."

"What?" Melnor says.

Wildcard studies him intently.

"What?"

"Is that what you want?" Wildcard says. "The black thing? After all, he used it to assassinate people too. Just a drop of blood. So you see, you're already thinking beyond order. What do you want, Melnor? What do you really want? Tell me. What face would this country assume if it were under your control? I need to know. It's important."

Melnor's face reddens as he struggles to speak. "What I don't want is for Qarash to revert to the Faldor days," he says. "Before your time. You have no inkling what this country was like. So I'll ask again, and answer before I lose *my* patience. Can it be controlled?"

Wildcard's fingers perch on his temple. "It's possible, if you believe Boran. That is, if Mesmer had a son or daughter still living. A daughter, I think, though I couldn't say why exactly. Just a hunch."

"Then why does no one remember?"

"He must have placed a barrier on her, a barrier that only failed if she left. That Renue took someone, that's for sure. I saw two pairs of footprints. I even found a few traces of the Gift in the Market. But I can't track her if she doesn't use it."

"What does any of this matter?" Debeau says. "A Pattern, a daughter. Mesmer fucked this country. He didn't crush the Damaskers when he had the chance. He allowed the Blanks to spread. He let this country crumble like stone."

Wildcard applauds lazily. "Half a point for potential. And another for the simile—not the best but I *like* that you try."

"For the last time—"

"Then shut the fuck up," Wildcard says. "If he had a daughter, you waste of flesh, it means he would have linked her to the Pattern too. No doubt that's why the spy kidnapped her. You know, this reminds me of an old story. Once there was a time before the black thing, when a brutal dictator realized that the poor hearts would always have the numbers. So he ripped the country to pieces, exploiting religious beliefs and cultures, and he started a war to—"

"—leave your story telling to your boys, Card."

Wildcard turns to Debeau slowly. "I didn't like that," he says. "I didn't like that, and I'll remember it."

"Only until your next bliss break."

"That's enough!" Melnor pounds his fist on the table. His

hands are trembling. "He hid her from us. Which makes her important. That's all that matters."

Wildcard yawns. "Let's just announce he's dead. Maybe I'll do it tomorrow."

"You will not." Melnor takes a breath. "Sometimes, I don't know if you were nicknamed to suit your habits, or if you simply act to keep up that fucking nickname."

"Possibly a little of both."

"And you call me stupid," Debeau says. "If we announced the assassination, there'd be revolts across the country."

"Who cares? Even the strongest forest has to burn every so often to regrow. A little revolution can be a healthy thing. Or we could take on Boran and Rady, together."

"Don't underestimate Boran," Melnor says.

"You're the weakest, Card."

"But my people like me. Your cities are veritable wastelands and sewers, Red Beard." Wildcard spins a chip on the table. "So what does it matter if shit burns?"

"Veritable wastelands . . . " Debeau stutters.

"Oh dear, fetch a dictionary, will you, Melnor? I forget that I don't need to speak in inversions or Blank or slants to sound like code to our friend here. It just takes a word over one syllable." Wildcard sighs. "The problem, I think, is that you don't read. Didn't your father teach you? How can you expect to govern an entire country if you don't read? You're as bad as Rady. Really, it astounds me!"

Melnor frowns. "Is it raining?"

Wildcard looks up. "That, or Debeau's women are tinkling on the roof because they have no beard—"

"—enough!"

"Yes, please," Melnor says. "It's getting tiresome. We have to find this daughter. Blame the black thing's recent . . . indiscretions on the Damaskers or the Blanks."

"Both," Debeau says. "If their animosity is so high."

"Am I dreaming?" Wildcard says. "That was a good word, my fellow." The buildings below are striped with splotchy yellow lights.

"Perhaps the Damaskers can be bargained with," Melnor says. "And we could draw their kin from other cities to help capture the thing."

Debeau grumbles. "Mesmer relied too much on that pet of his, if you ask me. This country's been in shit storms for decades. He did us no service by silencing the thinkers."

Wildcard looks up slowly, then stands. "I'm touched to hear you say that."

"We'd better throw in together, now."

"On my word." Wildcard approaches the fogging window.

"Your word?" Debeau says. "I'll believe your word when I see you with an actual woman in your room."

"I'm taking note," Wildcard says. "Remember that one day from now, when your own people have that thick neck of yours in the noose." His eyes shift. "Does anyone else feel a draft in here?"

The three listen to the rain.

"It's nothing," Debeau says. "Come to my cities and you'll see real storms."

Wildcard pouts. "And you've never invited me."

"This isn't a city," Melnor says, joining Wildcard by the window. "It's a graveyard."

Wildcard rests a hand to his cheek. "I hate Ashkareve."

"Then give me your support."

"Bullshit!"

"No," Wildcard says slowly, his hand to the glass. He wipes the window with his sleeve. "No."

"Why?"

"They say there are only two classes of men, Melnor. Those who are content to yield to circumstances, and those who aim to control them."

"Control circumstances? And what circumstances haven't we considered?"

"Not circumstances," Wildcard says, breath fogging the glass. "Other men."

Chapter Seven

Snow blankets the lawn and forest, but it doesn't appear as magical anymore. Still, Sophia runs to the back of the Manor and presses her hands against the windows, watching the flurry. Winter used to be her favorite. Now the Manor feels cold, no matter the season. Her father doesn't seem to recognize her anymore. Since her mother's death, his door is always closed.

Hearing the floorboard groan, Sophia crawls beneath the long hallway table and gazes up through the glass at the figurines. Father is walking the hallway, observing the tables and rugs and phones as though they are foreign objects. His dress shoes stop at the far end of the hall. She can hear him mumbling. In the past months, his actions have become even more erratic. Once, he ordered all the Krylight out of the Manor, and for the next few weeks after the sun went down there was only candlelight that transformed rooms into caverns and servants into wraiths and ghosts.

As he passes, she starts to ask him something but he continue on as though he hasn't heard. She repeats it as he vanishes behind the corner.

It's my birthday tomorrow, she says. Remember?

In the morning, she wakes to a knock at the door.

Hello, an old man says, something hidden behind him. Do you remember me?

She recognizes him. One of her father's advisors, the one who walks in the garden and behind the Manor, usually alone. Yes, Faldor, she says. I remember.

He holds up a present. This is for you.

What is it?

A surprise. Go on.

Slowly, she unwraps a kite shaped like a butterfly, purple and yellow. Wow. It's beautiful.

Get your coat, Faldor says. Let's go see if it flies.

Though Sophia spends most of her time with Faldor, she also begins to follow her father. She adapts, learns how to listen, to puzzle out from the cooks and servants where in the maze-like Manor he could be hiding: his study, the den, the medal room, the garden, the basement.

One night, she catches him eating a piece of bread up on the parapet overlooking the city.

Are you okay, Father? I never—

I told you not to call me that anymore.

Why?

He stares past her. Please, he says. Please, Sophia. Just leave me be.

♥

The veins of Goramon Avenue bulge. Will Mesmer finally appear? What will he say? Who attacked us? Will there be war? Thousands of louts have been waiting for hours in the blinding midday sun, slowly reduced to slabs of baking flesh. Many have taken shelter under tents and canopies, some under the shadow of loved ones. The wind carries the odor of grilling onions and greasy meat, fried dough frosted with powdered sugar, the salty aroma of coins, perspiration, the tang of crushed fish eyes clinging to boots.

High above, the bell sounds, once, twice, and thousands watch the podium. Spades are positioned around the stage, more on the rooftops, rafters, even balancing on the clotheslines, possibly. Two disheveled louts hold newspapers over their heads. Lots of them. Why? Show of force is strongest when the enemy is weakest. Who says? Pestras. Who? Some old fart.

Mesmer has not been seen for ages, though not a day has gone by when his presence has not been felt: his eyes in statues, his heartbeat in laws and proclamations, his gait in the whirl of spades storming into a house. Once there was always someone watching in Ashkareve, but since the Scream, the apparatuses of surveillance have clearly lessened. In the last two weeks, people have begun to speak again—about almost everything, the etymology of tremblers, the term Manor, the name Mesmer, the man himself. They remember how in the beginning, he actually sought out their love. He walked the streets then, would drop by a house in the middle of the night and you'd have no choice but to let him in. He would even arrive bearing presents, a rare plant, a beautiful fabric, a figurine from a far-off land, a bottle of liquor, a brand new car. Mesmer wanted to be loved, but love was always the costliest thing he could ask for. A month ago, only a suicidal fool would speculate openly why he retreated to the Manor, why he has appeared so rarely in the last years: the loss of his sons perhaps, or his wife, or the failed war. Which took from him the most?

Suddenly there comes a thunderous applause, hooting, whistling, and hollering as Poten Rady takes the stage. His black hair is combed and parted neatly to the left. The Poten's bushy eyebrows nearly meet above his smallish nose. A slight, nearly undetectable smirk widens as the clapping swells. From behind the stage, Wildcard watches as Rady waves generously.

"Hope you didn't have to wait too long," Rady says, rolling up his sleeves. "Though I sure could use the tan."

The people laugh.

He wipes sweat from his forehead. "Thank you for coming. I know the last few weeks have been difficult ones, but let me assure you, we will never, never, forget the victims of the Scream. Yet we must also remember that because we live in one of the strongest nations on this earth, there will always be those who will seek to destroy us. Now, my intelligence tells me that the Damaskers and

Perenians were behind the assassination attempt. Now, I've given the Perenian leaders a deadline to respond to these allegations, but I won't lie. This situation fills me with . . . consternation." Rady shakes his head sadly. "If you see something suspicious, go to the police. We must take this new and unique threat seriously. Our very way of life is at stake. But we can never relent, not in the face of terror. In the next weeks and months and years, we will all make sacrifices, and come together." He stands tall, raising his chin. "This is *our* country, never to be taken away from us. But only in unity can we endure the brutality of evil, and so I say, if it comes to war, it comes."

The people applaud vigorously. But from somewhere in the expanding crowd an old woman is shouting. Those closest to her step back as though she carries a terrible disease. The crowd presses up against each other, making a passageway for several spades who grab the woman by her arms.

Rady squints. "What was I saying? God, it's toasty today. Man, I can't wait until this speech is over, so I can get a cold one!" His face grows somber. "But this Perenian threat is very real, very, you know. And the Damaskers. And possibly the Blanks. Now, I don't want to frighten you, but we are living in an age of uncertainty and fear. Only with your cooperation will our gentle ship survive this storm. We must do this for our children. If we must fight and die for them, then I say, hand me a gun. A big one!"

Clapping, the crowd begins to chant Rady's name.

"Actually, that reminds me of something my pops told me before I joined the guard," Rady continues. "Son, he said. Try to look unimportant—cause the enemy might be low on ammo."

The applause swells.

Rady winks. "Another thing he said. Teamwork is essential, son, because it gives the enemy more targets."

Wildcard studies Rady and the enthusiastic crowd. Near the bell tower, an old woman wrapped in a brown shawl is yelling.

Why does the black thing . . . she starts to say, but her words are swallowed by the crowd's applause and hollers. Another woman springs up twenty yards away. Why is it taking innocents? What crime was my son guilty of? Why the unmarked? What about the laws? Wildcard can't tell whether Rady simply doesn't hear the women, or is merely pretending not to.

The Poten leans into the microphone. "This is a time of faith, and God is on our side—whichever God or gods you believe in, they're all on our side. Remember, it is our faith which separates us from our enemies, our faith that makes us ensure . . . er . . . endure. You know, we endure. We ensure. Those monsters who attacked us. We'll hold them responsible. We will seek them out. And always remember the victims of the Scream, so we must be strong for future generations. For our children."

Wildcard clings to the side of the stage, watching as Rady takes a pair of glasses from his pocket. More of the protesting women have become isolated islands amid a sea of louts. Black uniforms seep through the crowd like oil. The Poten is supposed to rally support for a war for the sole reason of taking disgruntled louts off the streets while the regime consolidates power. Now, Rady is trying to explain the Scream, the moment at which the black thing became both untraceable and unaccountable. He will then mask the failures of the Manor by creating a fictional conflict with the Perenians, one of the oldest and more effective tools of the regime. Mesmer is dead and buried but the people will never know it, and Debeau has been bought off with the promise of leading this new phantom war, a war he has longed for since his father was killed in the last campaign. Wildcard catches Rady's eye as he glances behind the stage where Boran and his shadow advisors wait.

The Poten's voice reaches over the crying mothers, grandmothers, daughters. "Well, of *course* no one *wants* to go to war. Another thing my pops told me—the only thing more accurate than friendly fire is—no, the only thing more accurate than enemy fire is . . . is friendly fire."

Only the louts in the first few rows chuckle, and hesitantly. A woman is wailing. *Why did it take my daughter?* She repeats the question as the spades approach but as they drag her off two more women take her place.

" . . . so you see, while he recovers," Rady says, "I have been given me additional responsibilities. In the coming months, there will be curfews and new laws—necessary, I assure you, to root out Perenian spies and allies in Ashkareve and throughout Qarash." He claps. "Now, I know it's hot, but we happened to bring a keg or two of Amber's Brew. And it's sweet and cold, boy! Ramsden's for the kids, and there's even gonna be a special tournament of smashball this weekend for those with ribbons on their doors. Maybe even a surprise or two. To me, the best way to respect the dead is to be faithful to the living. So thank you for being faithful. As always, I am your—"

Sections of the crowd are cheering, but turn quiet as in the center of the avenue, a young lady with an ugly scar across her face begins to shriek.

"Quiet. Hey, quiet her up now," Rady says, pointing to the women. "That's rude—hey, I'm trying to talk here."

Seven spades lift hands to their earpieces simultaneously. As the woman reaches for her dropped handbag, seven tremblers unload on her in bursts and her head splits open like a gray mush melon. A young man kneels, taking a blue flower from her hand. He holds it up for the crowd to see. Rady barks over the microphone for the spades to hold their fire, the impact of his voice driving people to their knees. More soldiers pour from side streets as barrels roll down the avenue and over a hysterical fleeing crowd. A keg cracks open and brown foam erupts. People are soaked in blood and beer suds. One lout is drinking from a geyser, and only feet from him, another lout is bleeding in a pool. Bodies are bumping, running, scrambling, tripping, falling, away from the stage and the tower.

Wildcard fights against Melnor as the older man drags him towards a towncar. He watches the dispersing crowd from the window. Two captains quickly escort Rady to the door, slam it shut behind him, as the car takes off. Boran and Melnor sit opposite Wildcard, who crosses his leg and opens a book.

"What was that?" Rady says, rolling down his sleeves as the car speeds up the avenue. "What the hell was that?" He wipes his brow with red, blotchy hands. The Poten turns to Boran. "Your men were supposed to *control* the crowds."

"They are, now."

Rady sneers at Wildcard, who smiles, then licks his finger to take the next page. "Why are you so damn silent? This was your fault too."

"Are you sure?" Wildcard says. "My recollection is that I argued for telling them you had overthrown the Manor. Boran's the one who wanted to pretend like our dearly departed still lives. You might do well to ask yourself why."

"Shut the fuck up," Rady says. "And stop smiling, so help me God."

"You first." Wildcard shakes his head as passing sunlight pauses over his troubled face. "You think you're God's messenger, don't you? So, how does it feel to be at the head of a country decomposing from the inside?"

"Get your eyes off that book," Rady says, swatting it from Wildcard's hand. "I looked like a damn *fool* out there."

Wildcard stares at Rady for several seconds, glances over at Melnor, then slowly bends over to pick up the book from the floor. "A damn fool?" he says in a low, level voice. "People just died. Women and children, no less." He holds up his book. "Poets will capture this day, Mr. Poten. And you will live forever. That's my hope. That they capture you." Wildcard stares at the emptying streets. "And then perhaps we will discover what that smirk of yours really meant."

"This is no time for jokes, Lisande. Read what I gave you."

"Why should I?"

"You'd be more cooperative if you knew the extent of your father's crimes."

"So you believe me now?"

"Read the testimonials. I assure you, such suffering and misery cannot be made up. I am not so talented."

"Answer *my* questions. Did I have brothers?" she said. "Did you kill them, Alkor?"

"No." The old Damasker paused at the door. "But don't take my word for it. Read for yourself. Please don't let Renue's death be in vain."

"He's dead?"

"He might as well be."

Snuffing out a candle, Lisande curled on the floor around the new stack of books. Her toe brushed the spine of a hardback. Darkness in the underground was more complete than she'd known, so intense it magnified voices. Often she thought someone was speaking to her when she was alone. But at least in the darkness she wouldn't have to see the books piling in her already cramped room. Alkor had insisted she learn the truth about her father's regime and delivered more historical accounts each day. Lisande did read, briefly, about her father's rise to power twenty-nine years ago. She had also read that Mesmer had two sons who were killed, which once would have seemed impossible. Now she was not so sure. Trying to remember anything her father or his advisors had told her quickly proved futile, and the servants rarely talked at all when she was around. Even Faldor never spoke about history or politics, as though she had been deliberately been kept in the dark.

Bardon hadn't come to see her in days and she didn't trust Alkor. She found herself thinking constantly of escape. Three days ago, as a meal was being delivered, Lisande had pushed the Damasker inside and ran down the corridors, searching desperately for an elevator to the surface. Eventually Granges found her, and now a guard was always posted at her door.

She could hear him outside, humming. How long had she been underground? After the attempted escape, the Damaskers wouldn't even let her go to the sunroom. Lacking that brief natural light, she often felt weak and had trouble sleeping. When she finally slept, her dreams were full with childhood memories, mostly her parents fighting and comments by hillborn guests about the animalistic louts. They might not have taught her about the history of Qarash, but they certainly made her distrust, even fear louts. Alone, Lisande struggled to make sense of this accumulating rush of memory. Only last night, she had woken and called, "Alaine." How long had it been since she had said her mother's name out loud?

Lisande stubbed her toe against another pile of books as she made her way to the door. When she turned on the light the room was spinning. "I don't feel well," she said. "Really. I'm sick—let me out."

The humming stopped.

As she closed her eyes, images and sounds began to blend, her father's face with Faldor's, a rotting melon rind, splattering, clippers snapping, metal grinding against metal, a scratching against the door, wood splintering, the deep groans of the underground elevators. She was standing in the middle of a cobblestone road flooding with rain, her green dress soaked through and clinging to her chilled skin. A mob of louts marched towards her, holding red torches flickering in the downpour, illuminating their ghastly faces orange. They began to chase her. She reached the underground and ran through the halls. Stopping to catch her breath, she saw the narrow corridors brimming with rake-thin bodies, shouting her name, calling for her execution. Their voices followed her as she reached her room and locked the door. She held her marked hands out, peeling black with each brisk stroke of her fingernails. Dreams are never dreams, the louts yelled, battering the door and then she heard her father's voice, they'll murder you like they murdered your brothers.

Lisande lay on the floor, eyes tightly shut, rocking herself. The door creaked open.

"This is how I found her."

"What happened?"

"A panic attack. Don't use the Gift."

"What would you have me do, then?"

"Hold her tongue or she'll choke. Granges, fetch me some borage juice and feverfew. What are all these books doing here?"

"I . . ."

"Remove them, Alkor. Now."

"Fine."

"She's not through the worst of it. Lisande, can you hear me? Try to calm down. Lisande? Squeeze my hand if you can hear me."

"We need her healthy for—"

"If you can't keep your mouth shut, then get out."

"It was merely . . . "

"Call Dora. We have to tell her."

"Why? No. We don't need to complicate—what? What?"

"For God's sake, look at her hands."

Chapter Eight

Wildcard sits in a wooden chair on a veranda overlooking Ashkareve. "It's watching me," he says. "Even now, pulling at my memories. I can *feel* it."

"All in your imagination." Melnor's fingers perch on his forehead. "Fucking hell, I've got a headache."

"Condolences, I've got the black thing following me." Wildcard gets up and leans over the balcony. "If we can get her before the Pattern unravels completely, then fine. Otherwise, I have to go by myself."

"Do you have any pain relievers?

Wildcard fishes through his pockets. "Rady. That man could put a lively face on a corpse. Oh right, he is—here."

"Thanks. He's well-liked, though."

"He's a fucking moron. And grossly incompetent. And he speaks like a buffoon, even if it is all an act." Wildcard's chair rests flat on the floor as he leans to Melnor. "We're different from them, aren't we? Neither of us would have done what Mesmer did. Right?"

"Of course not," Melnor says. "Though I must admit, Boran's effective."

"I don't trust him," Wildcard says. "Seriously, though, with respect to Rady. Couldn't we have found someone less . . . overtly unintelligent?"

Melnor breathes on his glasses, fogs them, wipes with his shirt. "They like him. They don't like you. It's as simple as that."

"You either."

Melnor flicks a bead of water from the glass. "Is something bothering you, Card?"

Wildcard's eyes are soft with yellow light. "I don't know. Mesmer, I guess. It's all so . . . fucking pointless, how he managed everything. I want to understand him, to understand why he did what he did, but now it's too late." Sighing, Wildcard taps his teeth together. "That smoke is really too much. If Boran would only let me go up to the Manor. It's probably just a joke."

"Be patient."

"Patient," Wildcard scoffs. "He must have been a pessimist at heart. Mesmer, I mean. Boran I understand, but Mesmer, he was more complex. He had a mind." In the faint light, Wildcard appears conflicted, his jaw tightening, bright eyes shifting. When he takes his hand off the balcony, bits of red-orange rust cling to his palms. He dusts his hands together. "You're awfully talkative tonight. Something on your mind?"

"No."

"No? Tell me, Melnor, what were your parents like?"

Melnor turns his head slowly. "I don't think so."

"You . . . don't think so what?"

"You just want something to mock. My parents are mine, not yours."

"You won't tell me? Really?"

"Find out for yourself. Not from these lips."

Wildcard leans over the balcony again, the wind gently tugging his hair. "My mother meant nothing to me. Hardly said a thing. It's a wonder I can speak at all. She was worthless, basically. Didn't cook, didn't work. She forgot to feed me sometimes—I mean, when I was little. Three, four years old. I remember having to climb onto the countertop to get something to eat—our cook left all the time, took advantage of my mother's ineptness. That's my first memory. Making myself a small plate, crackers and cheese." He shakes his head. "It's a mystery, sometimes, how people become who they become. It's no excuse, but three and half, four. Valadrine was more dangerous than Ashkareve, back then. I turned to books early. My mother, she never even left the house. Not that I can remember, at least."

"Never left the house?" Melnor yawns.

Wildcard glances back. "You don't care."

"Your fictions don't interest me, Card."

"Fictions? What fictions? I'm serious. If you know where someone's from, you know everything. What I'm trying to tell you is, I don't know where I'm from. Not exactly. The wild card's my father. I want to know."

"Your father was Andrius Libran," Melnor says briskly. "A lawyer turned politician. Only he lost the election that counted and committed suicide. You grew up rich but alone, given every privilege wealth could muster. You've led a ridiculously unencumbered life. Luckier than most. Luckier than mine." He massages his brow. "There are no secrets in this day and age, Card. At least none that matter. You could know everything about me, if you wished, and I already know everything of you. Your mother was a secretary, and your father a failure, and—"

Wildcard lunges at Melnor, grabbing him, but the older man twists, throwing Wildcard to the ground. Melnor quickly pins the younger with a knee.

"What do you know of my father, you arrogant fuck?"

"Calm down and I'll let you go."

"Get the fuck off me."

"When you stop struggling."

A click. Wildcard aims a small trembler squarely at Melnor's chest. "Now get the fuck off."

Melnor stands slowly. "We're almost reached a deal with them." He grabs a briefcase. "So you'd better wise up and stop playing games."

"Then the next time I tell you something, listen."

Long after Melnor has left, Wildcard continues to watch the

city. "I know you're there," he says. "What do you want from me? Could it be the same thing I want from you?"

♥

Bardon gave her herbs and teas, burned incense, candles, ran baths, but for days Lisande could hardly sleep more than a few hours. When she did, she had constant, nauseous nightmares of louts storming the underground and basements filled with screaming women. Bardon began to teach her meditation techniques, to take a living thing at one extreme and imagine it returning to the other, and after a few more days, she calmed down some. But left alone, she continued to stare at her hands. They were no longer black, except in her mind.

A knocking woke Lisande one morning, but to her surprise it was not her guard or Granges. Instead, an older woman waited at the door, adjusting her straw hat from which fell graying red hair.

"Hello."

"You look familiar," Lisande said. "Who are you?"

"Dora Bemoss."

"There's a print of you in Renue's room."

"I didn't know that," the old Drailer said. "Must be Bardon's— well, let's get you out of here for a bit. Sound good?"

"Outside? Really?"

"Of course. You've been cooped up here too long."

As the two women walked down an alleyway, even the shadows appeared beautiful and lively to Lisande, and she found herself excited by the sunlight ahead. She purred as the warmth hit her face, though the sunlight hurt her eyes and as they emerged on a deserted street. "Where are we going?"

"Two places, actually," the old Drailer said. "Latchtown, then the university. And I think we'll get some exercise first. Don't worry—you're safe with me."

Dora led Lisande through a quiet neighborhood. After fifteen minutes, they came to an empty field that overlooked a vast flat of glinting metallic shacks. Further to the south east, factories spewed a constant, thick smoke, and behind those were several power plants.

"Is this Latchtown?"

The old Drailer nodded. "Let's get a bit closer."

As they descended, the light reflecting off the roofs became so sharp and blinding that Lisande had to plant her eyes on the dirt below. "It's so bright."

"Fuck—sorry, excuse my language." Dora placed Lisande's hands on her shoulder and helped her down the hill. "That was stupid of me. Should have remembered sunglasses."

At the bottom of the hill, between the closest shacks were fires overlaid by grills and spits of grisly meat. Adults huddled around the fires, turning the spits and chatting, while children in little more than rags kicked a green ball back and forth on a patch of concrete. Lisande folded her arms and watched as a lanky youth kicked the ball towards them. A smaller boy sprinted after it. Nearing the two women, the child spat up a little and fell down. His nose was plastered in snot and his upper lip stretched awkwardly, exposing gray gums. The little boy reached for Lisande's blouse. She stepped back and he bumped into her leg, leaving snot on her pants. Behind the boy, a girl had appeared, dragging herself towards Dora, using her arms to pull her legless body along the ground. The old Drailer reached down and rubbed the girl's head and scratched her chin. Lisande felt sick. The girl cooed.

"What happened to them?"

Now she could see a group of children lying in the shade beneath the closest roof, watching the ball game. An older woman by the fire saw the two children and stormed over to the bottom of the hill. She yelled and rapped the boy on the head, then looked directly at Lisande and Dora. Holding her stomach with one hand, she began to drag the boy with the other. The boy started to cry and ran behind a shack as the woman picked the girl up and took her over to the spits, putting her down in the shade with the others.

"The lost children of Latchtown," Dora explained. "That'd what Lyle called them anyway. We give to them through charities, but the money can't bring them back."

Lisande felt sick but she couldn't look away. "But why are they like that?"

"The Dousings."

"The Dousings . . . "

"You know about them? Alkor said you had refused to read anything he gave you."

"Well, I lied."

"In any case, it's never the same to read about something like this, is it?" the old Drailer said. "We'll go one more place, if that's still fine with you."

Lisande continued to watch the children until minutes later when a brown car pulled in front of the shacks. They stopped their game as the two women hopped in the backseat. As the car headed north, she brought her heart-shaped necklace from beneath her blouse and kissed it, wishing that Renue would wake up. She went to push her hair behind her ears and pinched the two inches of hair she had left.

"What's wrong?"

"I forgot," she said, cheeks flushing. "My haircut."

"Ah." The old Drailer bent closer, examining the locket. "Did your father give you that, or—"

"—Renue."

Dora held up her own necklace, a crescent moon, broken into fragments. "Touch it." The necklace was uncommonly cold and Lisande had to take her fingers off it after a few seconds. "Protective barriers are very difficult," the old Drailer explained. "This took a year off my life, maybe more. But worth it. You can instill the Gift in anything, if you're willing to pay the price. That's why I asked."

"You killed someone?" Lisande said.

"No, but the black thing can see the Gift too. Now it can see more, apparently."

"Why doesn't Alkor have one, then?"

"This barrier only hides women. Alkor tried—still tries every night. It's more difficult for men, for some reason." The car continued northward. There were so few people on the streets, and those who saw the car quickly disappeared into shops or down sidestreets. "I know you don't trust him," the old Drailer said, continuing to stare out her window. "But you should have seen Alkor in his youth. Inspiring. Selfless. Brave—handsome. A truly great man." Dora tucked the necklace beneath her shirt. "We've all had to make sacrifices. There's a reason this moon is only a sliver."

"You're barren," Lisande said. "Is that how it works? If you use too much of the Gift."

The driver pulled over and let them off by a gas station. As the car sped away, the two women began to walk up a street with a slight incline. Dora crossed her arms. "When I was younger I cried and cried," she said. "Well, it's this way. Unfortunately, we don't have much more time until they find us."

"Find us?"

"My counterparts."

The old Drailer stepped up on the sidewalk and glanced back quickly. Across the street, two men were dumping garbage into an overflowing container. Lisande watched them as the old Drailer grunted and bent down to rub her knees. "I know you won't tell Alkor," Dora said. "But I have to ask. Did your father teach you the Gift?"

"No."

"He never taught you?"

"I just said no."

"Easy. I was only making sure."

After several streets, they hiked a small hill and a great bowl of a stadium appeared. Lisande was hoping to see the twilight forest as they climbed further, but the stadium blocked her view. "Alkor thinks I'm hiding something," she said. "I'm guessing you're no different."

"No, I believe you." The old Drailer paused. "Why do you think your father kept you in the Manor, then?"

"Maybe he thought someone would kidnap me—like you have."

"We did protect you, didn't we?"

"If you call imprisonment protection, then sure."

"You're not grateful?"

"For *what*?" Lisande said. "Sending someone to kill Faldor? Holding me underground like a common criminal?"

"Maybe that's fair. I apologize. But don't blame me. I didn't find out about you until very recently."

Expanses of cultivated grass surrounded exquisite stone buildings, and a winding set of stairs ran between them, segmented by islands of neatly clipped bushes. Green vines crawled around the tall pillars, and behind the buildings were clumps of mossy green boulders. A thick layer of wispy clouds drifted slowly over the mountains above.

Dora gestured to a grassy hill to the west, overlooking a field with two netted goals in the corners. "I studied biology and chemistry right there," she said. "Thirty-five years ago. I didn't do very well. Couldn't concentrate. I had the Gift. It can be very alienating. I had my first date there."

"You didn't bring me out here just for exercise," Lisande said. "This is all some trick or something."

"Lisande, you have every right to distrust us. But please, I'm trying to show you something important." She led Lisande to a set of stairs that zigzagged up to a small tower. Nearby, an elderly couple sat on a bench. The older man coughed into his hands. His spouse flipped his collar up and kissed him on the neck.

"Lisande, most people live their lives seeing with a limited palate of colors, a limited view, a single perspective. But those who cultivate the Gift can often hear voices long past. Glimpse the very patterns of life itself. Which is why you sometimes find those with the most talent for the Gift in mental institutions. Comforting, I imagine. Come on, up the stairs. That's what I want you to see. It's a beautiful view."

"You're not coming?"

"Go on," the old Drailer said, catching her breath. "To the top. By yourself. I'll be up in a moment."

Lisande took the stairs quickly, feeling the strain in her legs. Reaching the top, she leaned over a metal railing. To the south, the city stretched into the blue line of the ocean. She could see Latchtown, shining brightly like millions of crowding stars. The old Drailer's voice startled her.

"They used to call Ashkareve the Glittering City," Dora said. "But as you can see, names can be misleading."

"Latchtown seems so beautiful from up here."

"Doesn't it?"

"What do you want from me?"

"And she doesn't play games either," the old Drailer said, resting her chin on her fist. "The Manor doesn't control the black thing anymore. Did Alkor or Bardon tell you this?"

"I don't remember."

"When the black thing was first created, Boran tested it in a town called Shilogh, a few hours north of here." Dora gestured to the mountains. "Heavily Blank. Within a week, almost four thousand vanished. A demonstration of its power, so no foreign powers would invade. As potent as any bomb, and perhaps more so."

"It killed them all?"

"No, actually. Most of those who died were killed by fellow

townspeople. It doesn't take a bomb to destroy a city. The Manor proved that. But now, the regime can't restore the laws. Otherwise, they would have done it by now." The old Drailer coughed. "We suspect your father placed a barrier that would open only to those with his family. His final safeguard against assassination. So I'll be blunt. We can make a deal to get you up to the Manor, to the Pattern. To restore it, and hopefully to destroy the black thing. Before Ashkareve becomes another Shilogh. You're not the only one who's been held captive."

"That's why you've been keeping me?"

"It should be your decision," Dora insisted.

"Not much of a choice."

"Today, it is. You can leave, now, if you want. I could say the spades ambushed us. In my experience, you rarely get the choice you want in life." The old Drailer gripped the railing, her hands blotchy. "You won't find your mother in many of the histories," she said. "But Bardon told me you wanted to know about her. Well, I did some research for you. She was from Latchtown. And she went to the university around the same time as I did. I never met her. The Manor was always extremely secretive about both your father and your mother, but I would be happy to help you."

"What about my brothers?"

Dora answered after a moment. "The Damaskers took one—Andal. Canden was killed by the Blanks."

"Was it Alkor?"

"A Damasker named Grethen. Boran found him eventually, if that's of any comfort."

"Alkor said he won't be able to keep Renue alive much longer," Lisande said. "But I'll make you a deal. If you do all you can, I'll help. Otherwise, you're on your own."

"Thank you, Lisande."

The two women took the stairs down. At the bottom, the older couple had disappeared, and a car was parked on the curb, where Granges and two other Damaskers were waiting.

"You think Mesmer really could keep her secret all these years?" Wildcard says. "I can't sleep anymore."

"Not much longer." Melnor places a corkscrew on the kitchen counter. "We'll make this country whole again."

Wildcard pats Melnor on the back. "The good guys win."

"We're not good."

"Better than some. Don't blame yourself. It's a damning profession."

"You're right about Debeau," Melnor says. "It'll be bloody."

"If we have the thing, then perhaps not. Grenore hates him, with reason."

Out of the room, into the cloudy sky and upwards until it can see the Manor perched on the hills. This is the place from which Mesmer reigned so tightly he bloodied his own hand, his robust tenor dulled by silencing the voices of others. A prison he made for himself. In Faldor's time, this land was home to no man, these white and green grassed hills where elk roamed and mountain wolves tackled deer. Then, the moon itself appeared closer. The Blanks tell their children the moon is a father holding a sleeping orphan child curled into himself, a remnant of the ancient, fecund world before the evil of humankind was born. Some priests say the moon is the essence of God. Perhaps the moon is a manifestation of the collective human imagination philosophers speculate, far enough away as to never become real. These are the seedlings of another myth: why Mesmer chose to build the Manor just so. To block the independent moon, the dictator blotted the sky with reaching towers. That man would have blinded the stars themselves. Close to the street, two louts sit on a stoop, drinking. So do you think he's really dead? Who knows? Stars sure are dull tonight. I hope he's alive. Why? I'm not sure. Follow the road snaking beside the dreaming forest and down to the yellow hills where the hillborns plot. Some have already begun to align themselves with the three, Melnor, Debeau, and Wildcard, club, spade, diamond, though no suit fits exactly. Who will be able to stop the black thing? It sees death like stars, they say, with malicious intent the brightest, like a white dwarf, and supposedly the most practiced assassins have literally gotten away with murder. Yet in Ashkareve, murder has long been considered unnecessary, ostentatious even. Now coffers are opening and money exchanging hands as coffins fill with poisoned bodies, blue-tipped and green-rotting, poison, dripped in the ears, in lamb chops and garlic-mashed potatoes, in wine the color of blood, in veins the color of wine. The bodies of once promising men lay mute in basements, fingers twitching, breaths but hisses.

On Goramon Avenue, a group of nightwalkers collectively shiver at the stream of smoke escaping a high Manor tower. The black thing is loose, they whisper. Fear itself is loose. You can feel it in a passing glance, as a shudder, a frosted word, like the stumbling into consciousness from sleep, in confusion, as anything inexplicable. Why did he create the black thing? Because the most powerful fear is intangible. The threat, the promise.

Just off the avenue, a pair of louts are discussing old rumors of Mesmer. They say his war against those who command the Sickness stemmed from his most profound loss, and of the promise the once-called Gift could not meet, the undiscovered cure for his dying wife. Two groups became the target of Mesmer's full wrath. The Damaskers and Drailers have burrowed to hide from the thing that sees not only murder but also the Gift, a slower kind of death. They hide in cellars peppered throughout the city, behind counters, masquerading as candy shop owners, booksellers, engineers, professors, cargo-unloading dockies, all gradually withering, weakening.

Southwest of the bell tower below the Inverts is a section of the city called the Blanks, a high walled, winding concrete maze where tinted windows designed to obscure inside shadows. These double-mirrored windows recall the first years of Mesmer's rule, when the regime did not have its supernatural arbiter and conducted affairs with blunt violence and assassination rather than surgeon-composed fear. The Blanks remember those days when rebellion burned instead of the poor coals and swirling ashes of resistance that now wait only for the wind to change direction. They bitterly stew in their untaught, sick Gift. They despise the Damaskers as much as they despise Mesmer, and some betrayals time alone cannot heal. Behind their stone-colored walls, the Blanks teach their children that it is better to be silenced while standing than sitting and rotting. Their faith endures. They embrace the thing. They worship it. And they are unafraid of death. They only wish to choose on what terms they meet it.

Down a side street, louts huddle next to rats picking through a spilled vat of lard. Nearby, cats and dogs eye each other while nudging an overturned trashcan. Watching the cats and dogs are two elders, sitting in a café called Spiderhouse. They hunch over their seats, these two gnarled centennials. Open-mouthed, sunken-eyed, the old men speak freely, unaware that anyone is listening. Why'd it take her? Norma never hurt a fly. Killed a fly. No, she didn't! Well, maybe a fly, but she didn't kill. The thing's been twisted since it Screamed. Always remember, Rady says. What? I don't remember.

What the two old ones sense is the blood of the city thinning, beginning to crack and flow like melting glaciers. What will be born, they wonder, with Ashkareve on the verge of rupture? Will it be a beastly thing, a blotted, ugly child? There can be nothing good born in a city of men, said the poet Lyle. I hate that poet. How does it go again?

The face of the city is always cruel.

The face of a city is always human.

At night, the city is more beautiful.

And the city is stunning, tonight.

It feels itself pulled back to the hills where Melnor is pouring wine. He hands a glass to Wildcard. "I didn't sleep well last night either," Melnor says, taking a long drink. "Twelve hours and the nightmare will be over."

Wildcard holds his glass up to the light. "Good color. Yes, then we can . . . " Melnor's glass shatters on the floor. His face is dabbed in purple and green, with splotches tracing his veins, like skin-colored tomatoes emptied of their flesh. Wildcard quickly reaches in his pocket and pulls out a pill, stuffs it in Melnor's mouth but the pill dangles on his tongue then falls to the ground with a rush of saliva. The phone is ringing. Wildcard lays Melnor down gently, then walks over to the counter. "Yes?"

"My men will pick him up in an hour. Wrap him up in a blanket and leave him downstairs."

"Boran?" Wildcard eyes his glass a second time. "Suddenly, I'm not so thirsty."

"Two types of men. Right, Card? I know about the exchange. The country's mine. We'll talk once the girl's secure. And don't do anything stupid."

"You know, it's difficult when—"

"Downstairs. Make sure the tongue's not blocking his windpipe. I'd hate for him to die."

Wildcard hangs up, then quickly pours the wine out the window.

♥

"I'm leaving tomorrow. They're taking me back to the Manor. But I'm glad you got me out, even for a brief time. Dora showed me some things the other day that make me realize that you were right. I had to find out for myself. Maybe I always knew, though I'm still not sure why I can't remember. I shouldn't have said what I said. It's a hard thing, to admit that the people you loved were like that. It doesn't seem possible. After it's over, I'll have to leave Ashkareve. The country. Faldor always spoke highly of Perenia. Maybe I'll go there. It's what I want—not what you want, maybe, but you've got Bardon and he loves you. Forgive him, please." Lisande rubbed her throat. "I'm scared. At least I'll see the forest again—that will bring up memories." She leaned in to hear the faint putters of his lips once more. "Why do I tell bad jokes? I saw this elderly couple yesterday, holding hands. When you wake up, look at yours. You got a second chance. Both of us. Thanks for saving me. Thanks for trying. Goodbye, Renue."

III

Chapter Nine

He flipped on the bathroom light and saw his unmarked hands for the first time. After washing his face, he approached the mirror hesitantly. Beneath his eyes were harsh age lines and constellations of black spots spread across his neck. He drank noisily and washed the remaining water through his graying hair, stared at the strange image a few minutes longer, then left the room. As he came out into the hall, a passing Damasker slowed, then ran away. Renue continued stiffly down the corridor, balancing himself against the wall. He felt weak and dizzy as he attempted to find his way to Lisande's room.

"Bren," a voice called from behind. "Good to see you're—"

Turning sharply, Renue lunged for Granges. "Where the fuck is she?"

"The Manor," he said, stepping back. "Easy. Just relax, she's safe."

"What did you do to me?"

"Nothing—don't fight. I always beat you on the playground."

"Fuck you."

"Calm down and come with me. Alkor will want to see you. Looks like you're a hero again."

Granges led Renue to an elevator and the two descended to the bottom floor. At the end of the hall was Alkor's office. The old Damasker sat behind a meticulously ordered desk of books and pens. A wide smile appeared on his face as he closed an enormous red book. He tipped his glasses, fingers tracing the arc of his jaw line to his hairless chin.

"My boy! So it's true. Come back from the dead, I see." He glanced at Granges. "Word from the caravan?"

"Any minute now," Granges said. "I'll let you know."

"Leave us." As the door shut, the old Damasker came around the desk, observing Renue closely. "You've gone gray. Funny, I didn't notice. Then again, my eyes were watery as an onion-peeler's every time I saw you." He touched Renue's shoulder. "How are you feeling?"

"Weak. Shitty," Renue said. "What happened?"

"We weren't sure until of course your hands lost their color."

"Is there water?"

Alkor heaved a pitcher onto the desk and poured a glass. "What do you remember?"

Renue drank quickly and held his glass out for more. "Where's Lisande?"

"Safe with Dora and Bardon." The old Damasker set the pitcher down and reached for Renue's hands. "Truly amazing."

On the wall behind Alkor stretched a map of Ashkareve, with a bold red line starting in Latchtown and proceeding to the docks and up Goramon Avenue up to the twilight forest, where three Xs were scrawled. A second blue line led from the Slants to a section of the hills above the University.

"We'll be sending you to Valan as soon as possible of course," Alkor said. "A brilliant, if evil man. We were contemporaries long ago, during Faldor's war. He lives in the hills. Lisande said she went there as a child. A dangerous hermit, but he *is* the only one still living who might know how to control the thing, and he will no doubt be curious to see you. Imagine it. A survivor! There must some powerful barrier protecting you, my own, perhaps, or some piece yet unexplained of this magnificent puzzle. But, the important thing is that you are alive and that we are on the verge of something wonderful, and it is all your doing! You were right. We checked her blood against Andal's. She is Mesmer's daughter!"

"What's happening now?"

"Personal escort to the Manor," Alkor said. "The veil is about to be lifted. Perhaps I'll even see the sun soon." He laughed. "Ah, I'm feeling wonderful today!" The old Damasker took out a bottle of brown liquor and set it on the desk. "Let's celebrate your good health, and the success of the mission. Taking his daughter, infinitely more valuable than the deed." He raised a glass. "To Melnor."

"Melnor?"

"Yes, Melnor. Our glorious defector." The old Damasker downed the drink and poured another. "We're striking while the hot iron sings, or whatever those blasted Inverters say. Found a tunnel Boran didn't know about. Captured one of his agents the other day—they haven't been able to get into the Manor, but we have the key." He took Renue's hand again. "Oh, we are in the soup of things, my boy! All because of you. You're a hero."

Granges burst through the door, trailed by five Damaskers. "Alkor."

Alkor clenched his teeth. "Don't interrupt—"

"Ambush in Frake Square. I pulled one team, but we're overridden. Someone found out about the exchange."

"Boran's not so stupid. If she's killed . . . "

"The Blanks."

"God damn it," the old Damasker said, slamming his fist against the desk. "Any word from Bardon or Dora?"

"Silent."

"Bring the girl back here. *Here,* I said. Not the Vines."

"Got it. You healthy, Puker?"

"Yes."

"No, he is *not*—"

"Come on, then," Granges said. "We're stretched thin as it is. I could use your help."

Alkor whined, spinning around to the map. "Not now, not now."

"What have you done?" Renue said, approaching the old Damasker.

"Puker, let's *go*. On foot—Blanks are rocketing cars."

Alkor knocked over his glass and buried his face in his hands. Renue followed Granges and the Damaskers out of the room to the elevator. In a matter of minutes, the group reached the surface and began to head westward. An expanse of dark gray clouds drifted over the city, muting the sunlight. As the group passed a restaurant called "The Green Onion," Renue located himself in the lower Slants, near a Damasker safehouse. Granges stopped as the other Damaskers disappeared into a covered parking lot.

"You see him, Puker?" he said. "The lout in the brown shirt is tailing us. Careless. See?"

"Yes."

"Take care of him, will you? Then meet us at Frake. No more loose ends." Fishing in his pocket, Granges produced a small vial. "I told him—that stupid fucking old man. Don't argue with me." He handed Renue a small trembler. "You might be a hero, but I don't bite. Prove to me it's not about you. *Please*, Bren."

"Fine."

"See you there. Be careful."

Renue nodded, then slipped behind a row of vendor stalls. A beggar grabbed at his ankle but he shook him off and surveyed the crowd through a translucent pink drape. After a moment Renue spotted the lout, heading after Granges. Renue touched the cork, thinking of Faldor, then pocketed the vial. Quickly closing the distance between himself and the lout, Renue placed a firm hand on his shoulder. "Don't turn around," he said, leading the lout out of the crowd and past the stalls, into an alleyway. "Now get lost."

"What the fuck. I know *that* voice."

" . . . Piek?"

The lout turned around. "Yeah, that's right. Get the fuck off me."

Renue released him and took a step back. "What the hell are you doing?"

"Been watching out for her, Face, like I *said* I would. Where the hell have you been?" Piek spit. "Followed her doubles earlier today. Saw the Maskers taking to the tower tunnels. Boxes of tremblers delivered to the swamps. They're making a move, and it involves her. Right? So where is she?"

"Get the fuck out of here." Renue started to run after Granges."

"Not so fast, *Newcomer*."

Renue turned. "Fuck."

"Or *Renue*, perhaps? That's my arena, *knowing* things." Three men ran past the alleyway as Renue came back to Piek. "The Perenian stole something, the Manor said. A weapon. Damaskers were responsible for the Scream, they said, and all those people who died the last weeks. Figured that was bullshit, Then I realized they might be telling some truth, for once. Always a sliver. Only the weapon's her, isn't it?"

"She's in trouble," Renue said. "Go home."

"Damaskers never trust louts, do they? Tell me where she is and I'll decide for myself."

"Why do you care?"

"Because night after I met her I didn't drink a *drop*," Piek said. "And I *always* have to drink to sleep. My mother. Besides, I love this city. More than you. More than anyone, maybe. So if the Manor wants her, I'm gonna make sure they don't find her. Know where she is? Good. Get moving."

♥

Lisande watched as Bardon crawled over the driver's side and knelt behind the car. Shots ricocheted off the roof. Something had hit their car and the windshields had shattered. The driver had died on impact. Dora opened the passenger door as far as it would go and Lisande followed, covering her head as an explosion sent bricks raining down. The air smelled like fireworks and an itchy heat wafted from the green-tinted dust and ash. The old Drailer led Lisande along the brick wall, and after returning fire, Bardon limped after them. In a whining rush a projectile exploded against the building and the air was thick with gray particles. Bardon pushed Lisande away and told her to keep running as Dora dragged her into an alleyway. The two women ran away from the Square and across a dozen side streets before turning north. The old Drailer slowed their pace as vines began to cover the buildings, twisting around the nooks and crannies, leading like clotheslines from apartment to apartment, down from the rooftops. Ahead Lisande saw a concrete archway, several stories high, and on the far side of the street seemed like another world entirely. Young people strolled amid colorful artisan booths and craft islands and the far line of shops and bars were brimming with crowds. Light, lazy strumming of guitars flitted through the humid air. Sitting around café tables, middle-aged men sipped iced tea and stared as the two women caught their breath. At the next intersection, the road was closed and in the center a woman with a short aqua skirt read poetry to a bevy of teenage women wearing summer skirts. Then a few young men sprinted past, shouting that the Slants were rioting, and the cafes quickly emptied. Jewelers hurriedly gathered their wares in blankets. Dora and Lisande passed a bearded man stuffing glass pipes into a satchel on the corner.

Finally, the old Drailer stopped and pointed to a store across the street with blue adornments and a wooden carving of trees with leafy eyes and branching arms. "We made it." Dora clamped a hand over her mouth. "You'll be safe here for a while." Lisande wiped her face. On her cheek were several small cuts but the blood had already dried. Far south, beyond stacks of buildings, dark green and black smoke filled the sky. "She's expecting you, but don't tell her *anything*— I'll be back soon."

"Where are you going?"

"To find Bardon," she said. "You'll be fine."

"Are you crazy?"

Before Lisande could protest, the old Drailer ran back in the direction of the Square. A middle-aged woman stood in the bookstore doorway. "Afraid I can't come out to greet you," she called. "So you'd better come in."

The woman locked the front door and disappeared into a room beyond the counter. The bookstore was lit with a soft white light, and wide, though with the squat ceiling made it resembled a book-filled cavern. Lisande took a seat on a stool and caught her breath. A few minutes later, the woman emerged with a damp cloth in her hand. "Amelia Stout," she said. "Welcome to Breventine's." She began to wipe the cuts on Lisande's cheeks and arms. "And you are?"

" . . . Sophia." Lisande could hear a constant hiss coming from the other room.

"Beautiful name—one second."

The woman walked into the room and returned with two steaming cups. "Thought you were a boy with that hair," Amelia said, handing one to Lisande. "What happened to you?"

She blew on the tea. The warmth felt good on her hands. "An accident—a car accident."

Amelia quickly closed the blinds. "Read at all?"

"A little."

The two walked slowly as the Amelia showed the various sections of the bookstore. At the back she paused in front of a brown corduroy couch. "Help me with this, would you? I'd like to show you the good ones. Something to get your mind off the accident."

Together, they dragged the couch to the side, revealing a trapdoor with a padlock. Amelia brought out a set of crowded keys, unlocked the door, and lifted upwards. A set of narrow stairs led to a basement, and Lisande followed Amelia downwards. At the bottom, Amelia took a few steps and flipped a ceiling switch, lighting the basement, while Lisande rubbed her arms. The air was cool and very dry. A machine hummed from the back right corner. Row upon row of near ceiling-high segmented bookshelves ran perpendicular to the stairway. Bending down near the closest shelf, Amelia took a few book and began to sort through them.

"How about this one? Boy navigates his dreams and returns to a town he visited thousands of miles away. Not sure why it's down here. Not a bad book, but a tad dreamy for my taste." Amelia restacked the remaining books. "Banned, all of these," she said. "This one's about a hillborn and a Blank who fall in love. Just beautiful. Taken by the Manor, of course." She handed Lisande a paperback. "*Burblie Rebellions*, taken by the Manor. Those are testimonials and transcripts of the tortured." Amelia walked to the next shelf, tapping her lip. "Most of these are biographies of *him*. Those over there are speculations on the color code. Any interest?"

"Why would anyone ban books?"

"Not from around here, are you? They've always taken away anything that's seen as a threat. Even in the book business, you have to be careful. Not just newspapers. But don't worry, there's a slight barrier so you forget titles when you leave. Drailers helped me with that. So, feeling any better?"

"Yes, thanks."

"Haven't shown these to a stranger since I don't know *how* long. But a friend of Dora . . . well, you know." Amelia frowned. "That reminds me of this time—a man came by a few years ago, sniffing around for some of these books. Of course, I suspected he was working for the Manor. But it was a *fortune* he offered, and I was a little desperate then, so I took the chance. Stupid, in retrospect. I remember that night, though, sitting down here to take inventory. When I looked at the list of books he bought, sure enough they were mostly about Mesmer. Not just the Manor, not just confessions—but *novels*. Fictions. About the black thing, about the dictator. Mostly trashy, if you ask me. But that night, I did have this funny little thought. Amelia, I said. Well, wouldn't it be just funny if old Mesmer ordered all those books for *himself*?"

♥

State your last name clearly into the recorder.

Rinehart.

Occupation.

Wrote for a paper, worked in real estate. Taught primary school. Sold cars for a while.

Current Occupation.

. . . unemployed.

Unemployed, thanks. Very well, let's begin. Can you remember when you were taken, Mr. Rinehart?

In the early morning.

Good—that's rarer. What can you recall?

I didn't even hear them open the door. That's the first thing. Completely took me by surprise, not that I was expecting them. They were ghost quiet though. Real experts. Now you see them, now you don't, that kind of thing. Neighbors probably knew I was taken, regardless, but I guess the point is so you don't know whether it was the thing or not.

Why do you say that?

That's the paralyzing fear, the not knowing.

Mr. Rinehart. What happened next?

Yeah, sure. So, I woke up just as they were putting the bag over my head. They taped it shut and I could hardly breathe. First thing I thought, thank God Aleve is at her sister's. Then I almost shit myself. Aleve, the shitting, thinking about being taken. But I heard people escape sometimes—Blanks mostly. I wanted to know where I was going, just in case. I'm the survival type, on account of my father. He was real into camping.

Any idea where they took you?

Not really. When they put the bag over your head, you can't do anything but focus on sounds, the van starting, backfiring, tires, humming, the wind, accents. Told me a bit. Even little noises, like, like spoons scrapping against bowls. That helped. They had stopped the car for something, and I heard those scrapping bowls. Knew then we were near the docks—too early for most to be up except dockies. They led me to a room, then, left me for days. Four by four feet. I'm not shitting you. Four by four fucking feet. Legs cramped the first day. Couldn't even lie down. Had to crouch. Gave me food through a vent. Had to shit and piss where I sat. Bread and beans and filth. Will never touch the stuff again.

When did the interrogation begin, exactly?

They won't find me, right? This is safe?

Of course. We're professionals. It's just lucky we found you first, Mr. Rinehart. So what did they want with you?

Names.

Did you give any?

See for yourself. Toenails gone. Arms don't work the way they should, only a couple of angles I can move them. Other stuff. Nightmare stuff. Damn, sorry, a little skittish.

I understand. Let's get off the incident for a moment. You look a little unnerved. Can we get you a tea? Tea? Coffee? Mr. Rinehart? Tea?

Coffee.

Any preference?

Hot. Doesn't matter. Anything hot.

Very well. Take a deep breath, Mr. Rinehart. Now I want you to relax. Think of this session more like a psychologist, alright? Have you ever been to a shrink?

No. Look, I really—

Mr. Rinehart, I'm going to have to insist you keep your voice down. Take a breath. Another. First question. What do you love most in the world?

Is that a fucking joke?

No.

Then why—

We do it for two reasons, Mr. Rinehart. First, those we find are often in too bad shape to tell the truth. They tell us what they think we want to hear, just to get our help. We've found it's . . . healthier not to just go to the heart of the matter. To find out a bit about the individual. It's a terrible thing you've been through, I know, but at least you're here to tell about it. Understand?

And the other reason?

Well, as you can imagine, I hear a lot of gruesome stories over the course of a week. And so it's for my well-being too. Life isn't all torture and violence. It helps me to hear about the lives of those I interview. Don't want to go home to the wife with only bad thoughts. Breeds unhappiness. Like policemen. They always have failed marriages. Wife can't understand the husband's world, and so on. So it's for my benefit too. Something good to tell the wife.

That makes sense, I guess.

Ready?

Yes.

Calm?

Sure.

What do you love, Mr. Rinehart? What keeps you going?

Aleve.

Your wife. What about Aleve?

Honestly? Her smells, I guess. I thought about her constantly in the darkness, in that pen. Little things mostly, the smell of her on my fingers those first few dates, when I rode home from her parents' house. Her on my fingers. Put them to my nose, the music blaring. Just smell them. Love that smell. Her smell. Probably sounds sick to be thinking about sex when you're about to die.

What else?

I don't know. It's hard to think.

Try your best. What else about her?

I mean, she's just beautiful. Got lots of freckles. Man, I like freckles, always did. Always went for redheads. Freckles. Around the nose. Aleve's got plenty of them. Like constellations. They seem to spread when she smiles—I like to make her smile. Tell me, did they get her? I didn't want to ask, but you know everything. Did they get her? Did they?

Mr. Rinehart. Relax. How do you make her smile?

But—

She's fine.

You're sure?

Yes. So how do you make her smile? I could use some tips. Please Mr. Rinehart.

Okay, okay. I get you. Horsing around, that kind of thing. I play a bit of guitar. Make up, make up songs about her. Funny songs. That kind of stuff. And I cook her breakfast, bring her flowers. Same as everyone else. I love her.

I haven't brought my wife flowers in years. Not even for anniversaries.

Well, you should.

See, this is good for me too.

Yeah, alright. What next?

Fondest childhood memory.

Fondest memory?

Yes.

Well, there was this one time. I was just a kid, and my folks took me and my brothers up to a cabin in the mountains. That was nice.

Where?

The Gennies. Ever been there?

I'm a city person.

Gennies are beautiful. Swear those mountain tips are blue at night. Something about the way the moon reflects off them. Icepeaked, probably. Yeah, folks took me up there—this was, you know, a few years before . . .

Before the?

Before the, you know . . . before him. The regime.

Mesmer.

Yeah. Sorry, but that name.

Don't dwell on it. So, the Gennies. What about them?

We went up there. Camping. Me and my two brothers and the folks.

Older brothers? Where are they now?

I'm the youngest, but they're gone now, both of them. In the war. God, I haven't thought about them in a while.

Really?

It's weird, when you sort of forget people existed. I wasn't even so close to them, but still. Anyway, went hiking up in the blue peaks, made a nice fire, roasted marshmallows, that kind of thing.

Would you say you had a happy childhood?

We were safe, if that's what you mean. Not much money but we got by. Folks taught me right. Nothing too terrible

Let's change focus for a moment. Mr. Rinehart, what is your opinion of the Mesmer regime?

Why?

We have to keep up on public opinion. Gauge what his support is like. So tell me. What do you think about Mesmer?

Fuck, I don't know. Never really thought about that either. That or the brothers. Not for a long time.

Why's that?

My opinion didn't seem to matter much, that's all.

Some day things might change.

I don't believe that.

What about your father? Was he a supporter?

My dad? He liked Mesmer at first. Found him, what's the word he always used? Personable. Supported the whole takeover.

Dad hated Faldor, used to rage about him, said Faldor fixed elections, that he was corrupt and whatnot. But he—my dad, I mean—died a few years into Mesmer's regime, so he didn't really get to see the war or anything. God, makes me nervous, talking about him in the open air like this. I mean, people don't *do* that, you know? Maybe you Maskers do, but not me. Don't know what to think. I was a businessman in the old days, and can't say I approve much of anything on that end. I mean, Manor chokes the country with those damn laws. Businesswise, it's insane, this country. Other countries, they have flights that any old citizen can take. People travel. You know? They *go* places. But not here. Stale as pond water.

What's wrong?

Made me think of the swamps. The pond water did.

Ah, here's the tea.

I ordered coffee.

Did you?

Yeah, I did.

Take a sip.

Got sugar?

Do we? No, sorry, all out. Just try it. It's a relaxation blend.

Alright.

How is it?

Hot.

That's all you wanted.

Guess so.

Continue.

Oh, well, yeah, it's just, no offense to you, but the Gift, I never really got it. People got planes and radios and televisions and all that, and I know we've got 'em too, but if we stopped worrying about the Gift and focused on technology, we'd be able to defend ourselves just fine, I'll bet. Manor outlaws something one day, then uses it the next. What's the point? I mean, think about Krylight. We're bathing in the shit.

What did you think about the assassination of his sons, Mr. Rinehart?

His sons? I don't know. It's war for you guys, I guess, but fuck, seemed wrong to me, even if I . . . I mean, they were just *boys*. I never heard of them doing anything too bad—at least, the younger one. Old one, he was worse, I heard. Rapist, took whoever the fuck he wanted to his little palaces. Glad I didn't have a daughter. Still, they were just kids.

You're getting a little riled up, Mr. Rinehart, so we're going to get back to this in a moment. Can you talk about something purely good? That is, something *without* violence?

Are you fucking nuts? I answered your questions, now where's Aleve? Tell me. You said you'd find her. Is she in here? Let me see her, just for a second. Please. I beg you.

Calm down, Mr. Rinehart.

Just for a moment, dammit.

Drink your—

Don't tell me to drink my fucking tea.

Calm down.

Yeah, alright. Calm. Calm as a pond, okay? Sorry, got a little angry, that's all. But you're asking me to remember something purely good. But that's not the way it works. Not in this city.

♥

Spades were patrolling north of the clocktower and had set up roadblocks on all the major streets leading to Frake Square. Piek navigated the Slants, slipping through long stretches of connected buildings, but by the time Renue and Piek reached the Square, it was deserted. In the center, a statue of Mesmer with a wolf by his side had been bowled over, the concrete basin ruptured. For a time, the two men stood, speechless. The air was full of swirling white particles and smelled of corroding copper and over-cooked liver. A layer of ash covered much of the cement. Thin black lines contoured several human figures, though the bodies had obviously been removed. Several scorched bodies remained, a young woman holding the wire basket frame, an older-looking man laying on his stomach, holding the remnant of a cane. Renue crossed the bodies and approached a car, wrapped against the southeast corner building. Broken bits of brick sprinkled the roof and windshield. He recognized a Drailer, slumped over the steering wheel, but the back seat was empty and the far door ajar.

"No sign of them," he said. "Where the fuck is Granges? Too many tracks to tell where anyone went."

"Can't you, you know, *talk* to them?"

"I don't have the Gift, Piek. They'll have to find me."

"Well, aren't you fucking useful? I'll contact my boys and see if they've—" Piek gagged. "Holy fuck."

"What?"

A low whine was coming from the bloodied mouth of a young man beneath the lout. Half a tattoo of a yellow bird with a blue beak covered the wrist and on the skin was blistered on what remained of the man's arm.

"They took his hands."

Renue bent down but the man had stopped moving.

"He was a Damasker."

"Fuck."

"Let's get out of here."

"Yeah."

"Where to?"

"North," Renue said. "Closest safehouses are north."

Abandoned cars littered the roads in the vicinity of the Square, but none had keys. They tried four safehouses in the Slants but all were empty. Strangely, there were no spades around. For several minutes, the sky was a seamless gray blanket of clouds, but then all at once rain sheets came down. Caught by the blinding gusts, Renue and Piek took shelter briefly in the mailroom of an apartment building.

"I can't see a fucking thing."

"Let's get inside," Piek said. "We'll never find her in this—a place with a phone. I'll call my boys."

"Where did they go?"

"No clue. I know that bar over there. Pumpkin Patch, something like that. It's a bit hilly. Probably safer right now."

They crossed the street and entered the bar. Most of the stools were occupied but there was a free wooden booth in the corner to the left of the door. In the far back, six men crowded around a red billiards table, illuminated by soft blue lamplight.

"Close the fucking door," the bartender yelled.

Renue shut the door as Piek held up two fingers. "Sabs." The bartender poured the beers quickly and with too much foam. "Pay, will ya?" Piek said, grabbing the beers. Renue checked his pockets as Piek blew air out in disgust. "A lout paying for a Face. Now I *know* we're fucked." He slapped a bill down and headed for the empty booth.

"I was born in the Slants," Renue said as the two men sat.

"Yeah? Your sis sure seemed pretty hillish." Piek took a long drink. "Fuck, two aren't gonna do it today."

The beer was thin and bitter. In the Manor, Renue had been served foreign brews sweeter and flavored with citrus fruits. "That's right."

"Damn," Piek said under his breath. "Finally got a good look at you. What the fuck happened? Remember you being younger."

Renue touched his face, recoiling at the slight age lines. "I was sick."

"Still look it." Piek scratched the glass. "So your sis—she the only one?"

"Yes."

"Parents?"

"No."

"Think your sis could like me? Sorry, bad taste." Piek glanced around at the bar. "You're sort of a dark fellow. Mom spit in your milk or something? What?"

"Both my parents were taken," Renue said. "When I was a kid."

"Oh. Well, shit, I'm sorry. My ma was doused, Pa's was a drunk. Runs in the family." Piek stood. "I guess we all have those stories. Want one?"

"No."

"Suit yourself." He downed his beer and promptly ordered another.

♥

After they were done softening us up—that's what they called it, softening us up, they questioned us. Were we plotting against the regime? What did we know? If you named ten people they said they might let you off. They had a list of names they were looking for. They kept repeating them, over and over and over.

Do you remember any names?

No. I think it was all bullshit, personally.

Why do you say that?

Because they just kept fishing. It was just an act. Hoax. I mumbled once and they said a name and I said yes. You know, to make it legal. That's a tricky word. Legal.

Do you remember the name you gave them?

Does it matter?

Probably not by now. Continue.

They brought a group of us together in this warehouse type deal, asked us to identify the others in the room. Could have been well out of the city by then. They drugged us when they had to move us. Put it in the food, or they'd jab their fucking needles . . .

186

Mr. Rinehart, please.

Sorry, alright. Well, the ones questioning us wore masks, children's masks—looked like frights. So I didn't see their faces. The people who talked the quickest the Hands seemed to think were lying. I don't know if they were, but I'm sure glad I talked slow. If I had anything to tell them, I would have. They tortured us in front of each other. Gross shit. Sexual shit. Electrodes. Testicles. I'm not a brave man. I don't have principles. I just want—wanted to go home. Home. They asked us more questions, and I told them what I could, I don't even know what. Anything to get them to stop. I play the mandolin, I said. Not sure what the question was. They took a few fingers. I don't even play.

We'll get a doctor for that. I know this is difficult, but details. Precise locations, if possible. This information could help us.

Sure. After the Hands were done, they loaded us all together in a van. It stank. Crammed in, just arms and limbs. Out into the boonies. I remember the birds, cawing as though they knew where we were headed, the kinds of birds you don't get where I live. Maybe they were used to it.

Who?

The birds. Seeing us. Maybe we were just another van of bodies to them.

But eventually you reached the swamps. You mentioned that earlier.

Did I?

Yes. The pond water, you said. Tell me about it.

Right. The swamps. That's where we were headed. They let us out and there were big mosquitoes buzzing around. Hands were tied. It would have driven me crazy not being able to swat them, but by then I couldn't really feel anything, like when you sit on your hand or your leg—what's the expression?

Falls asleep. The leg falls asleep.

That's it. Fuck. Right. My words are fucked.

Do you think you gave them anything useful before the swamps?

No. Like I said, I don't know a thing.

Very well. Continue.

Everything I've ever heard is the swamps are the worst, though I also heard they make you eat Krylight in the mines and then as it travels through your intestines and it warms up with the friction. You melt from the inside. But the swamps, there's just something about them. All that life. They feed you to alligators or let snakes bite you. But by the time we got there, I was numb. Blank fucking numb. Nothing was working. Not my brain, nothing.

How many of you were there?

Twenty or so. And a few were speaking languages I didn't recognize. Some asked me questions but I didn't say a word. Kept my mouth shut. Sometimes when you can't see, you can't tell who's a prisoner or who's a spade. A buddy of mine, well a friend of his was asking questions and they had known each other for like ten years or so. A long time. But he turned out to be an Ear. Just like that. Hell, everyone is nowadays. Maybe I'm one and I just don't know. They're good with voices. People think the dialects were made to trick the Ears, but that's crap. If you're around something for long enough, it becomes natural. Dialects. Hell, even the fear.

Why's that?"

I don't think people are as afraid as they used to be. I don't even think I was *that* afraid when they took me, only thinking about Aleve and stupid things. Maybe that's Mesmer's problem. Running out of ways to scare people. That's why it's called the black thing, right? If it had a real name, it'd be familiar after awhile. That's what people are most afraid of. What they don't see. Know.

Maybe—you mentioned stupid things? What did you mean by that?

Yeah, stupid things. Near-death stuff. How I'd never smell Aleve again. How I probably wouldn't get to grill my onion sausages anymore. I love those damn sausages. Stupid things. A smashball game I saw as a kid with my folks. The Gennies. Brum—this beer I like. You know Brum? Yeah, and—

Sorry, Mr. Rinehart, but now that I look at it, we've got a hectic schedule today. So I have to ask again. Were you involved in any of the crimes they accused you of? Or did you actually know any of the names?

No.

Please, I can tell you're holding something back. Please. Mr. Rinehart.

. . . Aleve's cousin Grody fell in with some Blanks half a year ago.

Brody?

Grody. Blake Grody. There was word they were trying to set something up. Weapons. In the North, not Ashkareve. Grody, I don't even like him. Warned him to quit, but he's family. Couldn't give him up. Aleve would just die.

Thank you. That's helpful to know. Now, take us back to the swamp.

Okay. They pushed us out of the van with the butts of tremblers, into this grassy field. High grasses. Snakes, I thought. I brushed by a willow tree or moss or something and could feel those little mites crawling. No one said a damn word. Just some guy, whimpering. We walked for maybe twenty minutes, then they shouted for us to stand in a line. I bumped into something knobby, a cypress knee, I think. Couldn't really feel it. But the guy next to me started to scream. They shot him, carried him away. Then everyone hushed all at once and we weren't sure what had happened. They made us hike a few minutes more. I could hear new voices, whispering, near us. A different group. Then they went quiet and I could hear the swamp. Gurgling. It's a strange thing, those insects. They brought us close to the water. I thought they were going to drown us. When we stopped, I noticed the wind. It sounded different in the swamps, not so harsh. Softer, like a reed flute, almost beautiful—if you're not waiting to die.

Of course. Go on.

Someone started barking at us. Executed, he said, as traitors of Qarash, but if we confessed our bodies wouldn't be mutilated. Returned to our families. One said chop-chopped. That was the word. Chop-chopped. Asked a final time if we knew any of you guys. Maskers. Drailers. Dumped and returned to our families, they said. Like it was a present, a reward. I could hear the other men, crying. Except for this guy, this grumbling guy next me. Must've been insane. Hands probably broke his head. I tried not to whimper. Be a man, at least at the end. Stand tall. That was a mistake. No reason to act tough. Must have been the one calm guy there, and I got a trem to the face for it. Broke my nose. They have it down, those guys. Like a performance.

What happened next? I'll just say, it's rare to interview someone in as good shape as you. You're lucky.

Don't feel it.

Trust me, you are. Continue.

Right, so the tremblers clicked on. Then I was afraid, afraid for all the things I'd never do. Climb Little Wolf, go camping with Aleve, not that she'd have gone. Maybe she would now. Wanted to start a café. My whole body was sweating. Then the grumbling guy pissed his pants. We could all smell it. I thought that'd be my last thought, why the fuck did the guy have to piss his fucking pants? That spade was counting down from ten, and asked if we had anything to confess. Last chance, he said. Seven. Enemies of the regime, he said. Some of the others cried and screamed. Seemed pointless, but I didn't want to be singled out, so I screamed and cried too. Four. It smelled so sour, the air. Urine. That fucking guy, pissing. Two. The tremblers clicked again. Wild confessions. Everyone was blaming everyone else, trying to make deals, but the spades didn't care. One. When they fired we all dropped to the ground and there was a steady whimpering, to Jore and God and Mesa. Grown men. Crying. But then something *clicked* in me. A hidden trigger, and I just couldn't pretend anymore.

Couldn't pretend what?

That's the funny thing. I don't even know. That there was a God? That life mattered? My dad, he was religious. Mom too. But I couldn't pretend anymore. Something was wrong. Inside me something was wrong. I gave up. I went real quiet, listening. It was odd, but I couldn't *feel* any bullets in me. Like I said, my body was numb so I wasn't sure. Maybe it was a trick. Maybe I was dead, passed to the other side. Then came the laughter, in front of us, twenty yards away, maybe, and then more laughter. They had missed, I thought. The fuckers had missed. On purpose, maybe. Maybe not. Then I figured they'd put a knife through my heart just to make sure. We did that in the war. Field clearers, we were called. I'd rather be shot than stabbed any day, so I started to stand, felt dizzy. I stumbled forward. Just kill me, I said. Kill me. Spades were laughing. That's when I knew.

Knew what?

That I was really alive. The laughter. It's a fucked up feeling, when there are two things that don't fit, like a baby crawling through a battlefield. Made me uneasy, that laughter, like they were actually *enjoying* it. God. Reminded me of this time I saw this dog die in a street, just fall over, and the second it died some teenage girl was singing. Beautiful voice, like some spirit. Dead dog. Teenage girl. The two don't fit but they were side by side. You see? That's how I felt. Dead dog, girl. The both.

Perhaps I missed something, but I don't understand why they would keep you alive.

Just hold on. It's my story, isn't it? Feels good to tell it. Maybe I'll be able to sleep. Therapy, okay? It was like those moths in light—I had to head to the laughter. Don't ask why. I just did. At least they'd kill me outright, I thought. Then all of a sudden spades ripped the bag off my head. I hadn't seen for days and everything was white, just the outlines of faces. Just whiteness. Dead whiteness. Then I could make out Krylight lamps. Thought I was in the other world. He's the winner, someone said. I told you, someone else said. I could make out some of the other prisoners now. They were trying to stand and still begging for mercy. Pathetic. You didn't believe I could bring a man back to life, did you, another man said. He looked a bit familiar, that man, but my eyes were so watery it was hard to see. I kept looking at him. Then he looked at me and my insides froze—not really, it just felt like that. I knew the face. That smile.

Who was it?

Mesmer.

You're sure it wasn't a double?

Double? Fuck if I know. Looked like Mesmer. He had an audience. They were all looking at me, applauding. I felt insect-small. They shot all the other men right there, shot them laughing, shot them right in front of me and everyone dropped again. Mesmer's voice, that's what chills me. That voice. I can't get it out of my head. Even now. I'll do it again, Mesmer said. And sure enough, the other prisoners started to get up too. Not dead, rubber bullets. They'd began to crawl, hands still bound, like worms, all the way to him. To his feet. They were kissing spade boots along the way, sobbing, thanking him. *Thanking* him. Do you believe it? Dammit, I'm jittery now. Glad I didn't have that coffee—hey, why are you laughing?

Transcript of Black Hand interrogation #15.
Officer Bre— 145360
Type: Catch/Release
51, March 3rd.

Outside the rain fell thick, beating diagonally against the glass. While Piek played billiards, Renue listened to idle conversations, an old habit. Anything to avoid thinking about Lisande. He hadn't finished half his beer. At the adjacent booth, three well-dressed businessmen were sipping wine and talking loudly.

"Lower Goramon's closed. Were just putting up road blocks."

"Really?"

"Yeah. I couldn't get to her house. Had to leave my car."

"No fun because of a gas leak?"

"Better then *her* gas leaking."

The businessmen clinked glasses.

Piek returned to the table. "Fucking mid was good," he said. "Took five from me—still up twenty. Oh, come on. Just trying to keep my mind off it. They don't know anything, by the way. Manor said some bullshit about a blown pipe. Told my boys to cross over to the west side, just in case."

The door flew open and rattled with the wind, the roar of the storm briefly quieting the bar. As conversations resumed, a thin young man dressed in a drenched purple shirt staggered in, dripping on the floor. He ripped a thin white frill off his collar and wrapped the rag around his arm. The bartender immediately pointed to the entrance. "Out."

The youth swayed, tucking his hands in his coat pockets. "I just want . . . "

"Get out."

"Ah, let 'em have a drink," Piek said. "Come on, kid."

"He's drenched, man."

"Don't give me guff, Latchie," the bartender said. "This is my place and—"

"The boy's soused. Let him in. Fuck. Come on, kid."

Renue pulled Piek away as the bartender came from behind the rail, his fat stomach jostling as he moved towards the youth. "Shut it, Latchie," the bartender said. "That one's a worthless poet. You're lucky I let *your* moth-riddled ass in." The men nearby chuckled and exchanged glances. "I said out. Out."

"I wrote you a verse," the poet protested in a wandering voice. "You didn't like it?"

The bartender pushed the young man towards the door. "Bullshit crap didn't even rhyme—something for my kids, you said. Hell, it was about God-damn flowers. Kids don't give a shit about flowers."

"I'll buy him a beer," Piek offered. He fished through his pockets, frowning. "Fuck. Good luck, kid."

The bartender scoffed. "Big surprise—come back when you've stolen more."

"Found it." Piek took out a crumpled bill. "Besides, my friend's a hillborn and even his ass's made of gold. I can always pawn that in the Vines."

The drinkers at the bar hooted.

Next to Piek, a man wearing a long gray coat eased off his stool. "He said get out, pixie. I'm trying to unwind." The man turned to Piek. "You too, lout. And don't stand so close. You smell like a gutter whore."

"That's where your lady likes it," Piek said. "So I go. If I chose the place, it'd cost extra."

A few drinkers snickered.

"That so?" As the man approached Piek, Renue took a step closer.

Piek winked. "Smarter than you, stillborn."

Renue tugged at his shirt. "Come on. Listen, sorry for the . . . "

"Yeah, back to the docks with your old man. Lay with some fish."

"Big mouth," Piek said. "Small dick, always."

The man slammed his mug down on the bar. "Outside. Let's go, now."

"It's fucking raining, and I'd like your lady's smell to stay with me a while longer." Piek took a drink and wiped his mouth. "How about a bet instead?"

"Fuck you. Let's go."

"I can drink two beers before you can drink one shot," Piek continued. "As soon as I put my first beer on the table, you start. Whoever loses buys the drinks and a drink for our lavender little pixie here. If you try to cheat, it's double. If I lose, me and the kid will both leave. Name's Piek. You?"

"You don't have the cash."

Piek held up another crumpled bill. "What does this look like, your menstrual papers?"

"Real comedian here."

"Scared? A few rules," Piek said. "Neither of us can touch the other's glass. If ya touch the glass, ya buy pitchers for the bar." At this, the men within earshot perked up. "And I get a head start. Can't take your shot until after I've put my first glass down. Sound fair? What's your name?"

"Strom."

"So you in, Stromie?"

"Let's get this straight," Strom said. "Basically, you think you can drink an *entire* beer before I can drink one shot? Is that right?"

"As rain."

"And I get to choose the beer?"

"Be my guest."

Strom crossed his arms. "Alright, Latchie. Scally, how about two . . . Versumes?" The men at the bar shook their heads as drinkers at the closer tables turned towards the contest. "And give me a shot of Dresen."

The poet swayed slightly as the bartender filled up two glasses with a syrupy dark beer with barely any head. Then, he took out a thin bottle, pouring a shallow shot of light green liquor. He set the drinks on the bar. Renue found himself sizing up the men around Piek while scanning for alternate exits.

Piek picked up the beer, took a deep breath, then began to drink slowly. Halfway through the beer, he paused to wipe his mouth of froth. "Damn, this is *heavy*," he said. Strom grinned maliciously. "Okay, gonna put my glass down now." Piek winked at Renue, then quickly turned the glass upside down over the shot, trapping it. When Strom reached for the shot, Piek held up a finger. "*Remember*—can't touch my glass or you'll be buying pitchers for all these clowns." As the trick set in, everyone in the vicinity began to howl. Piek finished his second beer quickly and slid it down the bar. "I believe you owe my friend here a drink, and our kindly bartender for the beers." He lifted up the glass and bowed. "To your health."

"Fucking Latchie . . . " The bar erupted as Strom eyed the shot. "Think that's funny?"

"Ah, lighten up, Strom," the man at the stool next to him said. "The Latchie got ya. Hell, I'll buy him a drink for the show."

"Me too."

"And another round to forget the Scream."

"And another the war."

"Another for Perenia, those pasty lisping fucks."

"Bottle of wine on me, bartender."

Reluctantly, Strom extended his hand which Piek shook heartily. "Fair enough, Latchie. Fair enough."

"Lavender, my boy," Piek said, pulling at the youth's collar. "Come on. And stop polishing your ass, hillborn. Help our esteemed poet to the table."

"You're a fucking idiot," Renue whispered as the three made their way to the booth.

"You knew that trick too," Piek said. "Used to be more like me, huh? Besides, it's always good to have friends." They sat down. "You alright, kid?"

"Let me tell you . . . the future of this city," the poet said as he cupped his red face. "Find more secrets when . . . you watch a fountain woman pee."

"Damn he's soused. What's your name, kid?" The poet didn't seem to hear. "Lavender it is. Are you really a poet?"

Lavender took a sip of beer. "So breathes the sacred heart, the only heart I've ever known. We breathe . . . the world in parts, the endless mill of blood and bone."

"What?"

"That's Lyle," Renue said.

Lavender's eyes lit up. "You like Lyle?"

"Poetry?" Piek spat. "Take a good fiddle story any day over, unless—any money in verse?"

For a moment Lavender quietly studied Renue. " . . . only sludge."

"How does it pay, though?"

"By the word." The poet grabbed his glass so hard it slipped from his fingers and slid to the edge of the table. Renue stopped the glass and handed it back to Lavender, who proceeded to drink sloppily. "I wrote for birthdays, Hallow Day, Independence Day, *his* birthday, any day." The young man fell back, sloshing beer on the floor.

"Wrote?" Piek said. "And now?"

"Poet, clean that up," the bartender growled. "Or I'll use your pretty hair as a mop."

"Yeah, yeah," Lavender said. "Maybe I'll write your epitaph— he meant well . . . he smelled horribly."

The bartender cursed and went back to washing pitchers in the sink. Piek knocked on the table and left. "Pissing contest."

"Your hair," the poet said softly. "What happened to you?"

"Sick. You?"

"Yeah." Lavender reached into his pocket and pulled out a blue pill and swallowed it with a sip of beer. "Sick—take one."

"What's it do?"

"Helps you sleep."

Renue eyed the pill in Lavender's hand. "No, thanks."

The poet put it in his pocket and shivered. "You hear him too, though. Don't you?"

"I don't know what you're talking about."

"The *voice*," he said. "Speaking in your head at night. Telling you stories. The memories of others." Lavender stared out the window and swallowed. "It's searching . . . "

"Have you seen it?"

But the poet didn't answer and instead turned to watch the rain beat against the window. Renue finished his beer. He was back in the Manor hallway, running his hands over the lines of his mother's face, dreaming of murder.

♥

Lisande closed the book and turned off the lights, wondering how much her mother had known about the regime. Had her father always been a monster? She could still see him diving into a pool one afternoon, his athletic body, his hairy chest and legs, pushing himself up onto the mossy green patio. Earlier that day, Lisande remembered, her father had given Meera Rady a silver bow. She couldn't swim and he didn't want her to feel left out, her father later explained. Children had always adored him. Nestling against the bottom shelf, Lisande could still feel the slight warmth of jealousy, wanting him to watch her, to love her with even half the affection he lavished on others. She closed her eyes. He dove into the pool again and surfaced, black hair matted, his eyebrow scar visible. He winked at her, as though the two shared a secret. He walked over and kissed her mother softly on the check as she handed him a towel. Only after her mother was gone had Lisande started to fear her father and now, sitting in the basement, she wondered why she still feared him, even after he no longer had the power to hurt her.

The stairs creaked as Amelia came down, holding a small tin of Krylight. She placed the tin on top of the closest bookshelf and the basement began to pulse. "Guess you don't like the lights either," she called. "Don't blame you. Hurts my eyes, those cheap bulbs. Where are you? Ah." She came around the bookshelf and pulled a stool over near Lisande. "Rain must be slowing Dora— what's wrong, dearie?"

"Are your parents still alive?"

"Lord no. Passed when I was just a little older than you, actually—what are you, eighteen?"

"Twenty-one."

"Must be the hair."

"Can I ask you a question?"

"You just did."

Lisande tried to smile but her face felt rigid. "Did you ever wish you could ask them questions you were afraid to as a child?"

Amelia nodded. "Who *doesn't*? My father, for instance. He died so suddenly. A heart attack. My mother married a corporal. But in the Faldor war he was crippled, became a drunkard. Mother stayed with him. She'd get angry if my sisters or I asked about our father. My brothers knew better. He didn't dare touch us, though. He had other ways. My mother had hidden love letters in a box in the attic. One day, the bastard burned them. You know what I would have asked her?"

"What?"

"Who made her happier? Not that I didn't already know, but I wanted to hear it from her. Just once. My oldest brother was a soldier, died in the war. The other's a lawyer in Varsooth. We don't talk much. It's easier, I guess—I take it your parents are both gone."

"Yes."

"Was it recent?"

"They both died a long time ago."

"Any family?"

"I might have a brother."

"Might? Take my advice, dearie. Time makes strangers." Amelia stood. "I have some business I should probably attend to, but I'll leave the tin. Unless you want the ceiling light."

"That's alright. I think I might try to take a little nap."

"You can use my bed upstairs."

"I'm fine here."

"I'll bring you down a pillow."

Lisande laid her head against the ground. The pulsing Krylight felt soothing, and as she closed her eyes she thought how, in the spring, she and her mother would collect honeysuckle and hang the vines in wreathes throughout the Manor until the air was sweet. One morning, she and Faldor had hiked to the mountaintop where the clouds were so thick they could hardly see each other. For her mother's birthday, her father woke Lisande and her mother up and brought them breakfast in the living room, platters of eggs, melon, and fresh juice, and as they ate he played piano. That afternoon, they had picnicked on the hill behind the Manor. The air had been full of dragonflies that landed on her ears, buzzing. *They'll carry you away, Sophia*, her father had said. *They'll hold onto that beautiful hair.* And she had loved him at that moment and, even now, in the basement of the bookstore, she could almost feel the sun on her hair and wing flutter grazing her cheeks.

A crash jerked Lisande firmly awake and she held her breath, flinching as a door above slammed and a gun went off. She crawled down the row of shelves, heart loud in her ears. Heavy footsteps were heading for the trap door opening. Then Lisande heard Amelia sobbing. Quickly, she hid behind the closest shelf, watching from between two hardcovers.

"Sure you're alone?" came a voice from above.

"Yes, I . . . swear . . . "

"A young woman was seen entering this bookstore. Just cooperate. It'll be easier on you."

Black boots appeared at the top of the stairs. A soldier dragged Amelia by the back of her blouse, her jaw slamming on each step until her mouth was black with blood. Halfway down the stairs, the soldier flashed a light across the basement. Lisande's mouth ran dry. She flattened on her back as the spade hurled Amelia down the final stairs.

"What have we *here*?"

When the soldier reached for the ceiling light, Lisande kicked the bookshelf with all her strength and books toppled over him, knocking the gun from his hand. For a moment, the soldier was pinched between the shelf and the stairs. Then he twisted out from beneath the bookshelf. Amelia reached for the gun as the soldier pulled out a small pistol. Both fired. The soldier crumpled. Lisande's ears were ringing and full of white noise. Slumping awkwardly on the stairs, Amelia groaned and dropped her gun. Lisande moved the shelf, then picked up the gun. With her other hand she stroked the dying woman's hair.

♥

Renue leaned over the table. "Rain's letting up a little. Let's go."

"Not so fast," Piek said, glancing towards bar entrance where two spades had appeared, one with a red band around his forearm. The room quieted as the spade with the armband began to question the bartender. Suddenly, they put a black bag over the bartender and pushed him to the nearest corner. Renue eyed the entrance as the two spades addressed the room.

"I am Officer Bartles and this is Officer Clemsy. Has anyone seen this woman?"

"Good sign," Piek said softly. "They haven't got her—maybe she's close by."

"Don't do anything stupid."

Clemsy unfolded a poster sketch. A man in a blue striped shirt near the bar said something to his neighbor and Bartles dropped the man with the butt of a trembler. "Any other jokers?" He reached into his overcoat and pulled out a small radio, listened for a moment, then tucked it away.

"They're newbies," Piek said from the corner of his mouth while holding the beer mug up to his face. "See how they hold their trems?"

"So?"

"So watch."

"They'll leave in a moment," Renue said. "Don't be stupid."

Clemsy grabbed another man, bagged and pushed him into the bartender as Bartles moved to the center of the room, tapping his trembler against chairs. The two spades proceeded from table to table, showing the poster. Two additional men were bagged before the officers made it around to their table. Lavender's face was pale and he was still shivering. Piek lit a cigarette as the officers approached.

"Seen her?"

"No."

"Nope."

Lavender squinted, leaning over Renue to see the poster, and began to giggle.

"Something funny?" Bartles smacked him across the face. "Laugh again."

"Ignore him—he's plastered."

The poet covered his mouth and pointed to the poster. "The lines are wrong . . . "

"Get the fuck up."

" . . . Manor has the worst . . . artists."

Bartles hit Lavender again, this time bloodying his lip. "Move." He dragged the poet out of the booth.

"He's drunk, that's all," Renue said. "He doesn't know anything."

Bartles aimed the trembler at Renue. "What if I drew that, asshole?"

"Easy, easy," Piek said. "It's good—God-damn good. I mean, I'd fuck her."

"Listen," Renue said. "It's not—"

Clemsy stuck his trembler in Renue's face. "I wasn't talking to you, old man, so sit fucking down."

" . . . the lines . . . "

Bartles kicked Lavender to the floor and the poet lay dazed at the officer's feet. He kicked him again and the poet curled into a ball. "Shut the fuck up, fairy."

"Stop," Renue said. "He can't even see the poster. You don't need to take him."

"We decide who we take."

"Shut the fuck up."

"We'll take who we want."

"Gentlemen, gentlemen," Piek said, taking a drag from his cigarette. "It's nasty outside. Let me show you a trick. Rain's slowing, another few minutes, that's all. Let me show you a trick, and if you like it, let my friend stay. Deal?"

The two spades pointed their tremblers at Piek. "Fuck you, lout. Take a seat."

"Let's take all three."

The men at the bar shifted, watching silently.

"Come on," Piek urged. "You don't want to get wet any more than we do."

The spades whispered for a few moments, then turned back to Piek. "Fuck it—show us quick, Latchie," Bartles said. "God save you if it's bad."

"Yeah, God save you, Latchie," Clemsy added. "God save you."

"Alright." Piek took another long drag. "I call this trick, Black

Hands." He blew rings above their heads. "And there's that damn smoke." All around the bar, men watched Piek as he glanced at the bagged men in the corner. "Hold out your hands. If you can guess where the ash is, I'll buy you a pair of beers for your trouble. It can take a while to question everyone in a bar, right?"

"Sometimes."

"Sure. Right?"

"Shut up."

Piek clapped. "Hold your hands out. Palms up." He took a long drag of his cigarette and flicked the ashes into his lightly formed fist. "Now, do everything I do." Piek began to swing his fists up and down. "Repeat after me. Singing. Everyone. Or they'll shoot you—won't you?"

"Repeat after him," Clemsy said. "Do it."

Bartles waved his trembler around. "You heard him. Sing, fuckers."

Throughout the bar the customers nodded obediently. Piek took a deep breath. "My wife told me between her legs," he sang.

"Sing, you fucks."

"Or we'll bag you."

Beneath Bartles, Lavender began to cough violently. Renue watched Clemsy dangle his trembler at the edge of the table.

"My wife told me between her legs."

"Else she would make me dead."

"Louder."

"Else she would make me dead."

"I told her any other night."

"I told her any other night."

"Tonight her sweet spot's red."

"Tonight her sweet spot's red."

The officers laughed heartily and some men joined him in a forced chuckle. Now Lavender had stopped coughing and was staring up at the table quietly.

"She fucked my dear best friend."

"She fucked my dear best friend."

Piek took another drag. "So then I bought a trem."

"So then I bought a trem."

"Shot him right between his legs."

"Shot him right between his legs."

"At least no sex for them."

The spades roared as Piek brought his hands together, forming two fists which he held out dramatically. "Officers—where's the ash?" Bartles gestured to Piek's left hand but the palm was clean. He pointed at the other. Piek opened the first and shook his head.

"So where is it, Latchie?"

"Your hands—check 'em." There was a line of gray ash smeared across Bartles' palm. "Yours too," Piek said to Clemsy, who showed his hand to a light applause. In the corner, the bagged men were wheezing.

"How'd you do it, Latchie?"

"Magic," Piek said. "It's all an act. Misdirection. Now watch this."

"Come on," Bartles said. "Tell us."

"That's an order."

"Magician's code. Against the law too—watch this, though." Piek waved his hands around, producing a coin.

Renue reached for the trembler but Lavender had already grabbed it, aiming up at Bartles. As the safety clicked off, the spade captain looked down then groped for his gun but Piek pushed him over the adjacent table and stepped on his hand, then took his trembler. Clemsy watched Lavender stand slowly, continuing to aim the trembler. Bartles got to his feet and looked around.

"What happens now?"

"Our friend is sick," Renue said. "We just want to take him home."

"Take him home?"

"Yeah, home," Piek said. "We need to take him home."

"Home," Clemsy said. "OK."

"Shut up, Clems. Fuck you, lout."

"You alright, Lavender?" Piek cleared his throat. He stepped forward violently and Bartles jumped back, tripping over a chair. Piek kicked him once in the stomach, then punched him square in the face and Bartles fell hard, sputtering.

"Piek," Renue said. "Stop."

"Fuckers doused my ma." Piek's face was twisted as he continued to kick the fallen spade in the ribs. Clemsy's face went pale as specks of blood hit the chair.

"Hey," Renue said, grabbing Piek's shoulder. "Hey. Enough."

Piek spit on the fallen spade and kicked him a final time in the mouth. Clemsy flinched as Bartles spit out a tooth, groaning. A static noise came from his jacket pocket.

Piek bent down, grabbing the radio. "Report in," he said. "Ask if they've found her. Find out where."

Bartles struggled to regain his breath and wiped blood from his mouth. He mumbled and pointed to Clemsy. Piek gave him the radio.

"This second officer Gran Clemsy," the spade said. "Nothing yet. Anyone found her? Out."

"Subject spotted. Proceed to Lower Vines for backup. Breventine's Bookstore. With caution. Central Slants hot. Shoot on sight. Copy."

"Copy. Clemsy out."

Piek crushed the radio beneath his foot. A few customers stood guard at the bar entrance while others began to unbag the men in the corner. The bartender surveyed the scene, then limped over slowly and looked down at the bloodied officer.

"We should go," Renue said. "Now."

Piek tossed a crumbled bill onto Bartles' bloody face. "Sorry for the outburst—drinks on me."

"What the fuck am I supposed to do with them?" the bartender said. "You ruined me."

"Use this." Renue fished in his pocket and took out the vial Granges had given him. "Just a drop."

"What's it do?"

"Makes them forget," Renue said. "Make sure to leave them somewhere safe."

"Knew you were trouble, Latchie. You're banned."

Piek continued to watch Bartles.

"Lavender—do you know the quickest way to Breventine's? No main streets."

"Yes."

"Take us there—please."

"Enjoy your beer, gentlemen," Piek said at the door. "Show our friends here a good time."

♥

Plates of sandwiches topped with green olives, bowls of crispy potatoes and leafy green salad cover the blanketed table, but she's on her tiptoes reaching for a lemon square bordering a platter of fried squid. Sophia takes the plate and heads for her mother, sitting with the other wives in bright orange lawn chairs. There's music playing in the background, one of those stuffy dances by her mother's favorite composer, Ravta Demin. Her father likes Ravta's brother better, Benji, the popular songwriter. The women are dancing.

Her father is with Boran and some other men by the white grass hill, holding elegant rifles, examining them. Occasionally a rifle is fired into the air between musical notes. She tries to find her mother. Her father shoots and one of the men says something. Father is screaming. Sophia drops her plate and scrambles beneath the table. A little boy is hiding between the table legs. Two men hold her father's shoulders trying to calm him but he becomes further enraged and pushes them away. He takes out a pistol and puts it to the man's head. Hold him, he orders. Boran and a few soldiers take the man's arms as Sophia feels a hand on her shoulder. It's her mother.

What's happening?

Nothing, she says, bending down to rub Sophia's neck. Let's go finish that blanket we were working on.

As her mother leads Sophia down the long table, she sees brownies dropped in the grass. The boy beneath the table is twiddling his thumbs and blowing air out his mouth. Her father is still yelling. Up on the hill, flowers bloom in bursts of red and yellow. Her father still has his gun raised, tracking the man as several soldiers drag him away.

Where are you going, Alaine? Alaine?

Someone turns on the music but the women are slow to move. Her father orders everyone to get up and dance. It's a sad-sounding waltz. They dance. Father doesn't like the music and tells them to play something livelier, something by Benji. Mother's pulling her by the arm. Father charges over and whispers in her ear. They push Sophia away and begin to argue. He grabs her mother's wrist but she twists free and stalks off.

Alone, Father picks Sophia up and swirls her around. He asks her to dance but she can't stop crying. She wipes her nose on her dress. He sets her down and performs a card trick for her, then another, then pulls a coin from her nose.

It was more difficult because of all the snot, he says. If you stop crying, the magic will work better. So much snot. Slows down the magic. He kisses her on the cheek.

She's giggling now. He tickles her, then tells the children to gather around the table. They clap as he makes a piece of squid vanish. Disgusting, he says. Now what shall we make disappear next, children? he asks. The broccoli salad, perhaps? They all giggle.

Father swirls her in the air. Sophia, dance with me, he says. After a few dances, he goes over to the table and pours her a tall glass of lemonade. Condensation collects in a rim around her fingers and she drinks. He tells all the children to line up then plays stop-go with them. The boy hiding under the table wins. When the game is over, the children gather around her father again and ooh and aah as he juggles colored balls, green, purple, yellow, red. He flips on a lighter and lights the balls, juggling as colored smoke hisses out and furls. A rainless rainbow, he says, throwing the balls in a great arc across the field, leaving behind colored trails of smoke that slowly dissipate in the breeze. The children applaud. It's hot, he says, wiping his forehead. Let's go swimming.

Later, after the guests have left, he'll put her on his lap and play piano for her in the ballroom.

Where's Mother?

She's not feeling well.

Why?

Oh, you know your mother.

Now she's crying again, so he picks her up and lets her touch the scar across his eyebrow that a lot of the guards have too. How did you get that, Daddy?

The war. Did you have a good time today?

Yes.

What did you like the most?

She scrunches her nose. The lemonade?

Lemonade?

Yes.

Why the lemonade?

It was really cold.

♥

As the three left the bar, a group of spades were proceeding south towards a smoky mass rising out of the Slants. In the distance someone was barking orders over a megaphone. Fire trucks and vans sped southwards towards the crackling of gunfire. Lavender led Renue and Piek west down a side street lined with coffee shops, book, music, and antique stores. Wind chimes clanged in the strong wind.

"Damn," Piek said. "Never thought I'd see this."

Passing the Vines, the air began to smell less smoky and as they headed further west, the explosions and gunfire became fainter and the neighborhood more deserted. Only the rush of locking doors and clamping windows greeted them. Lavender stopped a few minutes later and caught his breath, pointing to a building halfway down the block on the right.

"Thanks for your help," Renue said, but to his surprise the poet continued to follow behind. Beside the entrance to the store, three Drailers lay in the shadow. Renue took their tremblers and handed one to Piek. The door was ajar. He paused to listen, but could only hear rainwater streaming into gutters. Inside, shelves were strewn about and books blanketed the floor.

"I'll call the boys," Piek said, moving quickly to the counter.

Renue walked down an aisle slowly. But a shot rang out from the back of the store and he ran over spilled books towards the sound. Lavender was squirming beside the couch, blood seeping from his side. Stairs led down to the basement, tinted a faint green. He could hear someone breathing heavily. "Shit," Renue said, clicking off the safety. "Lisande?"

"Renue?"

"Are you there?" In the poor light he could see her, holding a shaking trembler. "Lisande?" The poet sputtered. Renue glanced back.

"Lisande?" Renue called. "Put the gun down."

"Is that really you?" came a small voice.

He came down the stairs but she lifted up the trembler suddenly and he froze. A woman lay cradled in her arms. "Put it down," he said. "It's me." At the bottom of the stairs, he took the trembler from her. "You cut your hair." Her eyes were vacant.

Lisande tried to point but her hand shook violently. Holding the locket, she teared up.

"Come on," he said, pulling her to her feet. "We have to go."

"Is she dead?"

Renue felt the woman's wrist. "We have to go. Now." He took her hand.

At the top of the stairs, Piek was bent over Lavender. "Fuck," he said. "Relax, kid. Hold where it hurts. Is she okay? Kid, don't try to move. Help's coming soon."

"Please," the poet said. "Don't let it take me."

"Don't move."

"Don't leave me," he said. "Here."

"Hold where it hurts," Renue said, wincing when he saw the wound.

"We've got to get him out of the city, bud." Piek gestured to the black marks on Lavender's palms. "And forget the Maskers," he said. "Boys told me they're finished—found out in the bar."

"What?"

"Sorry. Didn't want to say before."

"We need to get them somewhere safe."

"Boys should be outside soon," Piek said. "Let's go." He supported Lavender and the four made their way slowly to the entrance. Outside, thick smoke rose from behind the bell tower, but the street was empty.

"*Pieky*!" someone called.

Renue spotted Benny, Kors, and Dego approaching on a motorbike. The louts quickly disembarked and leaned the bike against the building.

"Fucking about time," Piek said. "Where are the other bikes? I said extras."

"Just this one left. Other was rocketed."

"Rocketed? What's happening?"

"Blanks taking the city." Dego pulled out a narrow trembler and twisted the barrel in his hand. "Maskers were sneaking a bomb to Blank headquarters. Blanks were tipped off."

"Pieky," Benny sniveled. "I . . . "

"*Breathe*, Benny." Kors patted the young lout on his back. "We're proud of you."

"What's wrong with him?"

"You did good, Benny," Dego said. "Real good."

"He shot two Blanks sneaking up on us."

"Streets full of them."

"Free for all."

"Overran a few police stations, the Blanks did."

"Surprised the Manor. Almost took over south side and the docks already—been planning it for months, seems."

"I *killed*, Pieky." Benny's eyes darted wildly, then he lunged for Lisande and buried his head in her chest. As he pressed his nose to her neck she took him in her arms and the two embraced, rocking back and forth.

"Let's split," Dego said. "Wave of them just south of the tower. Bound to spill over to the Vines."

"Give me the keys," Piek said. He handed them to Renue. "How's the western gate?"

"Boran pulled most guards," Kors said. "Why, you want to bring something in?"

"Take her out of here," Piek said to Renue. "Them too. Kid's marked."

Renue watched Lisande stroking Benny's hair. "You're not coming?"

"Sorry, chief," Piek said. "No room. Besides, you know I can't. Keep her safe. If things calm down, find me."

Piek pried Benny off Lisande and kissed her on the cheek. Renue sat the poet and Lisande in front of him on the bike and turned the ignition. The engine revved as the louts stood to either side, balancing the bike. They rode west though the deserted streets and beneath the great arms of Mesmer that formed the western gate of Ashkareve, not stopping until they were out of the city.

IV

Chapter Ten

The motorbike ran out of gas a mile from Ashkareve and they proceeded on foot on a country road, occasionally passing houses with cobbled-together wooden fences. For a time there was only a violent wind that stirred and excited the yellow grass fields. To the southwest, Renue could see others fleeing into the flats towards the highway, but he wanted to avoid the major thoroughfares in case any spades were still searching for them. Out of the city, the poet's hands had finally unblackened.

Lavender collapsed as the road they were on turned to dirt, so Lisande waited in the middle and stopped a truck. Renue and the driver lifted the poet onto the truck bed and climbed in. The driver asked no questions. Soon Little Wolf Peak rose over the hills as the truck sped westward, kicking up mud and emptying puddles. Minutes later, the man parked by the side of the road near a clump of houses, told them to get out, then sped away. Renue approached a few homes, trying to barter for supplies, but no one was home or answering. The houses were neat with well-manicured yards, but because of the distance between them there was an odd, quiet presence that made Renue uneasy. He broke into one home and took some bread and canned food, a glass jar which he filled with water, some bandages, and rope, gathering it all up in a blanket, lugged the blanket over his back and quickly left. Lisande was stroking Lavender's hair. The poet's eyes were glassy, though there was a curious smile to his lips.

"We need to keep going," Renue said. "In case they're following us. Colver, maybe. Somewhere Boran can't find us."

Lisande wrapped Lavender's stomach and he managed to stand. The three headed up into wooded hills, avoiding the thorn bushes and brambles. At the top of the first hill, Renue glanced back at the city. Just a mass of smoke and fog softly glowing. Half an hour later, the group stopped to catch their breath beneath a gnarled oak tree, and Renue realized he had never really been out of Ashkareve, but he had studied maps enough to lead them away from the highways. Amid the rugged terrain, he found a narrow, crooked path which led into a stand of gray-needled pine trees. To the north were the Krylight mines and further northeast the twilight forest, though both were now obscured by the thick woods. Lisande paused at a fork in the path.

"What's wrong?"

"Nothing," she said. "I thought I . . . nothing."

When Renue felt they were far enough away, he suggested they stop and make camp and Lisande tended the poet's wound. For a time, Lavender spoke feverishly of loved ones, but as dusk approached the poet soon fell asleep. Lisande and Renue found a large stump nearby and the two sat down. A slow, cool breeze drifted through the forested hills. They could see only light flares down below, nearly obscured by a maze of yellow and green leaves. Renue stripped a few stripes of blue lichen off as they conversed quietly.

"Do you think he'll live?"

"No."

She looked down. "I killed him."

"No, you didn't," he said. "The black thing would have found him eventually."

"I don't want him to die, Renue."

"I know."

"I mean, isn't that the point?" she said. "Isn't it? The laws. Not to value your life more than any another?" She rested her head in her hands. "Maybe my father was right all along."

Renue coughed and touched his face, feeling the age lines on his forehead. "Did you visit when I was sick?"

"Yes."

"Even though you hated me?"

Lisande nodded.

"Do you still hate me?"

"No." Somewhere above the tree line a crow cawed and a flock of sparrows scattered beyond the tree ceiling. Lisande picked up a leaf and began folding it over and over, then tore along the vein. "I went a little crazy," she said. "Did they tell you?"

"No."

She took a breath. "What are we doing here?"

"The city's not safe anymore."

"What about Bardon? And Dora? What if—?"

"—Lisande," he said. "Stop. Let's just worry about us for now."

When they returned to camp, Lavender was writing in a small, leather-bound journal. Beneath the trees the light came down in faint orange bands. Renue put his arm around Lisande as the poet closed the book and attempted to stand.

"Lie *down*," she said. "Rest."

"But I want to see the city," the poet said in a weak voice. "I had this . . . dream . . . of a forest . . . around one of those old castles. It kept burning in a circle . . . regrowing after the fire." His voice fell softer. "Passed. Maybe cities do that too. Burn so they can grow back." Lavender frowned. "Why is she crying? Why are you crying?"

"She thinks she took your life," Renue said. "She doesn't understand."

Lavender tapped Lisande's shoulder. "It's not your fault. Miss? Miss?" He brought out a bag of light blue pills from his pocket. "I didn't want it to take me," he said, "so I took myself."

"Who did you kill?" Renue said. "Lavender?"

The poet murmured. "Strong pills. You two look like . . . these beautiful blurring lights, like two flowering stars."

Lisande sniffled. "Stars?"

"Will you stay with me?" His eyes closed.

♥

They found a tree upturned by the recent storm and dug dirt with their hands and buried the poet. On the way back to camp, Renue and Lisande came across a creek and splashed water on their faces. He filled up the glass jar, then picked up a leaf and told her to find one. He counted to three and they dropped their leaves together, watching them race in the water. His leaf was in the lead until she picked up a large branch and threw it into the water, submerging the two.

"That wasn't fair," he said.

"What's fair?"

Back at camp, they watched a cluster of flies hovering around a bush of yellow flowers. A stiff wind blew, scattering the bugs. The two sat together, silent, darkness settling in the woods.

"Renue?"

"Yes?"

"Do you think I could have helped him?" she said. "Be like he was when my mother was alive? Maybe I could have said something. Done something. I mean, how could my mother *be* with him? She was so . . . " Lisande brought her knees to her chest. " . . . good."

"I don't know."

"I'm not going to sleep tonight." She exhaled. "Tell me something nice."

"Like what?"

"What were you like as a kid? Granges and Dora and Bardon told me a little—I was curious, that's all." A line of shadowy trees blocked her view of Ashkareve, but the city still felt unbearably close. "It's just hard to tell when you're acting sometimes," she said. "I don't really know you."

"When I was a kid, we'd pour wax all over our hands and shoulders and then fight with wooden swords. A blow, then the wax would crack, another and it'd fall off. We'd steal candles from religious houses. I wasn't much of a fighter, but I was always clever. For some reason, it really *mattered* to me, winning. It made me feel good to win. But it was all a trick."

"I don't understand."

"I'd lead my opponent out into the sun," he explained. "Then stand back at the shade line, playing defense. Let the wax melt until it'd just slip off. None of the other kids seemed to notice."

"What about in winter?"

"We didn't play then."

As the night closed in, they listened to the birds and brown tree bats creep from their nesting places. Lisande had never known such wild nature. Life teemed all around them. The air smelled only slightly of smoke, but besides the smell and the distant crackling sounds it was possible to imagine she was thousands of miles away from the city.

"Renue?" she whispered.

"Yes?"

Bat wings flapped hidden amid the myriad of branches, and crickets were awake now and chirping. Lisande brought out the silver locket and held it to her forehead. It felt cool. "How do people do it?"

"Do what?"

"Survive for so long." She waited for a reply but when she asked again, he was already asleep.

♥

The room smells of sawdust and pungent chemicals. As she sneezes, her father finally notices her. Get out, Sophia, he says. Don't argue. Wait outside.

But—

I told you not to come down here.

She sits on a stool near the door, holding onto the sides and leaning against the wall. Her father comes out a few minutes later.

Sophia, don't kick the wall. You're scuffed your boots.

What's *wrong* with her?

She's not feeling well.

But why?

He straightens, running his fingers across the golden frame of a painting shaped like creeping roots. Her father's eyes catch in the poor lamplight. It doesn't matter.

No one gets sick in the summer.

He puts a hand to his head. I'm sending you to a doctor tomorrow.

I'm not leaving her.

Don't be difficult.

Why can't I *be* with her? We could bring down a cot. For both of us.

She needs to rest.

Why are you keeping her down here? Maybe if she could see the forest, she'd feel better. Let her touch the trees like she likes.

She needs to be down here, he says. Trust me.

Do I *really* have to go? Can't he come here?

He shakes his head. I want you to have the best.

Who?

The man that came by last week. You remember Valan. He lives in the hills, but it's difficult for him to travel here.

I don't want to leave her.

No, Sophia. Let her rest.

Her father always has to have the last word. Sophia starts to head for the door. I'll just be a second.

He grabs her arm hard and she freezes. Let her rest, I said. Now go pack your things. Boran will be by your room in an hour. I don't want you to get sick too. He kisses her on the forehead.

♥

Pine needles stuck to his face. "Renue?" He was breathing so slowly and she pulled down his shirt, revealing a black bruise on his collarbone. Lisande nudged him and his eyelids flitted. "If you're joking, I'm going to kill you. I swear." She jostled him. "Renue, this isn't funny. Are you alright?" She felt his pulse, his chest rising so faintly she could keep it down with a few fingers. Fetching the half-filled glass bottle, she splashed some water on his face. He sputtered, finally opening his eyes. "Get up."

"I can't," he said.

"What? You can't move? Are you serious?"

" . . . yes."

"You were sick yesterday too, weren't you?"

"Yes."

"Is that all you can say? Yes?"

He closed his eyes and smirked. "Yes."

"Come on," she said, prying his shoulder from the ground. "We're going."

"Where?"

"Valan," she said. "Alkor promised me he'd take you. He showed me where on the map—it can't be that far from here."

"Valan . . . "

"This is not a choice," she said. "You're sick. We're going."

"Fine. Just give me a minute."

Lisande led him north until they came across a path that cut along the hill line. Even before she recognized the scraps of white iron fence like the ribs of great beasts or the lichen that spotted the trees yellow and red, she felt a familiar presence. They walked beside the underbelly of a recently uprooted tree crawling with grubs, beetles, and worms. Then she recognized the flat cabin nestled between two trees branches sagging with purple fruit.

"You've been here before?" he said.

"When I was younger. My father sent me."

The cabin was sunken into the ground and thick lines of fire spikes rose around the perimeter. A white-speckled dogwood shaded one side and bronze-leaved camellia bushes cropped the other. Circular stones lined the walkway, rocky islands floating in a sea of thousands of dull orange and gray pebbles. When they were halfway down the walk, a boy appeared from the cabin and quickly closed the door behind him. He continued on the path, humming an odd, atonal melody.

"Excuse me," Lisande said.

The boy stopped humming and took a step back. Then he ran by them and disappeared into the woods. She knocked. A moments later, an old man came to the door, barefoot. From his head sprouted tufts of white hair in thin wisps, like the loose cotton threads her mother often used in blankets as filler. The old man tugged impatiently at his blue bathrobe. "What did you forget this time you—" He took a step back. "Who are *you*, and why didn't the thrashers thrash you? Dammit, that's what the thrashers are *supposed* to do!"

"Do you remember me, Valan?"

The old man pursed his lips and reached to feel her face. "I recognized the voice, but you can't be too careful. They can steal voices—can't steal a face. Not yet, at least." He frowned. "Who is the other?"

"This is Renue, my brother. He's sick. Can you help him?"

"Renue." Valan repeated the name a few times. "Sounds fictitious. I don't trust anything that can be made into its opposite. No, it's not a good name, not at all—no flexibility! Now Valan, *that's* a name! Means honey pot, I believe. What is the opposite of honey pot? You tell me." He sniffed. "Wolves should come back soon. I dreamt it. Any night now."

"Renue, show him your wound."

"A *wound*, you say?" The old man scratched his chin, then spit in his hand and wiped his face. "The wolves in the Faldor days could tear your arm out of your socket." He turned to Lisande. "It's not a wolf wound, is it?" he said excitedly. "Because if it *is* a wolf wound, I'll gladly treat him." Then he touched Renue's collarbone and pulled away. "The nightmare," he murmured. "Have you finally found me?"

"What?"

"Valan, he—"

"Come inside, quickly now. Lock the door. Take me to my chair."

The old man held out his arm and Lisande grabbed it, reaching back for Renue's hand. Her stomach rumbled as she entered. "If you please," Valan said. "Excuse the mess. There hasn't been a woman here in many years, if memory serves me—which it often doesn't. How is your mother, by the way? No, the red chair with the footstool. Grab it for me, Sophia. That was a present from your father, was it not?" Brick stairs led to a sunken living room with an L-shaped couch in one corner and a fireplace next to it. Puzzles and books were piled on a dining table and in the adjoining kitchen a sink brimmed with dishes and pots. "You— the fictitious one. Do you know how they made the city? Tell me how it was designed and I'll help you. Otherwise, leave an old man his fleeting moments."

"They made a . . . "

"Exactly!" Valan jumped. "Yes, a circle of fire, burned it into the ground, equidistant from the bell tower. That was the original palace, before it became a governmental body, before it became obsolete, but yes, yes, like spokes on a wheel. Did you know one of my contemporaries, Marland, designed a forest around his home? In the same manner. Easier to copy than to create, but oh, that feeling if you make something truly original! I know *that* feeling. Beautiful, eternally burns, Marland's home does, but without the smoke. Now tell me, why are you worth saving?"

"He's my brother, Valan. Please help me."

"Brother? Oh? Give me your hand then, sir." Valan snatched it and released quickly. "So you *have* come back to settle a score. I didn't think I would die today, but you've outsmarted my defenses. Very well, make it quick. I suppose I deserve it, though you did too if you remember. But you probably don't, and for that matter, I don't either. Ancient history." The old man smacked his lips. "Now, give me your hands, both of you." He shut his eyes. "Many deaths." Valan hobbled over to the kitchen and ran his hand across a series of glass containers. He opened one and sniffed deeply. "Here's a joke. You know the difference between the Sickness and politics? No? Same amount of power, but in politics, you only throw up on the inside." The old man pulled out a dried stem from the container and hobbled back to Renue and Lisande.

"Will that help him?"

Chewing a stem, Valan snickered. "Oh, no. This is for *me*. Don't worry, though. He's through the worst of it. I'd get some fresh air and stay away from the city for a while. I don't know who tried to heal you, but they did a terrible job. Probably took ten, twenty years off your life, if not more." He reached for Lisande's hand again and his face soured. "You, the sick one. If you have any family in the city, I'd warn them to leave."

"I don't."

"Just me," Lisande added.

"No, no," Valan said. "I might be blind, but I still can see certain things. Him? Brother? Not unless you mean metaphorically." He perched on the stool. "Now, in that drawer over there, by my spice rack—yes, I hear you, warmer, one more step. There are some herbs in there, twilight stems. If you feel it near, take one.

If you don't overdo it, they're quite nice. Wondrous dreams. But too much and you'll sleep forever. Your mother, what an addict! Your father too. Then again, it doesn't surprise me. Wolves. Ah, there used to be thousands of them. Like the Gift, those creatures are, leaving markers with sweat glands so they can find their way. Thousands. Then those idiot farmers butchered them all. Should have black hands, those farmers. To kill anything is the same. Kill a wolf, your male part falls off. So much for extinction!"

"You helped Mesmer make the black thing, didn't you?" Renue said. "Why did you do it?"

"*Renue.*"

"Lisande, it's a fair question. You know who this is? What he did?" Renue turned to Valan. "Don't you feel any remorse?"

"That *voice*," the old man said, hopping off the stool. He lead them to the door. "Something unsettling. Like two notes playing at once. Still a bit off." Then the old man burst into tears. "Want to know how it started, yes? Not for *death*—my misunderstood creation. No, not for death, but for tracking. He just wanted to find his family. Just wanted to find his family. No, not on my conscience. Now leave me be. Leave me *be*!"

"So he'll be alright?"

"I'm feeling fine, Lisande," Renue said. "We should go in case they check here."

"Thank you, Valan," she said at the door. "If I come back, will you tell me about my mother?"

Valan had closed the door halfway. "Of course I would," he said. "But you won't."

♥

They passed the lichen-spotted trees and heading southward. After hiking for another hour, Renue and Lisande set up camp. As dusk approached, they ate a little, then listened to the sounds of the forest. In the warm, moist air, the forest seemed even more isolated.

"What do we do now?"

"Colver is a few hours west of here. Maybe we can find a ride tomorrow."

"Can we make a fire tonight?" she said. "Right. It rained."

"We can still make a small one. Smokeless."

"Not that anyone would notice it," she said. She gathered bits of kindling that Renue split down the middle, shedding the outer, wet bark. He started the fire as the leaves around them changed from green to orange brown to black. "Can I?" She held up two leaves and he nodded. Throwing the pair in, she watched them peel back. She sighed.

"What?" he said.

"So . . . orphans once again."

He flipped the smoldering twig ends into the fire. "He was a crazy old man. What does he know?"

"I just sort of wanted you to be my brother," she said sadly. "In some stupid, impossible way. My father kept so much from me. There were so many secrets in that house."

Renue found a stout twig and pushed the coals closer together. "Yeah."

"You're not surprised?"

"Not really."

"Why did you come after me, then?"

"I felt responsible, I guess."

For an hour they watched the fire burn down to coals, neither speaking. Then Renue stood and covered the coals with dirt.

"So we're leaving for good?"

"Yes."

"Will you hold me?" she said.

He scooted over to her and she leaned back into his chest as he picked at her hair. "It was prettier before you cut it."

She sat beside him and rested her head on his shoulder. "Is it my fault?" she said. "I *killed* him, Renue."

"No," he said, unsure who she was speaking of. "*No,* Lisande."

"Okay."

He woke later with a slight chill from the night wind. Lisande had been crying in her sleep. "I love you," he said. "No matter what." He wondered if someone could hear a voice while dreaming. He said it again, then moved closer and saw her face, flooded with dark tears.

♥

She picks up a bronze vase inscribed with the founding myth of Ashkareve. Gifts from Gratar, Melusa, Perenia, and other nations grace the polished wooden credenza. A golden sword with a ruby-adorned hilt hangs from two silver placeholders. On the table across the hall, three ceremonial pools spill glacial-blue water in a continuous loop. The cage of a now freed Myree bird sits, empty. She imagines its long brown feathers and what it must be like to glide in currents so high. The last few weeks, she's been feeling particularly restless, and has even considered reviving an old childhood practice of running away, though when she was younger somebody always watched her and she never got very far. Maybe she'll try again, even if they eventually bring her back. It's the idea of running that's sustained her, she knows. Not escape itself. Footsteps coming from the marble hall give her goosebumps. Her father is dressed in a formal overcoat and a gray button-down shirt.

Was his death hard on you?

Of course. She stares down the hall past him. You?

Yes, he says, as though tasting soured wine on his lips. Surprisingly so.

Down the hall she can hear sounds of merriment, laughing guests, clinking glasses, lively conversation. A wake has turned into a party.

The service is at five.

I'm not going.

No? Why not?

Does it matter? She puts down the vase. I prefer to grieve privately.

I'd like you there.

Are you asking me, or telling me?

I have something for you. He takes out a small green bracelet.

I'm not a child, she says. You can't buy my happiness.

Put it on. It has sentimental value.

No.

It was your mother's. He lets it dangle until she takes it, instantly feeling eight again.

How long since we spoke? A year? How long since we even shared a meal?

I always set aside one day. I'm a busy man. It isn't an easy thing to run a country, you know.

It used to be two days, she says. But I guess you like birthday cake more than memorials. Sophia runs her fingers down the Myree cage bars. So, did you find Faldor's murderer, or did he slip through your fingers?

We'll find him.

But it doesn't bother you that Faldor's gone, does it?

I just said—

No. You didn't.

It bothers me that there was a murder in my home, he says. That troubles me, yes.

She nods slowly. When you find his killer, I want to see him. I want to see him and spit in his face before you do whatever it is you do.

There are leaders from twelve countries in these halls, so keep your voice down.

Going to send me to my room?

He straightens. I came to tell you something, he says. I'm leaving.

Leaving?

Will you miss me, Sophia, when I'm gone?

One day out of the year? I suspect my life will change very little.

Perhaps. His smile curls. There's some food inside, he says. I can have someone make you a plate.

How thoughtful. Like a match in winter, she says as he turns to leave. Father.

He pauses. What?

Why did you do it?

Why?

The lights seem to dim and the laughter beyond the hall fades, as though she and her father are alone in the Manor. He turns to face her. Because sometimes life steals from you quickly and without mercy, he says, buttoning his coat. And afterwards, you are never the same again. But they can't steal what you don't have. Remember that, Sophia. They cannot steal what you do not have.

♥

In the darkness, he felt her fingers closing around his neck and his ears were hot and full of white noise. Her body fought against his with surprising strength but in a final surge he pushed her off. She lunged at him again, scratching at his face, and her hands squeezed his throat again. His vision dulled and for a moment he thought to let his own hands fall. Then, something within him woke and he threw her off, struck her in the face as she bounded back towards him, wrestled her to the ground and pressed his knees against her arms and she spat. He pressed harder. Suddenly her body lost its life and her hands came down dead as broken limbs. Seeing that she was no longer resisting, he slowly edged off her and the two lay panting in the dirt. After Renue had caught his breath, he crawled to his pack and brought out the rope he had taken. In the moonlight he could still see the glare of her eyes, but no matter how many times he said her name she wouldn't respond. Even as he bound her hands she didn't flinch.

"Lisande. Can you hear me?" He touched her face and her eyes became strange and wild again. "Sophia?"

"He's dead."

Renue searched for a hint of recognition in her eyes. "If I could take it back, I would."

"No," she said. "My father."

"He can't hurt you anymore." Her body was stiff for another minute, but then she relaxed and he kissed her on the cheek, quickly untying the knots. "Those are our old lives, Lisande. It's time to forget them. We'll start over." She nestled against him and he put his arm around her. "We're going someplace new."

"Where?"

"Somewhere simple. A beach town, maybe," he said, aware the calm voice he was using he had learned from Bardon. "We'll sit by the surf in the evenings and watch birds peck at shells. We'll collect shark teeth and conchs, bring them home." As he held her, he thought about Bardon and the dinners they used to make together in his small apartment, all the memories he hoped would fade in the coming years. Lisande curled into a ball and slept but he couldn't. His eyes stayed locked on her. An hour later she rolled over on her side, mouth touching the dirt. "Renue."

"Yes?"

" . . . never mind."

"Just tell me."

"It's stupid."

"I can't wait."

She rested her head on his knee. "What's your name?"

"Renue."

"No," she said. "Your *real* name. Besides, you'll need a new name where we're going, won't you?"

"Bren. It was my dad's."

"Bren—is that why you chose Renue?"

"Sort of. What about you? Want a new name?"

"Lisande's enough for me." She sat up and held his shoulder. "What about Bardon? You never even asked what happened to him."

"So?"

"What's wrong?" They lay flat on the ground again, on their sides, facing each other.

"He lied to me."

"Only to protect you,"

"That doesn't matter."

"It doesn't?" she said.

♥

When he woke she was gone. A warm, stiff wind blew over the hill as Renue called for her. Lisande's sheet was bundled against a small oak tree. In the dirt beneath it he found her silver locket and dusted it off. He put it in his pocket, then followed her tracks up into the hills. Faint dawn light showed lightly through the fog drifting over the city. Her trail zagged erratically, as though she had been running blindfolded. Eventually, he came across the strand of gray pine, near where they had buried the poet. Then, Lisande had veered sharply south, crossing an empty two laned road, heading for the ocean.

Half an hour later he came out of the woods and onto a rocky expanse. Crouching in the powerful gusts, he spotted her in the distance, staring over the promontory. "Lisande," he yelled.

Flies fought against the breeze buzzing and struggling to find sheltered landing points. He crept slowly, weaving in between shrubs and rocks. Lisande reached out to grab something in front of her. When he came around he could see her lips moving. He approached the edge. Beneath the cliff face, waves pummeled the frothy rocks below. Three ice birds with their long translucent feathers glided over the waters as the waves crashed beneath as another powerful gust swept across the promontory, sending dead grass and dirt into the air.

"Lisande," he said, taking a step closer. "Sophia."

She turned. "Go."

"I don't understand."

"Colver," she said. From their vantage, a few freighters were visible, but beyond the steel barges there was only empty ocean. "You should go."

"Not without you."

She sat down, back to a nearby rock, and held her knees with her hands. "No, Renue."

"No—no what?"

"No," she said. "No, I can't go with you. I'm sorry. I know it's what you want but I can't."

He sat down beside her and crossed his arms. "Why not?"

"How much of me is me?" she said, staring off. "How much of me is my father?"

"You're nothing like him," he insisted. "Nothing. Can't you see that?"

She turned to him. "I could say I lived my entire life a prisoner. That I had no choice. That he kept me in the dark. It's not like you. You devoted yourself to helping people, and then Bardon betrayed you. He should have told you. I understand that. But it's not the same with me."

"But I failed him first, Lisande."

"How?" she said. "If you do something good, you do something good. It shouldn't matter why. You tried. You saved me."

"For selfish reasons."

"I don't think so—well, I'm going," she said. "Back. To the

Manor. To find the Pattern. I don't know what else to do, but I feel responsible and I just can't shake it. If I can do something, then I have to. Try. Or maybe that's just what I keep telling myself. I never did anything for anyone."

"That's not true," he said. "Me."

"I can't just become someone else," she said. "Not like you."

He sighed. "I don't think anyone ever can, Lisande. It's just pretend." He leaned out over the rocks, wondering how far the air would carry him. As the two stared down at the ocean, Renue felt a strange symmetry at the thought of seeing his mother's portrait once more, and found himself surprisingly afraid. But he hid his fear and told her he would take her back to the Manor.

V

Chapter Eleven

It took them the remainder of the day to hike down to the city's edge. At the western gate they passed again beneath the great arms of a statue of Mesmer. In the Vines, most of the shops and business were closed and hardly anyone walked the streets. Stray dogs and cats shirked in the alleyways and peeked out from behind dumpsters. Ashkareve was a graveyard.

"What's wrong?" Lisande said, squeezing Renue's shoulder. He had stopped and his eyes were shut tightly.

"Alkor just found me."

"And?"

"Bardon's dead."

A car barreled down the street and she pulled him to the sidewalk. She put a hand over her mouth. The sediment-coated air tasted like rust. "What do you want to do?"

"I don't know."

"Yes you do."

"We'll meet them at a safe house and wait," he said. "A bit south of here. They'll escort us to see his body."

Renue took her a few streets down to a yellow clinic, nestled between a grocery and a bookstore. The color of the building reminded Lisande of the lemon cookies they use to serve in the Manor. The floors of the clinic were green tiled and posters hung crookedly on the creaking walls. In a back room they waited, empty except for a pair of stools and a few cardboard boxes with medical supplies. Lisande sat cross-legged on the ground.

"What are you doing?" he said. "What is that?"

"A spade," she said, holding up her connected hands, fingers shifting. She flexed them in the opposite direction. "There's the heart."

"I think my father used to do the same thing." Renue grinned. "But he called it something else."

Lisande smiled at the hint of the boyishness in his voice, watching as his hands formed a slightly different shape than hers. "Really?"

"Look, a seagull," he said, joining all of his fingers. "And the waves below."

She giggled.

"What?"

"You're got this side of yourself you don't know what to do with." She held her hands up again. "My father used to do this, switch back and forth between spade and heart. He used to say, we're all a little of both. Except your mother, he'd say." She held up a finger and tried to mimic his voice. "Except for your mother," Lisande said. "She's all heart."

♥

As the car pulled up, Lisande looked up to the Manor. A thin line of smoke continued to drift out of the highest tower. On the ride to the underground, Renue sat in the front seat by Granges, with Lisande and Dora in the back. Granges told them on how the Damaskers had been almost destroyed by Alkor's botched plan. Boran still controlled most everything north of the bell tower, but the Blanks had taken the docks and southwest, turning the central Slants into a battlefield. Much of the Vines and Inverts had been marked by looting and violence. The city had effectively shut down.

Lisande watched Dora stare coldly out the window. "You shouldn't have come back," the old Drailer said. "They'll just use you. Like they used me."

They parked at a junkyard in Latchtown and took an elevator hidden within a cave of orange-rusting cars. At the bottom Alkor greeted them. He had deep bruises beneath his eyes and obviously had not slept in days. The old Damasker asked whether they were hungry but Renue insisted on seeing Bardon immediately. The body was being preserved in the same room where Renue himself had been kept. A gray cloth covered the fallen Damasker's face. Lisande paid her respects quickly then left, and Dora followed behind. A moment later, Alkor appeared and chased after the old Drailer. Eventually, Granges led Lisande to a small cot where she slept until dinner.

When the meal was over, the surviving Damaskers and Drailers met in the sun room to discuss the state of the resistance, and although they had invited Lisande to attend, she chose to wait outside. Dora had already explained to her about the tunnel they had found that led from the bell tower to the hills. With the city in chaos, Boran had consolidated his troops and called for reinforcements from Grenore, but they would likely not arrive for a few days. The Blanks had already started uprisings in several other major cities, further sapping the Manor's strength. For Lisande, the plans themselves did not matter. Renue had convinced her that this was their best chance, and she trusted him.

"Mind if I join you?" Granges' face was covered with deep bruises.

"Of course."

He held out a pair of brown bottles. "Thought you might be thirsty." Granges twisted off the cap and handed her one.

"Are you done in there?"

"No, but that meeting's got a different purpose," he said. "Alkor."

The carbonation tickled her nose. "Oh."

"Don't worry." He slid down into a sitting position, across from her. "If I were going to poison you, I would have done it a long time ago."

"That's so comforting." She swirled the bottle. "What is it?"

"Ramsden's Rootbrew."

"I've had this before. When I was a kid."

Granges clinked bottles with hers. "Probably in a nicer place than this."

"How are we going to get up the forest?" Lisande said. "Dora already explained the rest."

"Trust me, it won't be a problem." He took a swig. "Dora. You know, I used to think that if women were in power, they'd be just as corrupt as men," he said. "I believed that. Only it'd take a little time. But those mothers who stood up to Rady at the tower, we could have ended this whole regime a decade ago if we had followed our own fucking credo. Performers of the word and not listeners. Between you and me, Alkor and Bardon fucked up big time, but I suppose they both paid for it too." He put the bottle down. "Bardon's death still hasn't set in—I hope Bren's holding up."

Lisande took another sip. "Do you believe in an afterlife?"

"What, someone told you I was born a Blank?"

"I did hear a few people talking about it before dinner," she said, "but that's not why I asked."

Granges picked up his bottle. "I don't believe in all that God bullshit, but when I was a kid I did hear voices. I don't like the idea of God, though. Never set right with me."

"Why?"

"It's just an excuse. Like the black thing, like anything you can't see." Granges checked his watch. "Well, they told me to bring you in now. Alkor has something to say." He got to his feet and opened the door for her. "We don't deserve it, Lisande, but thanks for the second chance."

Sitting on the stone bleachers were Dora, Renue, and several other Damaskers and Drailers whom Lisande didn't recognize, all watching Alkor. "Thank you for coming," the old Damasker said. "As you all know, it's not in my nature to make long speeches. Sorry, gallows humor, I suppose. I'll be blunt. I assume full responsibility for myself *and* for Bardon's actions, and step down voluntarily. Dora will lead, and Granges will take my place." He glanced over at Dora, then turned back to Lisande. "We are forever in your debt, so thank you. Now, our purpose is straightforward. If we cannot control the black thing, Ashkareve will tear itself apart. The Pattern must be in the Manor, so there we must go. Tomorrow, we'll take the tunnel up to the hills. Granges has informed me that Boran has pulled all his forces to Goramon in order to control the Blanks. Get some sleep tonight, everyone. Tomorrow we climb the hill one last time. And, a final matter. To ensure our final mission's integrity, everyone in this room will go. Everyone." The old Damasker took off his gloves, revealing unmarked hands. "Even me."

♥

Sophia stands beneath a lone twilight tree, in front of a modest headstone engraved with twin vines reaching around a mother wolf. She folds her arms to her sides, feeling her ribs, counting them. The winter sky is a swirling gray, minutes before the season's first snow. Across the field, oaks and elms are stripped of leaves and hardly move. She touches her chest. The mountain beyond appears distant and hollow. What's on the other side? Anything would be better than this ghost house. It's been three years since her mother was buried and the even the adorning stone vines seem curious.

I don't like you out here by yourself.

Her father's face is tired, but she turns her attention back to the grave, following the inscription with her finger: *Alaine Treben.*

Faldor's just over there, she says.

It's freezing.

I like visiting in the winter. In case she's cold.

You're not a child anymore, Sophia.

Sophia rubs the top of the grave. She likes the coarse quality by the stone and often watches rain pound the grave. Maybe the stone will crack, she thinks, and they'll have to move her mother to the forest, like she would have wanted.

You need guards with you if you're going this far out, he says. I've told you a hundred times.

You don't trust me either? You're suffocating me, like you did to Mother.

What did you say? What? Repeat yourself.

Nothing. She shuffles her feet. When am I going to school? You *promised* mother—and you said I could take a trip with Faldor too. Remember?

I've changed my mind.

She comes around the grave, placing it between her and her father. I hate this house, she says.

It's dangerous down there. They're *animals*, Sophia. You have no idea.

At least let Faldor go.

I can't.

What are you afraid of? But he refuses to meet her eyes. I don't understand.

I love you, he says. I want you safe.

Love? Love? This is how you treat those you love? Letting them waste away? Let me study at the university. I could pretend to be someone else. Our secret. Please.

You're twelve.

I could be eighty and it wouldn't matter.

He smirks. Your tongue has sharpened overnight. Are you becoming a woman?

None of your business.

He takes a step towards the grave. God, I miss her.

She'd be alive if you'd just let her go, Sophia says. But you *kept* her here. Like you're keeping me.

That's not fair. You know, you'll miss a lot in life if you look only with your eyes.

She runs her hand against the stone vines. It was never enough to have people love you, was it, Father? You had to own them, too.

He raises his eyebrows. Don't say that.

She glances over at Faldor, standing at the top of the closest hill. Everybody knows.

Less than you'd think.

Because you shut them up.

Tell Faldor not to forget the guards next time, Mesmer says, turning sharply. Without you, I have nothing.

♥

Alkor sat on the stone bleachers gazing trancelike up at the ceiling, absentmindedly playing with his gloves, putting them on, taking them off. Renue watched the old Damasker from the door for some time, then entered the room. "You can't sleep either?" he said. "Don't need those anymore."

"Old habits," Alkor said, smiling. "Take a seat—what is it they say about old habits, Bren? Ah, never mind—do you know the play, *Ceiling Spiders*?"

"No."

"Three close friends, imprisoned in a bare room. They're told there's a monster waiting in the pipes and shadows of the ceiling. It's one of those choppy, speculative dramaticals. What is up there? Can we ever go to sleep? Eventually, the fear makes each character turn against the other, consumed by imagined, clandestine deals, aroused suspicions. Of course, this is a metaphor for Ashkareve itself, for all of Qarash, perhaps. In the end, only one player remains. The lights go up. The ceiling is empty. Nothing." The old Damasker took one glove off and laid it on the floor. "Sometimes, I feel that no matter what I do, I

can't escape the feeling that I am a victim of my own spiders."
He touched his face gingerly with his bare hand. "I was a better
man in my youth, though I was always the more ambitious of
Bardon and me. He was wiser, until only a handful of days ago
when he agreed with my foolish plan. Now he's gone." Alkor
cleared his throat. "But despite the Gift, despite my intellect, my
experience, I've realized I'm no use to anyone anymore. Just a
tired, old fool. And he's dead. My best friend is dead."

"It's hard to believe he's really gone."

"Yes. And now, I find myself with an . . . inability to view
the world in spiritual terms," Alkor said. "Bardon's death can
contain no solace for me. He simply vanished." The old Damasker
turned to Renue, his eyes sunken. "I will say, he did agree with
me to not include Dora in the failed take-over—that I *am* sorry
for. And now he's paid for it and yet my hands are unmarked.
Were he here, I know exactly what he would say." He stroked his
throat. "Only the dead can tell true stories."

"Pestras." Renue watched the old Damasker bring his hands
level with his eyes. Alkor's fingers were long, the type piano
players or guitarists have. Stretching, dancing, fingers. "Why
didn't he tell me, Alkor?"

"Bardon must have had his reasons," he said. "Forgive him.
Promise me. Blame me for it all."

"I'll try."

Alkor's fingers perched on the scars of his face. "You know, I
always hated him—Mesmer, I mean. But tonight, after so many
years, my mind has an ocean's quiet. Perhaps it's because I'm
in danger of losing Dora as well. She was with me until I came
down here, you know. I loved her. But it would have been no life,
for her to be with me. That was one of the hardest moments I've
hard, if you can believe it. Letting her go." The old Damasker
rose and walked over to the mantel where the flag of Qarash
hung. "It always seemed an inevitability, Bren, that each and
every person I ever loved would be taken by one man. I believed

the laws held no purpose other than for him to retain power, to fuel his wars, his ego, like those Krylight jugglers who have to rub their hands together constantly to keep away the afterburn." Slowly, Alkor returned to the bleachers and rested his elbows on his thighs. "I've endured these hands nearly every night for decades, dreaming of the surface. The natural sun. And now, on the eve of my parole, I'm not sure I can leave tomorrow."

"It's your choice," Renue said. "Might be wiser if you stayed. We've lost enough."

"But I *said* I would." Alkor looked up at the ceiling a final time. "Such grand distinctions, the forms of a verb. Did you know I wanted to be a grammarian as a child? I always thought I had a way with words."

"Did you?" Renue smiled slightly.

"Enjoy yourself. I only said it to lighten the mood." The old Damasker's voice drifted. "You and I have known each other a long time, Bren."

"Did you know my mother was in the Manor, Alkor?"

For a minute, the old Damasker's mouth hung open. "At one point in time, Bardon suspected as much, but because I could never discern your precise age, neither of us could say for sure. A year can alter much in a timeline, after all." Alkor expelled an awkward, hauntingly long laugh. "But I suppose we'll find out tomorrow."

Chapter Twelve

Standing water covered the ground. The tunnel itself was only wide enough for three to walk side by side. In the beginning, voices echoed from street level but soon faded as the path inclined, narrowing further. Only in the last few days as the Pattern failed had the tunnel become visible, protected up until that point by a barrier so subtle and powerful that it had not been discovered for decades. Renue wondered what Lisande must be thinking, taking a tunnel that her father had used during the regime. As a teenager, Renue had viewed Ashkareve in a similar fashion, methodically walking every street his father might have walked in the hope of somehow discovering some clue to the man himself.

The group fell to whispers after half a mile in the darkness, their voices no longer covered by the sound of water. Dora called for Krylight and Alkor lagged behind while she ordered scouts to proceed ahead. "Puker—a word." Renue let go of Lisande's hand and went to join Granges. When the two men were far enough ahead of the others, Granges slowed. "I'm not good with words, like you," he said. "Listen. Bardon never got to apologize. I'd hate for that to happen today. So the docks—it was out of line, and I'm sorry." Granges chuckled. "Nothing? We've never really seen eye to eye, have we, Puker? But we were *both* just kids when Mesmer took over. Hell, I don't even know what a normal life would be like. Maybe boring. Maybe boring could be nice. What I'm trying to say is, the docks were about them choosing you. Not what happened in the Manor."

"Alright."

"After today," Granges said. "I'm in charge of this shit storm, and I'll need your help. Maybe they should have chosen you, but I'm stuck with it. Between you and me, I don't think what we're doing now is going to help. I think the Pattern's already gone."

"Why's that?"

"You'll see." Dora called out and Granges immediately extinguished his Krylight. The group followed the soft beams of two Drailer flashlights. Natural rock now composed the tunnel floor and brown bricks lined the concave walls and ceiling. Alkor trailed far behind. "You didn't see the city these past few days," Granges said. "The Square was nothing. Spades cleared most of the bodies before you got there, efficient bastards. But the Blanks. The louts. If you ask me, it's just beginning. Scares the fuck out of me, how fast things fell." His fingers crawled over the tunnel wall. "Bardon."

"Bardon."

"I'm not sure exactly why you left that night, Puker. Alkor told me it had something to do with Bardon, but he wouldn't say why exactly." Granges cleared his throat. "Guessing it was about your parents. Everything always was—that's what I never really understood. I hated my folks, but I suppose hate's better than nothing. Even so, everyone's got an ugly side, and if you can't understand that, then you didn't really love him in the first place."

"Yeah, I guess."

"We'll either find your mother in the Manor, or we won't," Granges said. "Either way, I'll help you. Should have offered earlier."

Renue sighed. A cool, mossy smell filled the air. In the distance he could hear water dropping, and a few minutes later the path was marked by holes made from water erosion. "Okay."

"Remember that girl in Bardon's class? The one with the earrings?"

"Sure."

"Does Lisande remind you of her?"

"Yes," Renue said. "A little."

The scouts were waiting for the rest of them at the end of the tunnel by a metal ladder. Boran's army was still posted at the barricade in the middle of the market, they reported, but the surrounding hills and woods were clear. The scouts scrambled up the ladder with Granges, Dora, and the others close behind and they emerged in a forested cubby surrounded by white-leaved weeping willows. To the south, stately houses and mansions cropped the hills. Dora sent some scouts down to monitor Ashkareve, and the rest of the group waited near a tree. Swatches of gray clouds covered the sky, as though to bandage the hemorrhaging city below. Finally, Alkor emerged. Granges crossed his arms impatiently as the old Damasker stood unsteadily. Then Alkor fell to his knees and pressed his palms into the dirt, grabbing the earth in clumps. The tenor of his cries made Renue ill.

"Shut up, old man," Granges whispered. "Are you out of your fucking mind?"

The old Damasker didn't answer, and only watched Dora, who was keeping her distance.

"He hasn't seen the sky for two decades," Renue said. "Give him a second."

Granges gestured to the hills below. "Boran won't be so sentimental."

Lisande broke from Renue and bent down next to the old Damasker, speaking in his ear. After a moment, Alkor wiped his bloated eyes and stood, apologizing. Renue wondered what Lisande could have said.

Granges led them through the willows to a small path along a stone-piled fence. A veil of cumulous clouds overhead blocked the sun, so thick and complete the day reminded Renue of an winter eclipse he and Bardon had seen from a rooftop in the Lower Slants. The trail crooked north, upwards into the hills.

When Renue looked back next, Ashkareve was cast in a dirty-white hue, faint, as though in a blizzard. Finally, the tops of twilight trees appeared but the forest was not as he remembered. The trees themselves were withered and shrunken, and the black bark was flaking, leaving piles of black mush on the ground. As Renue grabbed a branch, it snapped in two. The once-lavender flowers were now faded like old photos in a forgotten album. He turned at a gentle touch on his shoulder.

"It's dying," Lisande said, reaching for a petal.

"I see."

"Road's a bit further," Granges called, "but let's stay off it. Just in case. Cut up here."

The group quickly climbed the forested hill. Soon, between the lines of swooping black trunks Renue could see the tip of the fountain rising from the clumps of brush and dead leaves which rested at the top of the hill. Suddenly Lisande grabbed his arm, panicked. Then he saw it, his own palms, blackening.

"Alkor," he said. "Problem."

The old Damasker turned. "There's probably enough death in the city to distract the thing," he said. His hands were now also marked. "I hope."

"What do we do?"

"It's not my decision anymore."

Granges eyed them skeptically. "Laws must still work up here, that's all," he said. "Alkor's right. Plenty of murder in the city now. Unfortunately."

Dora had removed her crescent necklace. "Take it," the old Drailer said, handed it to Lisande. "Please."

"But what if—"

"Just take it," she said. "We won't get a second chance here. Debeau's reinforcements could be here as soon as tomorrow. We keep going."

The same cars Renue had seen on the grounds the first night of the Great Game were now parked in a line, their tires shredded and engines exposed and gutted. The group followed Dora across the grounds, passing the fountain. At the stairs to the Manor entrance, the old Drailer paused. "Lisande."

"Be careful," Granges warned. "Last I checked, there was a barrier."

Lisande took the three stone steps, Renue by her side. "Help," she said, pulling the door. "It's heavy."

The Manor door groaned and a pungent smell of spoiled food wafted out. The red carpet was undisturbed and ran through the center of the reception room to the podium. Renue recalled his arms around a beautiful blond, spilling into the warmly lit room, and there was Faldor with his ledger, face illuminated by soft light.

"We'll post out here, Dora," Granges said. "Renue, Lisande, do either of you have any idea where he might have kept the Pattern?"

"I'm not sure."

"The statue," Renue said. "Faldor wanted to show me the statue." He sprinted across the lobby to the door, the others chasing behind, yelling for him.

Outside, the garden was thinned and stunk of vegetative rotting. The once stout blood tree trunks were snapped in two and all the flowers that had lined the paths were shriveled. The garden seemed so much smaller. Renue raced over a creek weaving though overgrown yellowing grasses and quickly found the mulched path, crushing decaying purple bulbs beneath his boots, passed the dying midnight trees and stopped at a small dirt clearing. A hundred hillborns were on their knees, blindfolded and bound, and standing in front of them was the disheveled man holding an ancient sword. At first Renue did not recognize Rady, leaning against a copper green statue of a man with his head in his hands.

"*Newcomer*?" Wildcard stepped from behind a statue, pulling out a small trembler from a wrinkled blue doublet. In the other hand he held a yellowed paper. "The first one to the party is always so awkward—why did you tell me you weren't coming? Oh right, you weren't invited. Forget something?" He waved the deed around, then tossed it to the dirt. "Worthless. You're not who I was expecting, actually, but welcome all the same. No, no, don't move. Not a muscle."

Renue glanced back.

"Don't worry, we have all the time in the world. Blocked the road. Didn't feel like entertaining Boran just yet." As Lisande, Dora, and Alkor came through the brush, Wildcard raised his trembler. Renue felt Lisande's fingers on his ribs. "Twenty spades follow my shot, so no Gift, got it?" Wildcard pointed to the parapets with the trembler and with his other hand flicked back his tangled black hair. Then he turned to Rady. "Mr. Poten, don't snivel. It's unbecoming of a head of state. After all, you *wanted* to know what it was like to lead this country, how it felt to have so many lives dangling at your fingers tips. Didn't you?"

Dora stepped forward. "What do you think you're doing?"

"My little experiment," Wildcard said, "to determine whether there is enough of the Pattern left to attract the thing. I'd like to have a few words with it."

"Why? You can't control it, Wildcard."

"I want to find my father."

"Your father?" Dora took another step forward. "Put the gun down and help us find the Pattern. We had a deal. Don't be stupid. Ashkareve's destroying itself as we speak."

"Country first, you mean?" Wildcard mused. "Can't I do both?"

"My daughters," Rady cried. "They . . . "

"Shut up, man. You should have thought of them sooner. You can't hide behind family." Wildcard smirked, his eyes falling on Lisande. "Isn't that right, long-lost daughter? A bit late, aren't you? The funeral was a month ago." He lowered the trembler, continuing to watch her. "Well, let's get started."

"Help us," she said. "Please. I know you're not like them."

"It's refreshing to meet someone who tries to see the good." Wildcard smiled sadly. "Once, that might have been true, Sophia. But not anymore. Not anymore." He clapped his hands. "Enough stalling."

"Don't do this," Dora warned. "You can't control it without the Pattern. We brought her. Where is it?"

"So you think," Wildcard said. "And Sophia, I'll bet *you* will help me get into the basement. So stick around, will you? Oh right. Why did you come back, may I ask?"

"I don't want innocent people to suffer. Please help us."

Wildcard scoffed. "Why? So these buffoons can replace your father? Don't fool yourself. They'd be just as bad, if not worse."

"You're wrong about them."

"Don't presume you know what *they* are capable of," he snapped. "They murdered your brothers, bled them dry. To husks. I saw the photographs. But did they show you? Not that I cared for them, personally. Neither shining examples of humanity. But boys will be boys. Canden and Andal. They were just children. Your *brothers*. Does that mean nothing to you? Butchers."

"What about you?" Alkor thundered. "For years Mesmer hunted us down and you did nothing. Nothing. How are you any different?"

"Wait . . . am I dreaming? Is that the legendary Alkor, or will the Butcher of Stalk Street do? What I would give to see Boran's face right now. For you, old man, I'd gladly answer a question." Wildcard gestured grandiosely. "A revolution waits between these two bone gates, this noble beating heart, this brain. Real change." He directed the trembler at Rady. "Now, I have a nightmare to reign in. Mr. Poten, if you please."

Rady choked and held the blade upright. "I beg you. My daughters, my wife. You, you can have anything you want."

"Not anything," Wildcard said. "Not anything. Besides, I gave you a chance. Don't make a monster of me too." He lowered his voice. "Mesmer had it wrong, you see. Only the man himself should pay for his crimes."

Wildcard splashed a clear liquid on the blade's tip and nodded to Rady who held the sword at shoulder level. As he ran it across each neck, the hillborns fell to the garden floor and immediately began to gasp in the mulch. Renue could feel Lisande's breath on his back. He squinted up at the parapets, then turned back at the dying hillborns. When the first man in line stopped moving, Rady dropped the sword, closed his eyes, and whimpered. An uneasy silence set over the clearing, disrupted by a sudden, brisk wind that made the rotting threads of blood trees whistle. A faint shade distorted the clouds above the Manor walls, swooped down, gliding over the tree skeletons. Rady started to beg for forgiveness.

"Oh, don't give me that," Wildcard said. "I gave you a chance to outlive your complic—"

The Poten opened his eyes looked around slowly. He smiled. "It didn't come. I'm free. You said, you said if it . . . " Suddenly Rady's back arched and it seemed like he were being pulled slightly off the ground, but just as quickly he collapsed like a string-snapped puppet.

Alkor stared at the fallen Poten's body. "They're . . . all there. All those I killed, as though alive again."

"Where is it?" Dora said. "I don't see anything."

Wildcard approached the statue. "The unmarked never do."

"Father?" Lisande exhaled, her breath frost white. She took a step and Renue tried to hold her back but she fought against him. "Is that you?"

"Lisande, it isn't him," Renue warned. "Don't." The shade of Faldor hovered over Rady.

"Stay put," Wildcard ordered, pointing the trembler. "I want to see what happens. Besides, it's me it wants, not her." The shade began to drift instead towards Lisande and stopped a few feet in front of her, its translucent limbs reaching. Wildcard edged closer as though hypnotized. Renue lunged, knocking the trembler from him.

"It's a bluff," Renue shouted. Wildcard came to and reached for the gun but Renue caught him stiffly across the face and flung the young Poten violently into the statue, crumpling him against the base. Lisande reached for the black thing but it quickly changed course, heading directly for Alkor. The old Damasker fell and tried to scamper back on his hands. Dora ran towards him.

"Stay back," he shouted. "I'm sorry. I loved you. More than words can witness."

As Renue watched the black thing near Alkor, he could feel the old Damasker's vigorous handshake when he had been chosen for the mission, convinced he had finally found a way to honor his parents; he pictured the shadow of Alkor on the stone bleachers, a defeated man craving redemption. Then Renue saw another old man in the garden who deserved a second chance. The shade of Faldor hovered behind Alkor as Renue briefly caught Lisande's eye. He ran at full speed towards Faldor and the two collided, embracing.

♥

Lisande bent down to feel his pulse, then twisted sharply. "Faint. What's happening?" she screamed. "Don't just stand there. *Help* him." Renue's body shook a final time then went limp as Dora rushed to his side. "I'm not sure. Alkor? Alkor!"

"The thing is in him," Alkor said, struggling to his feet. "There's nothing I can do." He nudged Wildcard with his boot. "We'll question the little muck when he wakes. I'm sorry, Lisande."

"Wildcard mentioned a basement," Dora said. "Do you know where?"

"I think so."

"Find it." Dora put her hand to Renue's head. "If you find the Pattern, maybe we can stop the thing. Alkor, go with her."

"But—"

"I'm the only unmarked one," the old Drailer said. "Just in case. Don't argue. Just go. Now!"

Lisande cut across the garden to the nearest door and entered a long hallway, passing the banquet table, covered with plates of moldy food. When she reached the first floor guest rooms, Alkor yelled for her to wait but she continued toward the kitchen and turned down a corridor full of paintings and statues. She slowed as she spotted the door that led to the basement.

It's best not to remember some things, isn't it, Sophia?

"Lisande?" Alkor said, voice echoing from beyond the hall. "*Lisande?*"

Remember now?

"Father?" she said, opening the door to a dark, winding staircase. "Is it really you?" She took the first step down and braced herself as the old Damasker clamored behind her, holding his chest.

"What did you say?" Alkor produced a clump of Krylight and stuffed it into a small metallic canister on the wall. "Here. Don't touch it. Go on. Quickly now. Show me."

She proceeded down in the dark green light, watching the stairs disappear beneath her feet until she came to a small oak door. Even as she turned the knob she felt sick but she hid the recoil and went inside. The basement was rectangular, with steel beams that ran at even intervals through the narrow room. A wooden footstool lay on its side in front of her. She stepped over it into the center of the room

"I feel something." Alkor pointed to the door at the end. "Your father's private study?"

"My mother died here," Lisande said. "I thought I had dreamed it."

"He must have hidden your own memories from you so as not to betray the Pattern's location."

If he goes through that door, he might die. Not that I'd care, but you've seen enough death.

"Why?" she whispered.

"What? Lisande, did you say something?"

The shade chuckled. *Your mother liked her privacy.*

Lisande spied a chalky contour of her father standing near the footstool, caught in the faint echo of Krylight. In the far right corner of the basement was a plush green reading chair. Next to it, a closet brimmed with large spools and threads. Alkor pushed in front of her but slowed at the door on the other side of the room, tracing the frame with his left hand.

"Don't open it," she said. "Stay there."

"Why?" the old Damasker said, stumbling back as his hand touched the doorknob. He winced and reached for the nearby chair, steadying himself.

The shade appeared on the other side, shaking its head. *Only trust a butcher with meat, Sophia.*

"Don't go any further," she warned. "I mean it, Alkor, stop."

The old Damasker paused, his eyes wild and shifting. "This must be the nervous system of the Pattern." He moved his hands closer to the door. "A powerful barrier—strange imprint. With some time I could unravel the pieces. We . . . we could have all of the tools of the Manor at our disposal. Stop the needless death. Control the city. End the rioting."

"Restore the laws?" she said. "Are you kidding?"

Do you see how it begins, Sophia? How easy it is?

Alkor attempted to come closer. "Only until the violence settles, of course—can you open this door? For Renue. Open this door!"

"Let me think."

"Open it." The old Damasker perched behind her but did not try to enter.

"Shut up." Her stomach churned as she approached the door. In the faint light she could make out a desk on which lay a typewriter and a stack of books. Then she saw a shadowy reflection of herself in a full-length mirror by the desk, short-haired, older. Lisande held the canister up and squinted. There was a small cot in the back corner, supported by a metal frame. The shade hovered beside her as Alkor approached the door hesitantly, coughing into his shirt.

"A powerful barrier," the old Damasker said. "Do you see it? Did Mesmer teach you? Lisande, unravel this barrier so I can seize the Pattern. There's no time. I can save Re—" The old Damasker spit violently and a small stream of blood trickled from his mouth.

You do remember.

As she shut the door, Alkor began to pound and howl from the other side, though his cries were muffled and barely came through the wood. Lisande set the Krylight beside a nearly exhausted spool of yellow thread and sorted through the books on the desk, mostly poetry and titles she did not recognize. A few composition books full of her mother's handwriting. A sewing needle kept the place of a book of Lyle's poetry. She felt the weight of the needle. The memory was still in her fingers, and she could almost sense her mother's slender hand over hers.

"What should I do?" Lisande placed the needle on the desk. She did not see any of the tapestries she had expected.

She must have shown you. The shade's back was to Lisande, staring at the small cot. *You saw the Pattern a thousand times. From her lap, no less.*

"You've never been in here before, have you, Father?"

The shade laughed. *Perhaps I should have asked for your help sooner.*

"But I'm not like you."

Actually, Sophia. You're quite like me.

"You're a monster."

Was I? You saw Ashkareve those last days. Just like Faldor's time. You want that? The shade hovered, pausing over the desk.

Lisande moved to the cot. It was small and cheap, the type a child would sleep on. Three blue candles were stacked on a night table. Crumpled papers and threads filled the wastebasket beside it.

The butcher's almost past the barrier. You can't hear him, of course. He's quite the animal, that one.

"You wanted me to take over?" she asked. "Is that it?"

Yes.

"Where you left off."

If you don't, someone else will. Don't play games. The butcher is almost through the bone, Sophia.

Lisande thought of her mother in her final days, alone in the dark silent basement. The shade had moved to the foot of the cot, watching her. In the crease of the sheet something glimmered in the Krylight, a single, long strand of her mother's hair. She ran her fingers from one end to the other, and let it fall to the mattress. "Mother died here," she said. "She died here, in this basement. And you let her. This room. Servants had bigger rooms. You kept her here. Down here. In the dark. Sleeping on this . . . this mattress." She spun to the shade and tried to grab it but her hands found only air. "Don't you have anything to say for yourself?"

Like most things in our marriage, this wasn't my decision.

"Don't lie to me," Lisande shouted. "Don't fucking lie. You're dead. Even dead you can't just admit it. You starved her, like you starved me. Renue was right. You're a monster."

Scream as much as you want. No one can hear you. It's a good thing you can't stab me again.

"You always had to control everything, didn't you?" she said. "It was never enough. Nothing was ever enough."

Your mother didn't want you to see her in such a state. That's the truth.

"You deserved to die."

With that I don't disagree. I made my share of mistakes.

"Tell me the truth. Damaskers. Blanks. You butchered them and then when you needed their help, they wouldn't. Was she an embarrassment to you? That someone could take something from you and there was nothing you could do about it. But you could never control life, could you, Father? Only death." Leaning herself against the bedside wall, she watched her tears fall to the poor, stiff sheets. "Renue was more family than you ever were."

The man who killed Faldor. Family.

"*You* killed Faldor," she said. "And Mother. Why did you do it, Father? Answer me." Lisande stood, gesturing around the room. "There's nothing here. No Pattern, not anything. Just a room." The shade was now in the far corner of the room, opposite the door. "What?"

Faldor took the photograph she used for this. I remember it.

In the small space beside the desk she found a canvas. Placing it on the desk, she brought the Krylight canister closer. The painting was crafted with gentle fluid strokes. At first Lisande did not even see the five figures, only the white Manor grounds where the fountain now stood. It was snowing, freshly fallen blankets, and footsteps led to the center of the painting where her mother stood, a bundled infant in her arms. Two boys were arm and arm with their father a few feet away, looking behind them at the twilight forest. Although it was clearly winter, the forest's lavender bulbs shown in the Manor floodlights, like a sea of phosphorescent purple jellyfish, like flowering stars.

I had forgotten that day . . . so many of those days.

"The forest is blooming—did you do that?"

Not me. It was your first snow. We wanted it to be extra special.

Lisande ran her fingers along the frame. "We were so happy."

Things were different in those days.

Her throat tasted sour. "Those were my brothers?"

Yes.

She pointed to the books on the desk. "These were all hers?"

Your mother rarely showed me her poetry. Just the portraits and tapestries. Maybe it was confessional.

Lisande placed the portrait gently on the desk, turned for the door. "I don't forgive you," she said. "For anything."

Nor should you. Your mother and I placed a terrible burden on you, Sophia. We fought about it constantly, but I always tried not to involve you. For that I am endlessly sorry. But you were always the strongest, Sophia. I saw that from the moment you were born.

"Don't try—I have to go, Father. Goodbye."

She opened the door. Alkor lay at her feet, panting on the ground. Blood had dried on his face and his eyes were sunken. "Is it done?" the old Damasker said faintly.

"It wasn't the Pattern," she said. "Come. Let's go help Renue."

♥

She found Renue at the base of the statue. His hair had turned completely white and he looked so weak Lisande doubted he could even stand. But at least he was alive, she thought. Renue's hand slipped from the statue and as he turned she held him. Lisande kissed Renue's wrinkled cheek. "Come on. We have to get out of here."

Dora stood over an unconscious Wildcard, bandaging a wound on his head. Granges and two Drailers appeared at the other side of the clearing.

"Did you find the Pattern?" Granges said.

"It's not here."

"Like I thought. Why were you two so quiet then? There's a God-damn lout army outside."

"An army?"

"Yes—Lisande, is there another way out?"

"Louts?"

"Yes, louts. Ambush. We're trapped."

"Help Renue, Granges," Lisande said. "I need to see something."

Granges glanced at Dora briefly. "Okay."

He supported Renue as they entered the main hall. The remaining Damaskers and Drailers watched from the windows as a cluster of louts milled around the edge of the forest. A hundred more gathered around the fountain, watching the Manor. Suddenly there came a faint cry from the forest and the louts charged the Manor, banging on the windows.

A lout pressed his face against the glass and squinted at Lisande. "Pieky," came a muted scream. "It's *her*! It's *her*!"

Lisande put her hand against the window. "Open the door," she said.

"Are you mad?" Granges said. "Why—"

"Just open it."

Dora and the two Drailers moved to the entrance along with Granges and unlatched the door. Benny spilled in, scrambling to Lisande. The young lout's face was red and beading with sweat. In his left hand he held a gun which he tucked into his belt as he hugged her. "Benny?" From behind the great door Piek appeared. "Knew you'd be here," he said.

"What are you doing?"

"Came to put out that smoke," he explained. "But you beat me to it. Just stopped." Piek reached to pat Renue on the shoulder. "Damn, Face. What the hell happened to you?"

"Forest line," came a cry from beyond the fountain. "Piek. They saw us—spades at the forest line."

"Fuck. To the trees, boys," Piek ordered. "We'll catch 'em climbing. How many?"

261

"Thousands. They're climbing now."

"Or not," he said. "Shit—can we barricade this?"

Lisande pushed past the louts and stepped out of the Manor. "Piek, tell your men to stay behind me," she said. "No shooting."

Piek clapped. "You heard her, boys. Follow close."

Lisande could hear the soldiers charging up the hill as she ran across the fountain towards the forest. The shade of Mesmer appeared beneath a rotting twilight tree as she reached up for the nearest branch.

You know what that might do to you, yes?

"Yes."

And you're willing to pay that price?

"The Pattern ends with me, Father."

So you think.

She could almost feel the forest swaying towards her as she reached for the branch. Slowly, the black trunks straightened, thickening, ripening, growing petals and leaves. The bark sealed first, almost immediately, sap crusting around bent-mark gashes as the first soldiers screamed and extended their guns. Then the trees rose higher, brown leaves filling with a lavender hue, sprouting, until the forest teemed with flowers and the limbs extended firmly upwards, towering over them. The frontrunners stopped as though frozen, then staggered back, knocking into the troops behind them. A few soldiers fired into the treetops but dropped their guns as the leaves spread, enveloping them. More soldiers pushed from behind but Alkor raised his hands and with a loud cry a great wind rushed forth, plucking petals and carrying them down the hill. Lisande glanced back. The old Damasker appeared to be conducting the wind, creating a blizzard of blue and purple and white petals rushing through the forest like a sandstorm. As the wind roared a final time sweeping the woods, the old Damasker collapsed. The nearest soldiers, only thirty yards away, began bumping into trees. Some sat. Others sang. They lay on the ground and slept. Behind her, the louts cheered and hugged each other as the forest floor was blanketed with black uniforms spotted with blue and white petals.

Chapter Thirteen

With the twilight forest in full bloom, it was impossible to return to Ashkareve, but they quickly discovered plenty of preserved foods in the storerooms. Piek told his men to clean the Manor and prepare dinner. No one knew exactly how long Boran's army would sleep, so they made plans to stay as long as needed. After setting Renue up in her old room, Lisande found a special cell for Wildcard. Alkor had insisted on placing the barrier himself, but by then the old Damasker could hardly stand on his own. Dora sealed the room, then ordered him to rest.

In the late afternoon, Lisande and Granges stood on the front parapet, watching the falling petals cast the city a delicate blue. Another harsh wind blew across the hilltop, filling the air with leaves once more. As the sun set, Lisande looked down at the fountain. The shadow of her mother was projected on the stones below, thin and elegant.

"Where's the black thing?" Lisande said. "Is it gone?" She looked over at her room where Renue slept.

Granges shrugged. "I'll check on him," he said. "Rest. We don't need to lose you too."

From her view she could see all of Ashkareve. With each breeze more petals flew. Even had she not known the room in which Dora and Alkor stayed, she could have found Alkor by the old Damasker's constant wailing. The old Drailer appeared at the door but refused to let Lisande in. So she left the two alone. But long after it was dark, Lisande could still hear Alkor screaming, his cries so constant that they had no choice but to move him to the basement.

When Lisande went to see Renue again, his breathing had slowed but he was awake. He wouldn't speak, so she stroked his hair and told him about the forest. A few of Piek's men dragged a cot into the room and she lay beside Renue until he slept again, but she couldn't. She sat in an old wicker chair by the window and watched the night sky. Dora had speculated that there were enough twilight petals to put Ashkareve asleep for weeks. A city deep with dream, the old Drailer had said. For now, Ashkareve was peaceful.

Lisande woke before the dawn and walked to the edge of the forest. Something was troubling her. In the thick of white and purple-dotted leaves, she couldn't even see the hills below, let alone the city. Maybe her father had designed the forest for exactly that reason.

In the morning, Lisande stayed by Renue's side, supporting him as he hobbled the long halls, staring at the paintings and tapestries. If she turned her back for moment, he'd wander out to the forest or the garden where she'd find him sitting quietly against the statue. But when he saw her he turned away and disappeared in the brush. She let him go. An hour later she walked the hall of portraits and found one missing. Later, in the kitchen, she would discover a frame, smoldering in the sink.

Alkor died just before sunset and Lisande led Dora and the others to a pair of gravestones resting in the mountain shade behind the Manor. In the grass grew orange umbrella mushrooms. She could remember picking them in the summers with her mother. The limbs of a lone twilight tree stretched over the field. They would place Bardon's grave next to it, the old Drailer decided, an uncomfortable, familiar intensity in her eyes. After they buried Alkor, Dora broke down and Granges took her back to the Manor. Lisande held Renue's hand and they stood by the recently upturned earth.

She ate her dinner at the fountain and afterwards she watched a cloudy gray dusk spread across the eastern hills. When it was dark she walked around the side of the Manor to the mountain edge. Finding a narrow path that snaked upwards, she climbed until she could see the city again. Ashkareve was so still she could imagine hearing the lapping ocean. She had felt her father's presence long before, but now, alone in the mountains, he appeared again, drifting beside her.

"What did you do to his father?" she said.

She could hear the animals of the woods, the night owls and black birds and overpowering crickets. Bats roosted amongst blackened branches and spread their quiet wings. With the city asleep, nature itself seemed to have rallied.

"And his mother?"

Her I fell in love with.

"Is that why Mother died?"

Not exactly.

Lisande climbed further into the mountains, past the brambles that in the late winter spotted yellow flowers. On a flat rock she stretched out and fell asleep, woken some time later by her father's voice carried in the air currents below. She followed the trail of his voice down from the mountain and across the grassy field to her mother's grave. In the Manor light, her burial stone was tinged a slight purple.

"How did she die?"

The Sickness.

Lisande tried to find the outline of the shade's mouth but couldn't. For a moment she thought she heard Alkor wailing, but it was only the brutal gusts coming from the mountains and racing over the Manor. She heard another howl, somewhere beyond the western hills. Maybe the wolves were returning.

"You didn't have any of the Gift, did you, Father?" she said. "It was always her."

Owls hooted in the black trees of the hills, stirring up rodents into the bramble and bushes. She wondered whether Renue was sleeping. She could almost sense him in the garden.

Clever girl.

"That's why they call it the Sickness."

Oh, it was called that long before. But aptly named.

She closed her eyes and heard Renue saying he loved her, and Lavender's parting words, two flowering stars, and then came Bardon's sorrowful, heavy voice, and finally her mother, reading fantastical stories by the fire, and sharing her strange and troubled dreams.

"And the smoke?"

So we'd know if you left the Manor. Besides, you'd always come back to me for a magic trick.

Lisande rested a hand on her mother's grave, fingers rubbing the coarse rock, tracing the engraved vines and the wolf. "I miss Faldor so much—can I see him?"

I'm afraid it doesn't work like that, child.

She wanted to scream but a hollowness filled her lungs. Crossing her arms at the summer chill, she finally turned to face him. "Why did you do it, Father?"

A question even I couldn't answer. But I did love you, in my way. You were always the strongest, Sophia. I was going to tell you it all, someday . . .

"Only I took you first."

You did what I could not. Besides, your friend was right. It's merciful, to take those with black hands.

"You mean . . . "

Yes, Sophia. Even I was not above my own rules.

♥

But how does it end?

As the trees sway in a summer night, the wind collects into a song that sings of a time irretrievable. Follow this song. Deep within a maze of concrete, the city is finally waking, taking its first breaths.

In the Slants a story blooms, the storming of the Manor, of a lout army that climbed the hills to do a simple thing, to put out a fire. Boran's spades had them trapped. A massacre was certain. But then a woman stepped in front of the army and brought the forest back to life, branches sprouting from her fingertips, flowers springing from her hair. She put the city to sleep and, in doing so, woke it from a decades-long nightmare.

In the morning, a pink light peeks through a window. On a deserted side street, two louts are retelling this story, embellishing it, as often happens. The myth of The Queen of Hearts grows. When she returns, we'll follow her, like a paper ball in the wind. Like what? Oh, nothing. Something I saw once, that's all. Just a stupid expression. Something beautiful and hopeful. Something rare.

Hidden amongst the walls and platforms, it awakens from years of dreaming murder, infant memories stirring, churning, brimming with consciousness and activity. Now, new frontiers loom in its mind. Starving, it takes the gabbing louts, stealing their breath, robbing them of the coals that are their essences. It has taken lives for years and will take again, but now it can feel itself changing, wretched and guilt-consumed upon the realization that dreams are never dreams. It discovers another fraying memory, of a wife traded like a poker chip. Again it screams. There is no greater loss than a loved one discarded, says Pestras, no more profound pain than an action that can never be undone. Yet is there within humanity an essence yet to be salvaged, any breath which has passed to the other side without chance of reprieve?

In the room there is a flicker and then a scream that once more shakes the hearts of frozen, waking, sleeping men and women throughout the city. Another myth is blooming. There is a statue in the garden of Mesmer where at night you can hear someone weeping, once a man, become Fear itself. Really? I swear. But why? To remind us. Of what? Our curse, maybe. Being human. But other nightmares will come soon enough— they always do. Will we *ever* know peace? Are we beasts, or something more? Look to the city, the lout says, his breath misting. The heart lies there.